KILLER'S CURE

THE DI SHONA MCKENZIE MYSTERIES

WENDY H. JONES

SCOTT AND LAWSON

Published by Scott and Lawson

Cover Design by Cathy Helms of Avalon Graphics LLC

To all the staff who work in the NHS, one of the UK's greatest institutions, all of whom are hard working and dedicated. I salute each and every one of you and thank you for what you do. You are what makes the NHS great.

1

The figure gazed in wonder as peace descended.

The body lay, calm, serene. As it should be. No more battles. No more war. All was, once more, well in this woman's world. No more pain. No more crying. No more cancer. No more sickness. This was as it should be. The natural order of things once more restored, her spirit would return to the heavens, her body to the earth. Ashes to ashes, dust to dust. They could almost see the spirit soaring above as they glanced at the ceiling. The figure pulled a crisp white sheet up to the woman's chin, took one last look, and left.

Blending into the surroundings they were swallowed up by the corridors, unnoticed by any other person in this vast institution. Why would anyone notice? No one ever noticed. Not here. Not now.

Once they had been noticed, looked up to, almost revered, but those days were long gone. Now they were merely one more player in the game of life. A tiny cog in the vast government machine. Pushed from pillar to post at the whims of masters far removed from them. They didn't care. No one cared. Not here. Not now.

2

Detective Inspector Shona McKenzie had no sooner swallowed two aspirin chased down by a restorative gulp of rocket fuel, otherwise known as coffee, than the phone rang. She groaned, knowing it would be the desk sergeant with news of a dead body. It was ever thus. No sooner had they stamped solve on one case than another came barrelling through the door screaming at her to leap up and solve it.

She was wrong. Not about the dead body part but about the desk sergeant part. It was Mary, the pathologist, who always had dead bodies tucked up in the fridges in the mortuary.

"Usually, it's me sending them in your direction. What's up?"

"I'm concerned." Silence followed.

"Could you elaborate?" Shona put the phone on loud-speaker and used her hands to massage her temples. She had enough murders to deal with without Mary flinging them her way. Communication, and dead bodies, should flow in the other direction.

"I've had several women admitted to the mortuary recently. All were in hospital when they died. All unexpected. All roughly the same age."

"I take it you're having difficulty defining cause of death?"

"Got it in one."

"Surely they died of whatever admitted them to Narrywells in the first place."

"You'd think so. That's not the only puzzling thing. They're not all Narrywells."

Narrywells being Dundee's gargantuan hospital, it kept Mary on her toes. Why was she bothering herself with bodies from anywhere else? She asked Mary that very question.

"We've a couple of pathologists off long term sick so everyone's picking up the slack."

Shona made a snap decision. "Let the Procurator Fiscal know, and he can decide if we proceed." It was probably nothing, but she didn't want to be accused of shirking her duty. The Dundee press would have a field day if they missed anything.

"So, you want me to report it to your boyfriend?"

"Yep. Pretty much." The thought of seeing Douglas, the procurator fiscal and, simultaneously, her fiancé, helped Shona's headache no end. She felt noticeably chipper considering she probably had another serial killer on her hands. She clicked end, slipped the phone in her pocket, and went to break the news to the chief. Better for her to break bad news than the fiscal. Oh joy.

As she suspected, the chief was not amused. In fact, he was downright grumpy, even for him. He was also rubbing his chest. She hoped it was indigestion and not a hear attack. She searched his face for the previous signs, but he looked to be in good health. Not that she knew a lot about it of course.

"McKenzie, I've had quite enough of this. Do you go out looking for cases just to persecute me?"

"Sir, they usually come to me."

"There seem to be an inordinate number of them when you're around. No one else has this ability to attract serial killers."

"There does, Sir. I'm not happy about that either."

"Don't get snippy. Let me know what your boyfriend has to say about it." He dismissed her with a wave of his hand.

Shona wondered if she could get him admitted to Narrywells with whatever was ailing him. He might come out via the mortuary. Boyfriend indeed. The Procurator Fiscal was much higher up in the pecking order than the chief. He ought to remember this fact when talking about him. Grumpiness was almost a pandemic this morning.

An hour later, she, Douglas, and the entire team were gathered in the briefing room. He'd declared the deaths suspicious, and they now had a murder enquiry on their hands. The strangest one yet, and that was hard going in the Dundee branch of Police Scotland. Since Shona joined the team, all their murder investigations were strange.

Sergeant Peter Johnston, the oldest and wisest of the team, wiped grease from his mouth with the back of his hand. He'd just devoured a bacon roll, his tie testament to that fact. "Here we go again." He picked up a napkin and wiped his hands. Shona wasn't quite sure why he hadn't wiped his mouth with it. But she had better things to worry her.

Sergeant Nina Chakrabarti, dressed head to toe in Gucci, added, "Yep. How do we investigate it?"

"With our usual consummate professionalism and expertise."

"So, we muddle through then." Roy MacGregor, Detective Constable, and self-confessed wit, who had uttered the words, laughed and high fived with Jason 'Soldier Boy' Roberts, another DC. A stint in the Territorial Army earned him his nickname and, strangely, his place on the team. He'd been instrumental in helping Shona with one particularly knotty strand of her first investigation as Detective Inspector.

"Don't be so cheeky or you'll find yourself being witty in traffic division." Then she added for good measure, "The pair of you." Outwardly stern, inwardly she rejoiced the pair were now on friendly terms. They'd been a nightmare when she started, even resorting to physical fisticuffs at one point. Thankfully things had moved on or one, or both, of them would have had to go. "We're going to be investigating the long, slow, and hard way. Track down relatives, nurses, doctors, and every damn person who works in any of the hospitals where these women were concerned."

"We don't know who they are?" Abigail pointed out the obvious flaw in their investigation.

"All will be revealed. I'm waiting for Mary to email me her thoughts and findings, including the names of the possible victims. I'll let you know the minute we've got it."

They dispersed. Douglas accompanied Shona back to her office via the kitchen where they grabbed coffee. Coffee might not make the world go round but it certainly fuelled Police Scotland. As did cakes but they were in short supply since Peter had a heart attack. The bacon rolls were a temporary aberration. Usually, it was all fruit and healthy eating.

Once they were ensconced in her office, in luxury chairs which enveloped their bodies in soft leather comfort – the boss still hadn't forgiven Shona for purchasing them with Police Scotland funds - Douglas moved swiftly on from murders.

"We need to set a wedding date."

Shona choked on her coffee, and it sprayed from her mouth. Coughing and spluttering she grabbed a tissue and mopped up the mess which seemed to cover a large part of her desk and a couple of police reports. She dabbed at the reports which remained readable. Shame. "Good grief man, we're at work. Wouldn't home be a better place to discuss this."

Douglas smiled, setting her heart ablaze and her insides

weak. "You're never home. As you're always at work, this is the perfect time to discuss it."

"Seriously, it's not." She smiled, taking the sting from her words. "I need to focus on the case."

Douglas sighed, took a sip of his coffee, and gave in gracefully. He'd have to pick his moment. This case might turn out to be nothing and she'd have a bit more time on her hands. Then he realised that with Shona involved this case would turn out to be something and then something more. They'd be awash with dead bodies before they knew it.

"The chief might want to have a chat with you before you go," Shona said.

"I already broke the news to him he had a murder investigation on his hands."

"How did he take it?"

"Surprisingly well."

Either he kept all his wrath for her, or he'd come around since she gave him the heads up earlier. Either way, Douglas got an easy ride.

"Fabulous. I'd love to chat for longer, but the procurator fiscal says I've some murders to investigate, so I'll see you later."

Douglas kissed her and left her with her lips tingling and her knees weak. Maybe it was time to consider that wedding after all.

3

Shona took a gulp of coffee and turned to her email. She clicked on the one from Mary who had given a succinct overview of the deaths which concerned her.

Diana Catchington. Age 58. Admitted with pneumonia. Recovering. Bertha Mallard. Age 61. Admitted for a stent. Recovering. Sarah McTaggart. Age 55. Admitted for appendicectomy. Went well. Recovering. Ann Treacher. Age 59. Admitted for bowel resection and colostomy. Recovering. Lara Moon. Age 57. Admitted following a road traffic incident. Critical initially but not life threatening. Had been in three weeks. Recovering well.

She had also sent the details of the wards they had been on and in which hospital, as well as a lot of other information Mary thought pertinent. They wards were Narrywells, Queen Elizabeth Hospital, Perth, and King Albert Hospital in Kirkcaldy. Shona was thankful they didn't stretch from Inverness to the Scottish Borders. This was just about manageable as Perthshire and Fife were pretty much on her doorstep.

She printed off several copies and called the troops to the briefing room. Peace descended and the only sound that could be heard was the slurping of coffee and the rattle of mugs on the large table as everyone took in the news they were reading on the printouts.

Peter spoke for them all. "Where do we start?"

Shona chewed her lip. "Even I'm not sure. The only person who seems concerned so far is Mary."

"The medical staff must have been concerned enough to send them her way in the first place." Abigail Lau, Shona's other sergeant, looked quizzical.

"Good point." Shona thumped her empty mug on the table. "Right, time for action. Peter. You and I are off to Narrywells. Nina, you're with Iain and can take QE. Abigail and Jason, you take Victoria."

"What are we meant to be doing there?" Jason asked.

"Cool your jets, Soldier Boy, and I'll tell you. Don't be in such a rush." She smiled. "I want you to speak to the doctors who referred the women to Mary. Their names are in the paperwork I gave you.

Shona kept the windows down as they drove to Narrywells. It was a beautiful summers day, warm with a light breeze. Of course, there was a breeze as Dundee must be the windiest city in Scotland. Today it was welcome.

"Do you think this will come tae anything, Ma'am?"

"I'm certain of it. Don't our cases always come to something?"

"Aye. They do."

Silence descended as they pondered the intricacies of such a case, far removed from any of their previous cases, yet eerily similar. The fates threw the dice and once again, they did not land in their favour.

Narrywells was huge. So huge it was deemed the largest teaching hospital in Europe and was rumoured to have thirty-two miles of corridors. Thankfully they didn't have to traverse all thirty-two miles, only a couple. Usually, Peter would be moaning about the walk but, after his heart attack, he'd embraced healthy eating and a more active lifestyle, so they were soon at the ward. They'd rang ahead to make an appointment but hadn't said what it was about. Shona flashed her ID card at the nurses' station and asked for Doctor Somers. It turned out the Doctor was busy with an emergency, so they were ushered into a cubby hole, optimistically called a staff room, where two mugs of tea and a couple of chocolate digestive biscuits magically appeared. Shona toyed with going to a different ward to interview another doctor but decided to wait it out. They could be trailing from ward to ward gaining nothing but a feeling of déjà vu. Mind you, the exercise would come in handy.

Fifteen minutes later they were joined by a young woman of about twenty-nine. Wearing scrubs, she looked both exhausted and harried. She was pulling her hair up into a ponytail and securing it with a rubber band. "These bands aren't what they used to be. Crappy things snap every two minutes. NHS cutbacks." She held out her hand then pulled it back. "Better not. Covid, infection control, and all that. Natasha Somers. How can I help you both?"

Shona inwardly sighed with relief. She'd managed to avoid Covid thus far. Goodness knows how but she was vaccinated up the ying yang and wanted to stay Covid free. "I believe you treated, and certified dead, a lady called," she glanced at her notes just to be sure she had the right person, "Ann Treacher."

"Yes. Lovely lady."

"I'm curious, what was the reason you asked for a post-mortem?"

"I'm not sure I am allowed to answer your question. Patient confidentiality rules."

Shona showed her warrant. "It says we can see all medical

records and all questions are to be answered." Shona kept her voice mild. The doctor was only doing her job and upsetting her meant they'd get nothing.

"I'd still rather check with my boss."

This started a house of cards with everyone passing the buck. They all, including the Doctor, had another coffee to pass the time. Peter had the look of a man who wanted another chocolate digestive. Shona had the look of someone who would kill him if he asked. Natasha had the look of a woman who needed to crawl into bed and sleep for a fortnight, not just sit and drink coffee. The coffee was worse than the station muck and Shona didn't think that was possible. Maybe this was what did in their current victims. If they were victims. She still wasn't pinning her colours to the mast on this one. It felt like a storm in a teacup.

4

They were draining the last of the brews and thinking of some other topic of idle chit chat to keep them occupied, when a woman strode in exuding perfume and confidence in equal measure. She was trailed by a short man who seemed to have been last in line when it came to dishing out confidence. Mice would complain if they were compared in timidity to him.

"I'm, Stella Barrington-Smythe, the CEO of the hospital. This..." she indicated the man, "is Jonathan Culpepper, the hospital's lawyer."

Shona stood up handing over the warrant with one hand and flashing her badge with the other. "DI Shona McKenzie of Police Scotland. Our warrant shows we have the right to any information pertaining to three patients." She rattled off their names.

Barrington-Smythe took one glance at the paper and, without saying a word, handed it over to the lawyer.

He took an insufferably long time to read it, adjusting his glasses every few seconds. At last, just as Shona thought she would take root, he said, "It all seems in order. The hospital will not be liable for anything pertaining to giving Police Scotland the information they require."

What a longwinded way of saying, we've legally got to give them what they want.

Shona refrained from speaking her thoughts out loud and said, "Thank you. Is there somewhere quiet we can go to chat to the staff." She rubbed her temples, although the headache was easing, thank goodness.

They were shown to an office that was probably a cupboard in a previous life. Barrington-Smythe spoke quietly to the occupant who stood up and said, "I'm Charge Nurse Anderson. If there is anything you need let me know." The entourage disappeared, leaving them to it. Shona sat behind the desk and Peter squeezed himself into a chair next to it.

"Dr Somers, please have a seat." The one remaining chair took up the tiny sliver of space left.

"It's Natasha. I get enough of the formalities at work."

"Natasha, can you please tell me why you felt it important to request an autopsy on Mrs Treacher?"

The corner of the doctor's lip curled up as though she was thinking. Shona gave her the space to decide. Eventually, her decision obviously made, she spoke. "As I say, Ann, was a delightful lady. She had cancer which we caught early. She had a section of bowel removed and a temporary colostomy stoma formed." She took in Peter's face and added, "That's a hole from the bowel through to the abdominal wall."

Peter paled and swallowed several times. Who'd have known it, thought Shona, all those grisly murder scenes and not a sniff of squeamishness, and now here he was going all peely wally at the thought of a bowel operation.

Natasha continued. "All was going well, and she was getting ready to go home. Then, I got a call at 6.30 one morning to say she had died in the night and could I certify her."

"What was the cause of death?"

"That was the problem. I didn't know. So, I asked for an autopsy."

"And the pathologist can't find a cause of death either?"

"No. Ann's family are, quite rightly, not happy and want answers."

"As do we all, it would seem."

"I certainly want one." A mobile phone rang. The doctor answered it and stood up. "I really need to go now. My work's piling up." She threw the door open and galloped off.

At this rate it was going to take the rest of the day to interview the doctors. Shona sent Peter in the direction of another ward to speak to a different medic. "Record the interview."

"Will do, Ma'am." He strode off, no hurry in his steps. At least he was walking thought Shona. His cardiac surgeon would be delighted. He might bang into her as he was off to the Cardiac unit to find out about Bertha Mallard who'd died following a routine stent insertion.

The incongruity of the unexplained deaths was amplified a thousand-fold by the fact none of the patients were on one ward or in one hospital. This would be downright impossible to investigate.

She sought out the charge nurse and asked her if she could have a printout of the staff rotas for the days before and after Ann died. The woman obliged – she'd obviously taken the 'help in any way you can' memo to heart – and within minutes Shona was clutching the pages. Charge Nurse Anderson was happy to talk to her but said as the ward was, quite literally, overflowing, it would need to be quick.

"Can you tell me what happened?"

"I wasn't on duty, but the night nurses told me they found Mrs Treacher dead when they went to do her observations in the morning."

Shona's eyes narrowed. "Would they not have checked on her overnight."

"She was fully recovered from her operation and going home the next day. They would have done her observations at about 10pm and given her a milky drink. Overnight they would have glanced through the window in the door to her room.

"And they didn't see anything amiss."

"There's only a faint nightlight in the room, so they would only see her sleeping. She was pretty self-caring at that point."

Shona made a mental note not to ever get admitted to hospital. Then she berated herself. From what she could see the nurses were rushed off their feet to the point of exhaustion. Still, they were dedicated. A lot like coppers if truth be told.

"What are your thoughts?"

"I don't know what to think." She lowered her head and shook it slowly. Then, she looked Shona straight in the eye and said, "Sudden or unexplained deaths happen. Sometimes it's just someone's time to go."

Shona remained silent, knowing the woman would fill in the gap.

The charge nurse shuffled in her chair, clasped her fingers, looked Shona straight in the eye, and said, "I would stake my life on the fact that none of my staff did anything to this woman."

No one said they did.

"So, why did she die?" Shona stared right back at her until the woman looked down. "This is something that must be answered, and I fully intend to find the answer."

The woman looked fearful. Shona fully intended to investigate the reason for that as well. This no longer felt like a storm in a teacup. It had the potential to turn into a full-scale hurricane.

What was that charge nurse hiding? Unfortunately, she would have to wait to find out as a knock at the door called the woman away. It would wait another day. Shona thanked her and said she would be in touch soon. That was a given.

. . .

Shona looked at her notes and headed back to reception for directions to the ward where Lara Moon had died. She put another few thousand steps on her Apple Watch on the way there. She wondered briefly how fit all the staff were with the number of miles they must walk every day. Lost in a reverie, she managed to kick a bucket full of soapy water and slip in the consequent deluge. Fortunately, the only thing damaged was her pride. She apologised to the cleaner, who said, "No speak English," and smiled. She smiled back, apologised, and went to find a hand dryer to dry her soaking wet backside. Not a good look for Police Scotland if her appearance suggested she'd had an unfortunate urinary accident.

There seemed to be people everywhere on the ward, all of whom rushed past at a dizzying rate. Despite having rung in advance there was no way they were able to speak to either the doctor or the charge nurse, Dave Carabiniere. She did manage to arrange times when they would come into the station and bring all the relevant paperwork, so she had to be content with that. *I thought my job was bad, those poor sods work for every penny they earn.* She texted the others requesting they get copies of the staff rotas for the period of the deaths. She hoped they'd managed to speak to the doctors involved.

She then called Peter, who was ready to meet her or would be once he'd got the staff rotas. Grabbing takeaway drinks from the café in the foyer passed the time until he appeared, and they headed for the car.

"Do you want an update?" Peter slid into the passenger seat.

"Nope, I want coffee and Radio Four. You can update us all back at the station." They listened to a gardening programme, Peter chipping in his own observations about what they should be doing with their tomatoes and cucumbers to protect against aphids and various other blights. Shona let it all wash over her, lost in her own thoughts. Despite the best efforts of her mother, she'd never been a gardener. The programme gave her time to think. She literally had no clue, or clues, as to where she should be going with this investigation. She was an 'attend the murder scene and move from there' type of gal. The sheer insidiousness of this one clutched at her brain and squeezed. Where did one even begin to solve it?

The others, who had travelled further than them, were still in the office – no make that the staff canteen – before them. "Are you lot eating again? For heaven's sake, get your backsides up to the briefing room now." She held up her hand as Peter opened his mouth. "Take a roll with you. You can eat it there. Get me an egg salad one as well." She rummaged around in her pocket and pulled out a ten-pound note which she handed to him. He watched longingly as the others swallowed the last mouthful of rhubarb crumble and custard and walked out of the door.

They all had similar tales to tell. The women had died unexpectedly, not all in their sleep. Some died during the day. There was no explanation and seemingly no common factor. They just died. Fear clutched at Shona's stomach. Could there be more, and it hadn't been picked up? As they didn't have the staff rotas, they couldn't compare them for patterns, so they were somewhat stalled. "I'm going to ring Mary. Give me five," and she disappeared through the door.

"Why's she so keen on the rotas? No one worked in the same place." Nina frowned and twiddled her phone stylus.

"Could be an agency nurse or a locum doctor." Abigail picked up her mug and peered inside. Empty. "Damn."

Shona reappeared and said, "Mary is ringing around her colleagues to find out if they've had any similar cases in the past six months."

Peter's mouth dropped open. "We've already five possible murders to investigate and you're looking for more?"

"I'm looking for patterns. If that means more cases, then we'll just have to suck it up."

By this point they all looked like they'd lost a tenner and found tenpence.

An hour later, the entire team were on the road again, this time to speak to grieving relatives. Shona pulled her car up at the front door of an imposing pile in the country. Stone built, with huge sash windows and a front door you could drive a carriage through. "I didn't know teachers were paid that well," Shona said.

"She probably inherited the house and curses every minute of her inheritance. The upkeep must be crippling." This, from Nina, who would inherit her own huge pile one day. The proclamation seemed heartfelt.

Shona rattled the lion's head door knocker. The sound seemed to echo through the house. She expected to see a butler; when the door opened it was a teenager sporting designer ripped, multiple piercings, and tattoos. Her voice quavering, with a highland lilt, she said, "We're busy right now. My mum says can it wait?" She attempted a feeble smile but failed.

Shona, keeping her voice gentle, said, "I'm afraid it can't." She showed her badge and said, "May I speak with your mum?"

Fear flashed across her eyes, and she hurried off. A beautifully dressed woman appeared in her place. Despite the makeup she looked haggard, her eyes full of unshed tears.

Shona showed her ID once more, introduced them both and said, "Please may we talk to you?"

The tears gave up their struggle to remain contained and dripped down her cheeks. "What's happened now? It's James isn't it? You've found James?"

Shona wasn't sure whether the woman sounded scared or hopeful.

"If we could come in and sit down, I will explain everything."

They were ushered into the kitchen. The woman offered them lemonade. "Normally I would make my own, but this came from Sainsbury's." She stirred the lemonade. The jug was cut crystal as were the tall glasses in which the lemonade was served. They accented the designer kitchen perfectly. It had probably made it to the front cover of Homes and Gardens or was an identikit of one of the kitchens in said magazine.

Shona and Nina accepted, more to make the woman feel comfortable than any desire for a drink, but Shona had to admit it was refreshing. Once they were all sitting down, she said, "It's not about James." She could see the woman deflate in front of her eyes. "We would like to have a word about Ann Treacher. Are you a relation, Mrs...?"

The fear reappeared. as did more tears. "Drummond. Anastasia Drummond. She was my mother. You think she was killed? I knew she died too suddenly." She dabbed at her eyes with a tissue. "I just knew it wasn't natural." The words tumbled out in a tsunami of nervousness and desperation.

"We are not sure what is going on at the moment, but the pathologist asked us to look into her death. It may be nothing."

The woman sat up straight and looked Shona in the eye. "I know it's something."

Interesting. "What makes you say that? She'd just had a major operation and deaths often follow those."

"Not so long afterwards. She recovered well, was dealing with the colostomy, and was looking forward to getting home. She would have been home, but they were having difficulty supplying some of the items she needed to bring with her."

"Did you visit her the day before she died? How did she seem?"

"She was bright, lively, and fed up with the fact she had to spend another night out of her own bed. She didn't even seem a teensy bit unwell or even tired." She looked Shona in the eye again. "There was no reason she should have died. I'm telling you; someone killed her."

Shona had to ask the next question. "Do you think it was neglect on the part of the hospital?"

Anastasia did not hesitate. "Not at all. The medical and nursing staff were nothing but professional and kindness itself. They couldn't do enough for my mother."

"So, who do you think killed your mother?"

"That I don't know." Her eyes flashed with fire. "It's what I want you to find out."

Shona looked at Nina and raised an eyebrow. Nina interpreted and said, "I am sure the medical staff were outstanding and all kudos to them. A bit like the police, there is always someone who doesn't quite fit that picture." She pulled out her phone and opened up the notes app. "Can you think of any member of staff who was different from the rest, even in the slightest way?"

The woman's eyes moved upwards signifying she was thinking. Interesting she took the question seriously, so a bit more hesitation. She opened her mouth, paused, then making the decision to continue said, "There was one nurse who was always a bit sharp. Nothing you could completely pin down, just not as nice as the others. Not unkind, just not kind." She looked at Nina and then Shona. "Does any of that make sense?"

"It does. Can we have her name?"

"He, not she. Xavier Peterson. He won't get in bother, will he?" Her eyes pleaded with them to say no.

Shona obliged. "Of course not. I'm sure you appreciate we need to investigate every possible angle."

The woman relaxed.

"Who's James." Shona asked the question nonchalantly, as though it was of no consequence.

"What? Why?" She swallowed a few times. "Why do you want to know."

"When we arrived, you asked if we were here about James. I'd like to know why you think the police would be interested in him."

"It was just a reaction. It didn't mean anything." She shook her head vigorously. "Just me being silly. Nothing there."

"If you're sure. Thank you for your time, Mrs Drummond. We'll leave you now so you can grieve with your family. Please be assured we are taking your mother's death extremely seriously."

"Thank you."

"Oh, one more question. When is your mother's funeral?"

"When the body is released." The woman's eyes narrowed, suspicion clouding them.

"I'm sorry for your loss. I will do my best to get your mother's body released at the earliest opportunity. I know how important a funeral is in the grieving process."

5

The minute they were back in the car, Nina asked, "What's the deal with James?"

"I've no clue but I intend to find out. There's something going on there; whether it's anything to do with our case is anyone's guess."

"Might be a bit tricky with only a first name."

"With Roy on the case. Are you having a laugh. He'll find out before we've had a chance to swig down our first cup of Brazilian blend."

"Of course. How could I forget."

Nina flicked on Radio 1 and they listened to mindless music for several minutes. Then, Nina asked, "What's with your interest in the funerals?"

"I fully intend going to every last one of them to pay my respects."

"Why? Do you need the free food or something?"

"I'm not going to the wakes. I'm going to the funerals. To see if there is any one person who is at them all. Keep up."

"That's why you're the boss and I'm a lowly minion." Nina grinned and they both laughed.

. . .

The station being devoid of any other member of the team, Shona drummed her fingers on her desk and made a valiant effort to control her impatience. Not able to put it off any longer, she turned to a stack of reports that did nothing more than depress her. Sometimes being a detective was frenzied police work and exhaustion. Other times it was mind numbingly boring. Boring was winning hands down right now. *The Police Constable's Report on Community Policing and the Effects on Crime Rates in Scotland*, was not a riveting bedside read. In fact, the tedious title was the most exciting part of the entire 127-page document. Yet, read it she must as the chief would probably expect her to trot out relevant parts of it at every opportunity. Sometimes she hated her job. Most of the time she didn't have time to think about whether she hated it or not. Sometimes she didn't have time to think, period. The only good thing she could say about the report was, it kept her occupied until the doctor and charge nurse turned up ready to be interviewed. It would also make a good door stop. How many trees died in printing hundreds of copies of this drivel. The Chief Constable probably knew if he emailed it no one would read it. If it cluttered up their desk, then they just might.

She plonked the charge nurse in the families' room with a cup of coffee, the doctor in the interview room with tea. "DI Shona McKenzie interviewing Dr Stephen Lorimer. DS Nina Chakrabarti in attendance." She rattled off the other formalities such as date time and Stephen was only a witness, and not under suspicion for any crimes. *Not yet, anyway*, thought Shona. *Depending on your answers you could be at some point in my investigation.* His voice weary, he said he understood. Goodness knows how long he'd been working for. She was only grateful he was able to speak to her during the normal working day. Although she was sure nothing was ever normal for him, just like her job.

"Thank you for coming in. We would like to ask you a few questions about..." She glanced at her notes, "Lara Moon."

"Of course."

This chap's voice was beyond weary – it was dead. Shona was beginning to worry about him. If he didn't perk up by the end of the interview, she would ring the hospital and tell them of her concerns. You could never be too careful these days.

"I believe you certified Lara dead?"

"Yes. I was the doctor on duty."

This would be hard work; Shona could tell. "What was the cause of death?"

"That's the thing. I couldn't really figure it out. I didn't know what to do." He clasped and unclasped his fingers. "That's never happened before. My boss said it was complications of the accident, but I wasn't so sure."

"What injuries did she sustain?"

Stephen rattled off a list of conditions the only words of which she understood were shattered pelvis, liver, kidney, and ribs. The rest of it could have been Chinese.

"Would any of those injuries be enough for her to die three weeks later."

He shook his head. "No. I wouldn't say so. That's why I wanted a post-mortem."

"Did you notice anything at all suspicious other than the fact she died unexpectedly?"

The nurses would be better at that. We don't spend much time with the patients, basically because we don't have much time." He looked at her. "It's gruelling."

His eyes looked a lot less dead, and his voice had perked up. Maybe he just needed a good night's sleep after all. She let him go and said they'd be in touch if they had any more questions.

. . .

"Do I need a lawyer."

That wasn't what Shona was expecting at all. Did Charge Nurse Carabiniere have something to hide. "Why? Do you think you need one? I explained you are a witness, not being arrested for anything."

"No. But it never hurts to be careful."

"Would you like one? You have the right to him or her being present."

"Yes."

Why didn't you say that earlier, numbskull, thought Shona. *They'd be here by now.*

"Interview ended at the request of Mr Dave Carabiniere who would like his lawyer present."

She switched off the recording equipment. "Sergeant Chakrabarti, take Mr Carabiniere to ring his lawyer.

Shona trudged to the main office to find out if the others were back. Roy and Abigail were in situ but there was no sign of Peter and Jason who'd gone the furthest. Also, Peter had probably stopped somewhere for sustenance; he couldn't seem to go five minutes without eating. She was jolly glad to see Roy. "I've a task for you. Use your genius computer skills to find out all you can about a chap called James."

"I might be a computer whizz kid but even I need more than that to go on."

"Hold your horses, sunshine. I've no surname but attach his name to a Mrs Ann Treacher and/or a Mrs Anastasia Drummond."

"In this area?"

"Start there." She had no actual clue where Anastasia Drummond lived. Given her daughter's highland lilt, she would bet it was the Highlands and Islands rather than Dundee.

She left him whistling, a man happy in his work.

She managed to fit in a mug of coffee and a stale doughnut before the lawyer arrived. She groaned when Margaret McCluskey strode up the corridor. The woman was a nightmare and represented every low life in Dundee. With the build of a challenger tank wearing lipstick, she seemed to storm through every case that ever landed on Shona's desk. She wondered why a nurse, who wasn't being charged with anything, needed McCluskey with him in a police interview. She also wondered how he could afford the eye-watering amount per hour she charged; money Shona could only dream of. Something else to look into. Roy would be busy today.

The lawyer was in her usual foul mood. "You can't arrest my client. He was merely carrying out his duties on the ward."

Her client sat, meek and mild, not saying a word.

"I'm wondering how your client can hold down a job as a charge nurse as he appears to be stupid. I keep telling him he's not under arrest, only a witness." She took a few deep breaths. McCluskey always made her blood pressure go through the roof. "The death happened on his ward. We are trying to ascertain what happened to one of his patients."

"He did nothing."

Shona snapped. "Are you even more stupid than him? No one is saying he did."

"You can't speak to me like that."

"I wouldn't speak to you like that if you would let me speak to my *witness*, and we could all get home for our tea."

"Ask your questions but one wrong word and I am stopping this interview." She sat back and folded her arms over her ample bosom.

Good God in heaven I must have been a terrible person in a previous life to have to put up with Margaret McCluskey, and her clients, in this one. "Of course. Now, Mr Carabiniere, can you tell me everything you know about the admission and ultimate death of your patient, Lara Moon?"

"I had nothing to do with that."

Shona banged her head against the desk. Literally. When she picked it up again, she looked him in the eye and said, her voice slow and deliberate as she suspected he only possessed two brain cells and one was broken. "For the umpteenth time, no one is saying you did. We are just trying to get to the bottom of what happened. We're interviewing everyone, or we would be if you would only answer the bally questions and let us move on."

McCluskey opened her mouth to speak but Shona held her hand up, palm towards the lawyer. "I know. I can't speak to your client like that. But I can and I will until we get a sensible answer out of him. Now, are you going to instruct him to tell us what we need to know or do I need to arrest him for hindering a police officer in the course of her duty?"

McCluskey threw Shona a look that could fell an elephant, then turned to her client and said, "Answer DI McKenzie's questions."

Thank heavens. A sensible move at last.

He leaned back in his chair, put his hands behind his head and smirked. "What was the question?"

This man was getting on Shona's last shredded nerve. "For goodness sake, you're taking the mick. Just tell me everything you know about a patient called Lara Moon."

"Off the top of my head, she was admitted three weeks ago with rib fractures, kidney damage, liver damage, a tear in her spleen, a pelvic fracture, fractured femur and fractured radius and ulna. Car accident. Not her fault apparently. She was going around a bend when a car came from the other direction on the wrong side of the road."

Shona swore she'd swing for the man. He was deliberately

telling her every minute detail. She kept her counsel in case he clammed up again.

"She was in ITU for three days then HDU for two and then moved to the ward. She was recovering well, although still in a lot of pain. The physios were working with her, and we were looking at her going to a rehabilitation centre for a couple of weeks, when she died." He stopped, leaned over the table and said, "Is that enough for you?"

Shona wondered why he was being so difficult. You'd think any nurse would want this cleared up and pronto. What was he hiding? Did every blasted nurse in the hospital have secrets?

"Who raised the alarm that she'd died?"

"Staff Nurse Faber. She called the crash team, but it was obvious the poor soul was way beyond resuscitation."

"What did you think of a post-mortem being requested?"

"I suggested it. I thought she might have had a pulmonary embolus and thought it was worth looking into."

It was Shona's turn to lean forward and lean on the table. "There, that wasn't so hard, was it? That will be all. I'll be in touch if I need anything else." He was almost out the door when she added, "I asked for the staff rotas.

"I emailed them to you."

The only thing she needed right now was a swift dram of Talisker Whisky. She'd have to make do with a coffee and another stale doughnut. Sometimes, life wasn't fair.

6

"I'm losing the will to live, and this is only the beginning of the case. I hoped we'd have it wrapped up quickly but that aint going to happen, is it?"

"With you involved, not likely." Nina scuttled off before the inevitable tongue lashing for insubordination occurred.

Wait until I catch hold of her, thought Shona. *Cheeky besom.*

The staff room was now at maximum capacity, and everyone hard at work. At what, was a mystery to Shona as their case was in its infancy and going nowhere. It turned out Peter had set them to, updating paperwork. He'd promised them cakes if they complied which was guaranteed to keep them nose to grindstone. He was scouring Home Office Large Major Enquiry system or HOLMES, as it was fondly known, for any other deaths in hospitals. It wouldn't be the first time a killer moved location. It kept them one step ahead of the law.

"Anything interesting?"

"Not a thing, Ma'am. A couple I might follow up on, but I'm no' sure anything will come of it."

Shona nodded her approval. "Roy, any closer to finding out who the mysterious James is?"

"I think so but want to double check a few things. Can I report back in a few?"

She agreed and asked them all to convene in the briefing room in one hour. She retrieved all the staff rotas and took them back to her office to study them in peace and quiet. An hour later, after checking and cross checking what felt like about a million names, she was no further forward. Who knew it took so many people to run a ward. Not one of them appeared on both lists. She rubbed her eyes and decided to ask the others to cross check. Given the sheer volume of names she might have missed something.

Shona photocopied the staff rotas and took them with her to the staff room. Her eyes were burning; she thought she might head down to Boots after the meeting to grab some eye drops. This was the beginning of an investigation that looked like it might be awash in paperwork, so sore eyes did not bode well.

"Peter, anything to report?"

"I've put a couple of calls in to the Met and Midlands Police and I'm waiting for someone to get back to me. I'll update you after that." Then he added, "If that's okay wi' you. Ma'am?"

"More than okay." Shona, who had been brought up in Oxford, was now a pro at deciphering his speech and knew that wi' meant with. She'd spent her first couple of years on the force asking him to interpret. It made for interesting conversations.

"Roy. What's your take on the mysterious James?"

"Looks like he could be James Treacher. He's been missing for two years. Well, according to his family he has. Turns out he's alive and kicking but not particularly well. He's a junkie and dope pusher. Been in chokey a couple of times for breaking and entering." He looked at his notes. "Perth Prison."

"So, how come his nearest and dearest think he's MIA?"

"Because he categorically doesn't want them to know. Oh, and he goes by Jimmy now."

"Can we get him in?"

"If we can find him." Roy shrugged his shoulders. "He could be anywhere."

Shona was about to lambast him for his nonchalance when Nina took one look at her boss's face and said, "Would you like me to see what I can find out?"

"Yep, and get him in."

"I'll take Roy."

"Good plan." *It'll keep him out of my way. Stupid sod doesn't know when to keep his mouth shut.*

They took Jason along, in case Jimmy wasn't keen to help with their enquiries when they caught up with him. She'd lay good money on the fact Jimmy would be lawyered up before they could say interview and his lawyer would be either Margaret McCluskey or her brother Angus Runcie. Despite the amount they charged, every criminal in Dundee had them on speed dial. She, and the remainder of the team, were checking and rechecking the rotas when her phone rang. It was the chief's secretary. Could she report to his office. As if the man couldn't come and find her himself. There were only four places she could be, if you didn't count the ladies loo that was. Surely it wasn't that hard. She stabbed at her phone to end the call and shoved her chair back so hard it almost tipped over. They all looked at her, but no one said a word. "I've been summonsed."

They grimaced and returned to their task, probably thinking rather her than me.

She stomped to his office wondering what she could possibly have done now. It was only day one of a case that didn't seem like a case, and she hadn't had time to upset anyone.

"I've had the Alexeyevs on the phone. Apparently, you are persecuting one of their employees."

The Alexeyevs were a couple of Russian brothers – Stephan and Igor – who were over all of Shona's cases like measles, only harder to get rid of. Crooks of the highest order they always seemed to get off the hook, whatever charges were thrown at them. "What? That's impossible. Unless they own Narrywells, of course, which I wouldn't put past them. They seem to own everything else in Dundee."

"Please don't be rude about the Alexeyevs."

Shona could swear she saw the corner of his mouth twitch into a smile. "Sorry, Sir. Who do Tweedledum and Tweedledee think I'm persecuting now?"

"McKenzie, I'm warning you." There was that twitch again. "Apparently you have had a Mr Dave Carabiniere in the station along with his lawyer, Margaret McCluskey. According to Stephan Alexeyev, you are trying to pin a murder on him."

This was the most jaw dropping statement Shona had ever heard. On many fronts. It took several seconds before she could utter a word. "The man is in charge of a ward up at Narrywells, how on earth can he be employed by the Alexeyevs?" The chief opened his mouth to talk but Shona barrelled on. "And I did not try to pin a murder on him. I was asking questions of him as a witness. You can check the video recordings." Her voice rose with every word.

"Calm down, Inspector. They informed me he is a security guard at their nightclub." He straightened the pen and notebook on his desk before saying, "I believe you about the interview. I will not be looking at the videos." He looked her directly in the eye. "Unless you give me a reason to change my mind. Do I make myself clear?"

Yes, Sir. Thank you."

"Stay out of the Alexeyevs way. That will be all."

On the way out of the door she asked, "Has Ex Lord Provost George Brown been in touch at all?"

The chief looked up frowning. "Why do you want to know about him? You haven't upset him as well, have you?"

"Not at all, Sir, but Pa Broon and the Alexeyevs seem to be joined at the hip."

"DI McKenzie, I'm warning you. Tone it down and keep on everyone's good side. I haven't got time to be soothing ruffled feathers."

"Sorry, Sir." She quit while she was ahead.

7

"You're telling us Cat's Eyes is back in the middle of our investigation?" Abigail spoke for them all. Peter and Iain appeared too traumatised to respond; the others hadn't returned from their trip to find Jimmy.

"Yep. And the Kalashnikov brothers."

They all sat and pondered this revelation. Shona broke the silence. "If Dave is in cahoots with the Alexeyevs I am going to be all over his business like botulism. The minute Roy reappears, tell him I need to speak with him.

"Aye, Ma'am." Peter's voice wasn't its usual booming self. Even her stoic sergeant had his breaking point.

Jimmy, a skinny little runt with missing teeth and greasy hair, did not look like a man who would be related to the elegant Anastasia Drummond. Nor did he look, or sound like someone who was keen to help them with their enquiries. They dragged him, kicking and screaming, into an interview room. Shona asked how they'd managed to get him here given the fact he was a witness, not a suspect? At this point anyway.

"He's been charged with assault to actual bodily harm of a police officer," said Jason.

"Good grief man, which part of your anatomy is injured now?"

"Not my anatomy - Roy's. He's currently icing his crown jewels in the toilets. Jimmy kicked him right in the todger."

She groaned. This pair couldn't seem to walk out of the office without sustaining an injury of some sort. It was usually Jason. They had more accident forms on him than the rest of Police Scotland put together. "TMI Jason. Is he okay?"

"He's fine. A bit of ice and he'll be a new man."

She sent Roy to Narrywells anyway. It never paid to be too careful given the plentiful blood supply to that particular area of a man's anatomy.

Shona switched on the video camera in the interview room and read the preliminaries, so he knew his rights.

"What the fu—"

Shona stepped in. "I'd ask you to keep it clean."

"Says, who? Since when did Dundee police get so prissy?" Despite his looks has voice held the cultured tone of a well-educated man.

"Says, me. It's my nick and I get to make the rules. Now ask your question without cursing."

"What have you dragged me in here for?"

"Originally, we just wanted to ask you a few questions. Now, you've been arrested for Assault to Actual Injury and hindering a police officer in the course of his duty." She threw that last one in just in case he somehow wriggled out of the assault charge. She also read him his rights again.

"I did not hurt anyone."

"You kicked my constable in the privates."

"It was an accident, and I won't have anyone saying otherwise." He fiddled with the toggles on his hoody, managed to look Shona straight in the eye for a microsecond, then said, "I want a lawyer."

"Do you have a lawyer, and do you have the money to pay for one?" Shona wasn't quite seeing this scenario. Knowing her luck the lawyer would turn out to be Runcie or McCluskey.

His foot beat a staccato rhythm on the floor. "I have a family lawyer and my mother will pay for her to defend me."

This was when it all went downhill. Fast.

"Was your mother Mrs Ann Treacher?'

"What do you mean was?"

"Please answer my question."

"Yes, she's my mother." His eyes flickered around the room and the beat of his foot grew stronger. This man needed a fix.

"I'm sorry to have to tell you your mother is dead."

Jimmy leapt to his feet, screamed, and grabbed Shona by the throat. Jason was on him so fast he, thankfully, didn't have time to squeeze. They soon had him, not only in cuffs but cuffed to the chair. He kept screaming. Shona pressed a button and called for extra help. And a doctor.

Jimmy was helped to a cell. A doctor appeared and injected him with something that calmed him down emotionally, and magically dealt with his withdrawal symptoms.

The doctor also examined Shona and pronounced her fit to carry on working. You'll have a few bruises tomorrow but, otherwise, you'll be fine."

She reported the incident to the chief who was, as she suspected, not amused. "Why does chaos follow you around like a noxious vapour?"

Pompous windbag. Everyone else would say bad smell. She, sensibly, kept her thoughts to herself and said, "This was unforeseen, Sir, but I will do my best to prevent chaos in the future."

"Don't make promises you can't keep." His voice gentler, he

continued, "Make sure you look after that throat. Whisky and honey will soothe it. Let me know immediately if it gets worse."

Shona's flabber was well and truly gasted. "I will, Sir. Thank you."

"Do you need to go home and rest?"

"I wouldn't dream of it, Sir." The chief looked sceptical, so Shona added, "I mean it, Sir. If I went home all I would do is worry about the case."

"Very well."

She sent Nina to buy several large packets of throat Lozenges from one of the chemists in the Overgate and poured herself a cup of coffee. It was time for fifteen minutes well deserved peace and quiet.

8

An hour later Jimmy was back in an interview room freshly lawyered up and with another charge on his sheet. The lawyer, who looked about sixteen, introduced herself as Krysia Nowak. Her name may have been polish but her accent was Scottish through and through. "My client would like to apologise for attacking you."

Her client sat, meek and mild, in a chair next to her, and did look genuinely sorry. Whether that was for himself or for Shona, she wouldn't like to say.

"He does, however, insist that the assault on your constable was an accident."

"I will need to talk to my officers about that and will get back to you." Shona shuffled the papers in front of her. This was more to give her thinking time than anything else.

She turned to Jimmy. "The reason we asked you to come in," then she emphasised, "to begin with was to talk about your mother."

The man's eyes filled with tears. He may be estranged from his family, but it appeared he genuinely loved his mother.

"When did you last see her or speak to her?"

He slouched in his chair but didn't say a word.

"Jimmy, I need you to answer."

The lawyer chipped in. "Answer the question, Mr Treacher."

A reasonable lawyer. Who'd have thought it. Shona wasn't sure she could take much more, first the boss being kind and now this. She was beginning to feel like Alice in Wonderland. If a queen had leapt out screaming, 'Off with her head', it wouldn't have surprised her in the slightest.

Jimmy slurred the words but answered. "I spoke to her four weeks ago."

Well. Well. Well. Shona wasn't expecting that. "And when did you last see her?"

"Four weeks ago."

Shona wondered if battering her head off the desk again would help her. Then decided the only place it would help her to would be the psychiatric unit up in Narrywells. That wouldn't exactly benefit the investigation.

"Prior to that, when was the last time you saw her?"

Jimmy shuffled around in his chair and worried at a hole in his jeans. "Two years ago." He looked up, his eyes desolate. He had the look of a man whose world had fallen apart.

Interesting, thought Shona. What was even more interesting was that Ann Treacher hadn't told her daughter that James was back in her life. She resolved to investigate that further. What were the family dynamics?

"What prompted the reunion after so long?" Shona straightened up some papers and picked up a pen as though ready to write notes. She saw the lawyer' eyes narrow, wondering what she was up to.

Jimmy looked down at his knees without saying a word.

"Jimmy, answer the question," Shona said, her voice sharp enough to cut through the drug induced stupor.

"I needed money." His voice was so low Shona had difficulty understanding.

"Can I clarify, you contacted your mother because you needed money?"

Treacher nodded.

"For the recording, the witness nodded his agreement."

"Surely, you must have needed money prior to this. Why this time?"

After several seconds of silence where the ticking of the clock was the only sound, Shona said, "Come on Jimmy, I'm growing old here."

He stopped the important task of making the hole in his jeans bigger and said, "Because my girlfriend's pregnant."

In the name of all that's holy, who in their right mind would sleep with the miserable specimen of manhood sitting in front of her. The aroma in the cell was enough to choke an elephant. Shona gathered her tattered wits about her and said, "How did your mother take the news?"

"She didn't believe me. She thought I was after money for drugs."

"Now, there's a surprise."

The lawyer perked right up, "There's no need to speak to my client like that."

"Like what? I was quite mild considering your client has just given us a reason for murder."

Her client sat bolt upright. "Murder. You said she'd died. No one said a thing about murder." His voice rose as he said. "You think I murdered her. No way." He started to get up.

"Calm down, and sit down, Jimmy. I'm not saying you murdered her or it would be on your charge sheet along with several other charges you've managed to accrue in the last hour. Don't add another one."

He slammed back into his seat again making it rock.

"Watch the furniture or we'll be adding criminal damage to those charges."

"She can't charge you with that, Mr Treacher, as you had no intent to cause the damage. It was an accident." The lawyer may look like a child, but she certainly knew her stuff when it came to the law.

Shona moved on. "So, your mother refused to give you money. What did you do then?"

"Told her she wouldn't be able to see her grandchild."

"And walked away. I find that hard to believe." Shona didn't give him time to respond. "Did your mother tell you she had cancer and was facing surgery?"

"No. She didn't. If I'd known, I would have tried harder to keep in touch."

Shona believed him. The man didn't know anything. "Do you want your family to know you are safe?"

"They know. Anastasia is paying my lawyer." He worried at a loose piece of skin on his lip. "She's also paying for rehab. I'm going into one when I leave here."

Shona wanted a police presence at that rehab centre, no matter how fancy it was. Jimmy was a flight risk waiting to happen and even if he wasn't guilty of murder there was no way he was disappearing and not facing those assault charges.

"You can stay in a cell until your sister turns up. You've still charges to face and you're staying under the watchful eye of Police Scotland until a court says otherwise."

Jimmy shrugged his shoulders, a man resigned to his fate.

It had been a long day, so Shona sent the team home. When she returned to her office for her coat and handbag there was a large jar of Manuka honey on her table with a note saying it was from the chief. Well, colour her surprised, the chief might not be quite so bad after all. At home she ate the Chinese takeaway she bought on the way home and prepared that whisky with honey. She then phoned her mother to catch up on all the news from Oxford. Sometimes Oxford seemed a haven of peace and quiet after all the goings on in Dundee. At the rate she was investigating suspicious deaths, Dundee would have so few inhabitants left, it would be downgraded from a city to a village. Shakespeare, her cat, somehow sensing all wasn't well in Shona's world, cuddled in next to her, purring fit to bust. The homely scenario brightened her world considerably. She considered ringing Douglas but decided her throat wouldn't hold up to more talking, especially wedding talk. She grabbed the TV remote and settled in for some mindless viewing.

9

The figure moved through the corridors with practiced ease, knowing every inch of every one of them intimately. Corridors others had forgotten. Knowing the terrain was part of their plan. Knowing who worked and resided under its roof was also part of the plan. Everything was meticulously worked out. The targets carefully chosen. Everything needed in place and available at any opportune moment. They blended into their surroundings seamlessly, one tiny cog in the giant machine that was the medical world. This was the perfect way to kill and get away with it. They smiled. The first in many years.

10

Usually, when Shona was knee deep in a case, she was awoken at stupid o'clock by a ringing phone or loud banging on the door. This time, much to her surprise, she was able to switch off the alarm, go for a brisk run, and scarf down breakfast and a couple of cups of dark roast coffee. She drove to the office with the windows down, listening to Radio 4. It was almost pleasant.

Almost. She'd no sooner put her handbag down and taken one arm out of a jacket than the phone rang; Mary had an update. There are a possible three cases from around Scotland. As they were isolated incidents, no one had bothered looking into them at the time. However, they could be part of a pattern."

"Did you need to ruin my perfect day?" Shona shrugged the coat off the other arm and, cradling the phone between shoulder and ear, hung the jacket up.

"Now you know how I feel. I'll email through the cases, and you can decide if they are worth investigating."

After hanging up she went to thank the chief for the honey, which must have cost him an arm and two legs, and break the news that the case might be a lot larger and more widespread than they thought."

"Why does that not surprise me. Nothing is ever simple or quick when you're involved. Are you going to be chasing around the country?"

"Not yet, Sir, and possibly not at all. I'll ask the local force to investigate."

"Just as well. Keep me updated." She was dismissed in the usual fashion by him ignoring her. Given his recent gift, she couldn't even cheer herself up by imagining his death.

She gathered the entire team in the briefing room, alongside various beverages and a couple of plates of bacon rolls. Shona, despite having breakfast already, couldn't resist a roll. It was healthier than the average as Doreen, in deference to Peter's previous heart attack, had grilled bacon medallions and not used butter. The roll was still perfection on a plate.

After an update on the previous day's progress, they agreed they had made very little progress. Most of the families were not particularly concerned. Death happened. It was devastating but they just wanted to get the funeral over with and get on with their lives. This was a blessing for the families but didn't help them in the slightest. They had all the funeral dates and Shona would be attending every last one of them. The thought of that made her stomach churn. All that grief.

"Roy, I want you to look into Dave Carabiniere. Leave no stone unturned."

"How deep?"

"So deep you can tell me the colour of his underpants."

Roy leapt to his feet.

"Not so fast. We're not finished in here."

He turned the chair round and sat facing the back. A man ready to make a fast getaway. Roy was never happier than when he was digging around in the bowels of the dark web. She'd suggested he become a forensic computer analyst, but he refused. Said he loved what he did here. Sometimes she wondered, but he had improved over the years and came in useful most of the time. When he and Jason were playing nice with each other that was. It was like working in a children's nursery sometimes.

She told them Jimmy's surprising news. "Nina and Abigail, I need you to bring the girlfriend in for a chat." She shoved a piece of paper across the table. "Here's her address. Her name is Sheila Baird."

"Is she a junkie as well? Might need one of the boys if she is as she might not come quietly."

"Iain, you can go with them."

"Right you are."

She handed a sheet of paper to Peter. "These are the names of a couple of patients who died with no known cause. Both were recovering well before they ended up on a table in the mortuary."

Pater glanced at the details. "Inverness and The Borders. What are we concerning ourselves with these for. They're no' our area."

"We're not. Still, do a general search on the internet – something might fall out. I'm off to ring my opposite numbers in both areas and ask them to dig a bit deeper. See if anything turns up."

They dispersed to the four winds.

The first call was to Hamish Strachan in Inverness. "It's yourself, Shona. How can I help you?"

"I've a strange case on my hands." She gave him a potted history. "I'd like you to look into the death of a fifty-nine-year-old woman who died in Raigmore hospital. Apparently, your pathologist couldn't work out the exact cause of death. She'd been in following a pulmonary embolism."

"My, lassie, you like to make work. Have we all not enough work on our hands without worrying about those who are buried in God's good earth?"

"You're right but I need to ascertain if there's a link."

"Of course, I'll help. You owe me a couple of glasses of The Balvenie at the next Inspector's conference."

"At five-thousand quid a bottle. I don't think so. I'll buy you a couple of Taliskers."

He laughed. "It was worth a try."

She repeated the scenario with the Borders then headed back to the main office. Roy was head down, fingers flying over the keyboard.

"Anything yet?" she asked.

Roy shook his head without looking up. A man focussed on his task. "Nothing much for either of the new women you asked about. The usual obituary – died suddenly, in hospital etc. One of them was big into raising money for charity. Put dinners and events on to raise money for cancer. The other, not a dickie bird about her."

"We'll leave it to the local police forces then. I'm sure they'll be in touch if they find anything suspicious."

She addressed the rest of the team. "See if you can work out any relationship whatsoever between all the dead women, including the ones in Inverness and the Borders."

Peter grabbed his mug and stood up. "That sounds like thirsty work. Anybody else want anything?" He took orders and headed to the kitchen.

Shona followed.

She poured herself a cup of sludge, that being all that was left in the coffee pot and slung it in the microwave. "What are your thoughts on all of thi?."

Peter shook his head. "I've no thoughts at all, Ma'am. All this silent killer stuff is no' your usual Dundee murder." He picked up the kettle and poured water in the pot. "I like something you can see. A body in situ at least gives us a starting point."

Shona sighed and took a gulp of coffee. "Flaming, Nora that was hot." She grabbed a glass of water and swigged it down.

"You might want to be careful wi' that coffee."

"You think. Anyway, I'm with you. There's nothing we can get our teeth into. It's all paperwork and interviews."

They gazed into their respective drinks for a few minutes. "Let's see if the others have found anything.

"It's only been five minutes. They're polis, not miracle workers."

Shona threw her head back and laughed. "I can always rely on you, Peter.

Not only had Sheila Baird come willingly but was a complete shock. Shona, expecting another down on her luck drug addict, was faced with a well-dressed, well-groomed young woman. The shock must have shown on Shona's face, because the woman said, "What were you expecting to see?"

Shona gave herself a mental shake. "Thank you for coming in, Miss Baird. Did my sergeants explain why we wanted to talk with you?"

"Yes. About James. I haven't seen him for weeks, so I'm not quite sure how much help I will be." She looked down then, her hands flying to her stomach, looked up and said, "He's not dead, is he?" Her eyes widened in fear.

They were back to James again. Also, another woman who cared whether he was dead or alive. Who was this man? "No, not at all. He's alive and in our cells."

"How is he?"

"He's fine, or as fine as someone who's in withdrawal can be."

Sheila's eyes clouded over. "He's been clean for over a year. He has a job. Why would he go back on the gear now?"

"That's something you will have to ask him." The next question wasn't strictly necessary, but Shona couldn't hold back her curiosity. "How did you meet him?"

"You mean, how did someone like me get knocked up by a junkie." Despondency had been replaced by anger. "I work with drug addicts, helping them get clean and staying that way. He was one of our success stories."

"When, exactly, did you last see him?"

Silence descended as the woman rubbed her stomach and thought. "Four weeks ago. I know it was then as we'd just started telling people about the baby." Tears gave up the struggle to stay contained and poured down her face. "We were happy. Why would he go back on drugs now? It doesn't make any sense."

It made perfect sense to Shona. She decided to throw the poor woman a bone. "It seems like he did it just after he met his mother."

This stopped the tears dead in their tracks. "Why would he meet his mother? He wanted nothing to do with his family."

"Why?" Shona couldn't get her head around any of this. "They seem fairly pleasant and respectable."

Sheila's voice rose. "Respectable? There's nothing respectable about a father systematically raping his son from the age of seven until he left home. There's nothing respectable about a mother who turned a blind eye to that rape. Think about that and then talk about respectable."

Shona sat back in her chair. Yet another reason for murder. She made a snap decision. "Would you like to see Jimmy." She took in the woman's face. "I mean James."

"Yes, I would."

Shona only hoped he was compos mentis enough to speak to her.

Walking back to the office Nina said, “I wasn't expecting any of that. What a surprise.”

“Surprise! It was mind blowing.”

“I thought you said Jimmy's sister was paying for rehab. I wonder if his girlfriend knows he's back in the bosom of his family.”

“I'd bet my pension on the fact she doesn't. Those women will be battling for supremacy in his life.”

“Poor sod.”

“Indeed. Although I'd like his tale to end with a happy family vibe.” Shona followed Nina into the main office.

11

"How are the searches going? Did any of the women have anything, or anyone in common?"

Peter indicated to Abigail she could take the lead. "Diana Catchington and Ann Treacher went to the same school but weren't in the same year. They might have known each other from groups or societies but I'd have to dig deeper into that."

"Good idea. Anything else?"

Peter took over. "Lara Moon and Sarah McTaggart go to the same church."

"Doesn't one live in Dundee and the other in Perthshire? How can they attend the same church?"

"People have cars these days, Ma'am." Peter threw her an are you barmy look. "And, just in case you hadn't noticed, Dundee City and Perthshire are snuggled up to each other like Siamese twins."

"And so are Dundee City and Angus." Roy chipped in.

"No need to be facetious."

Peter's look said he begged to differ, but he kept his mouth shut.

"What about you, Roy?"

"Do you think we'd get a warrant to look into Dave Carabiniere's bank account?"

"I very much doubt it, but I'll give it my best shot. Have you found anything else out about him?"

"Can I give you it altogether?"

"Keep me in suspense, why don't you. Sure, but today would be good."

She left them to it and tried her luck with the Sherriff.

"Have you gone out of your mind, Shona? The man is a witness, not a suspect."

"He's tied up with the Alexeyevs so I'd say he's got something to hide."

"Taking on an extra job to earn a crust is not an offence in Scotland. Even if said job is for the Alexeyevs."

"They're a couple of gangsters."

"Not according to their record – that states they are legitimate businessmen."

She sighed. "Thank you, Sherriff Struthers. I'll come back when I have more to go on."

"You do that, Shona, and I will be happy to provide your warrant then."

Roy just shrugged his shoulders. "Do you want me to go in the less legal way?"

"No way. Keep this strictly legal or we'll not only be doomed but sacked and facing trial."

"Okay."

It worried Shona that Roy was an expert hacker. She'd never had the nerve to ask how it came about. The possible answer scared her.

Back in her office she sat down and updated everything they knew about the case so far. Quite literally clueless, she had not one shred of an idea as to where to go next. She never thought she'd find herself longing for a dead body she could see and feel, the bloodier the better. This silent killer stuff was harder than her previous seven cases put together. And they were hard. She pulled out the staff rotas again to see if they'd missed anything. Nothing. She made a decision, stood up and grabbed her car keys. Poking her head around the office door she announced, "I'm off to see Mary."

A couple of them nodded but most were bent to their task.

Mary was halfway through a post-mortem, so Shona made herself a coffee and took it to the pathologist's office, where she plonked herself down in a comfortable armchair. She grabbed a couple of biscuits from the stash in Mary's drawer and picked up a magazine. Twenty minutes mindless activity would do her, and the case, a power of good. She settled back.

Mary soon bustled into the office, all four foot ten inches of her exuding professionalism and efficiency.

"Well, if it isn't the Grim Reaper herself. Come with me to the kitchen. I'm parched with a brain screaming for caffeine." Seconds later she poured herself a cup of coffee, topped up Shona's and set to refilling the pot.

Shona took a gulp and said, "You're the one swimming in dead bodies this time. I've nothing to do with them."

"They're in your orbit."

"Jeez. Everyone's a critic." Once they were settled back in Mary's office, Shona asked, "I'm curious as to what makes you think there's foul play?"

"I can't put my finger on it. There's nothing out of the ordinary, although I wasn't looking for anything out of the ordinary to start with." She paused and took a sip of her coffee. "One such death you let it slip past. Two and you wonder. Three and you start to see a pattern."

"Did you do any tests for suspicious substances?"

"Not to start with. I just put natural causes on the death certificate. By the third one, I was digging a bit deeper."

"And?"

"And nothing. I came up empty handed."

"I thought you were meant to be some sort of poison expert."

"So did I. This has me stumped."

"You and me both. Where do we start?" Shona stood up ready to go. "It would really help if you could find something that links all the deaths. Any substance whatsoever."

"I'm fresh out of miracles."

"Shame, I was in the market to purchase several."

I'll give it all I've got."

Shona left, no further forward but knowing if there was an answer, Mary would find it.

12

She returned to find Adanna Okifor lounging in her office sipping Rooibos tea from a chipped mug. Shona, who'd grown to like the woman, despite her loathing of journalists, said, "What are you cluttering the place up for?"

Adanna, the most cheerful person on the planet, laughed, showing dazzling white teeth. A beautiful black woman, she was a vision in yellow, brightening the room up in more ways than one. "Well, there's not much of a crime scene to attend, so your office it is."

"How in the freaking heck do you know we're working a case?"

The journalist tapped her nose with an elegantly French polished fingernail. "I can't give away my sources."

"And I won't be giving you any information."

"Touché." She took another sip of tea and said, "Someone at the hospital gave me a tip off."

"They're a right loose lipped lot."

"It's a hospital. The staff canteen's packed full of people chatting about their day. The art of conversation is alive and well and settling in comfortably in Narrywells." She took another soothing sip of the Rooibos.

"And a journalist who just happens to be drinking tea and eating cake. Oh, and don't forget listening in to those conversations."

"It's not my fault they allow anyone to use it. Any chance of a scoop."

"Sit tight. I'll be back in a minute."

"Have you solved the case?" The chief looked at her over the rim of his spectacles.

"I'm afraid not, Sir."

"Then, why are you bothering me? Have you any new information?"

"No, Sir." *Three bags full, Sir.* "I was wondering if we should put out a press release. The rumour mill is starting up at the hospital."

"Are you crazy? Have you finally gone stark raving mad? There's nothing to say in a press release yet and we don't want to tip our hand."

"That's what I thought, Sir. Best to be sure."

"Go and solve the blasted case and stop wittering about press releases." The chief went back to his computer, and she left the room wondering if she could possibly find whatever poison was being used and employ it on the chief. This thought cheered her up considerably.

She broke the news to Adanna that there was nothing to report quite yet, and the chief would have them both put up against a wall and shot if anything was reported.

Adanna's take on it was, "I'm a reporter and your chief doesn't own me." Her grin took the sting out of her words.

Shona wasn't fooled. The journalist would report something; she just hoped it would not jeopardise her investigation. If she was honest, she trusted Adanna to do the right thing. The woman had integrity. Yes, she reported the news, it was her job after all, but she did so in a way that didn't leave relatives, and the police, wretched and baying for her blood.

The staff room was completely empty when she got there. She looked at her watch and realised it was lunch time. She headed to the staff canteen which was also empty. Strange. She pulled out her phone which she realised was on silent. There was a missed call and a voice message. They'd gone to the pub for a different form of stodge. She sent a text saying she'd eat at the station and not to take too long. She bought a huge plate of steak pie and followed it up with dumpling and custard. She'd make the most of the fact Peter, and his healthy eating, were well out of sight. The case was moving slow as the Dichty Burn in summer and a short hiatus wasn't going to hurt anyone.

"Or would it?"

13

They were welcomed in, turned down a cup of tea, and went about their business efficiently and quickly. No stone left unturned. On completion, they waved goodbye to the occupants and left. That was the plan. But the plan changed. They did not leave but remained, hidden from sight, waiting for an opportune moment. Nature changed the plan once more. No longer able to hide they stepped from the cupboard to the hallway. The door creaked.

"Who's that?"

The figure moved into the sitting room.

"What are you doing back?"

"Did you forget something?

"Yes, he stooped as though to pick something from the floor and plunged the syringe into the nurse's thigh. He was dead before he hit the floor.

"What?" The woman tried to stand. The figure pushed her down, another syringe and the woman collapsed in her chair.

They stepped outside the door, went to a corner of the garden, and relieved themselves. Urges may not be acted upon immediately, but they were always acted upon. Always.

14

She'd no sooner scraped the last mouthful of custard from the bottom of the plate than her mobile rang. "McKenzie."

The desk sergeant was his usual cheerful self. "You've had a shout, Ma'am. Couple of dead bodies in a cottage just outside Liff."

"You've got to be kidding me. I've enough on my plate with the case I've got without adding any more to the pile."

"I hear you. Here's the address. She grabbed a pen, wrote it down and stood up."

Then she dialled Nina's number and broke the news they'd have to leave their steak and chips and head to Liff.

Once she was suitably suited and booted, Sergeant Muir, the POLSA, ushered her past the crime scene tape. The first of her team to arrive, she entered the cottage and, treading carefully, looked around. The home was pristine and seemed a haven of tranquillity; apart from the two dead bodies in the sitting room. Although even they didn't clutter the place up. The perfect epitome of 'she looked peaceful' the standard way of describing death. An elderly woman sat in an armchair, looking like she was asleep. The only anomaly was a bandage on her leg and a walking stick leaning on the chair. A young man lay on the floor. Not a speck of blood was to be seen. Not a wound to be found, unless there was a wound under the bandage, which was a strange place for attacking someone if you wanted them dead. *What the heck. Were they back to the embalming? Why did all her cases have to be as crazy as all get out?*

A human whirlwind blew into the room in the shape of an elfin woman who bristled with energy. Whitney the police surgeon was a force of nature who radiated joy despite her job. "Afternoon. Haven't seen you in a while. I was beginning to think you'd moved on and things had settled down."

Shona had a reputation as the Grim Reaper of Dundee but had long ago stopped trying to defend herself. She shrugged and said, "Nope. You're stuck with me."

Whitney examined the man, quickly and efficiently. She jotted down a few notes, ripped a page from her pad and handed it to Shona. Then she repeated this with the woman. "Definitely dead but I've no clue what killed them. A job for Mary. I'd hazard a guess, with you involved, it's nefarious purposes." She was out the door before Shona could open her mouth to respond.

She exhausts me. I must be getting old, thought Shona.

The team tipped up within about five minutes. They were as mystified as her. "I thought we'd maybe have something to get our teeth into." Peter spoke for them all.

"Do you think this is tied into the hospital deaths?" Abigail said, her voice tentative.

"Nothing is beyond the realms of possibility but I'm not seeing it at the moment." Shona shook her head and bent down to take a closer look at the scene. "Let's not rule it out though. Iain, I need photographs. Once that's done, look for fingerprints and look for blood."

"There's not a spot of blood to be seen." Roy stood in the doorway, looking on, as there wasn't enough space for even one more foot to enter, never mind a whole person.

"You're right, but we're treating this crime scene with all the respect it deserves."

"It disnae look much like a crime scene from where I'm standing."

"The two dead bodies say otherwise and as it's been reported as a crime, we treat it as such until we're told to drop the case."

They all cleared out to allow Iain to take photographs of the area, dust for prints, and spray luminol around. Then, Shona joined him again. Not a bit of blood to be found, except a bit on the corner of the television. She wasn't entirely sure that had much to do with the investigation, but she had to rule it out officially. Wild hunches didn't play well in court. Luminol highlighted every speck of blood, regardless of how well scrubbed a place was, so it was obvious nothing to do with blood had gone down here. Iain had treated the whole house and it was spotless.

Shona was beginning to wonder if Tesco was hiring. She'd had a gutful of her job.

"Who found them?"

Everyone shrugged. Shona headed in the direction of Sgt Muir to find out. "The woman's daughter. She's in one of the police cars."

"Do we have names for the victims and the daughter? "The female victim's name is Elsie Dalhousie. Her daughter is Faith Dalhousie. We've no clue who the man is." You knew where you stood with Sgt Muir even if he was a man of few words.

Shona headed in the direction of the police car the POLSA pointed out. A woman, her head in her hands, sat in the passenger seat. A young policeman, looking distinctly uncomfortable, sat in the driver's seat. He leapt out when she approached. "I'll leave you to it, Ma'am," and he bolted like a ferret after a rabbit.

He's not up for a career in police liaison then. More your chase 'em and catch 'em type. Shona had learned to read all types of coppers during her long career and had a hunch he'd be a fabulous beat bobby for her whole career.

"Ms Dalhousie?"

"Dr Dalhousie." She scrubbed tears from her eyes with the back of her hands.

Interesting. "Do you work up at Narrywells?"

"No. I'm a Doctor of Chemistry. I work at St. Andrews University as a Teaching Fellow."

"Thank you for clarifying. I believe the woman in the cottage is your mother?"

"Yes. Yes, she is." The tears restarted and poured down her face.

Shona rummaged around in the glove compartment, pulled out a packet of tissues and handed it over. The woman tugged one out and dabbed at her face. Mascara now well and truly covered her eyes and cheeks. Shona supposed the doctor wasn't too bothered about it smudging when she applied it that morning.

"I believe it was you who found them? Do you know who the man is, and did you call an ambulance?"

"Yes, I found them. The man is a stranger, and I did call an ambulance."

Shona wondered where the ambulance crew were now. She didn't have long to wait for an answer. "The paramedics called the police."

Shona made a note to contact the paramedics for interview.

"What brought you to your mother's house?"

The woman swallowed and answered fairly calmly given the circumstances. "She's not long out of hospital, so I try to visit every day. I took an early knock off to bring her some shopping."

Shona's spidey senses pricked up. "Was she in Narrywells by any chance?"

"Yes. Why do you keep asking about Narrywells?" The woman glared at her. "You're obsessed."

Shona kept her voice low and soothing. "I appreciate it may seem like that, but I need to ask odd questions to get to the bottom of things."

Dr Dalhousie took some deep breaths and said, "She was in hospital for two weeks with an infected varicose ulcer. She got out two days ago once we got home help, carer, district nurse and meals on wheels in place."

There must have been people crawling all over the place, each one of whom was a professional. None of them were top of the list as murder suspects but she'd have to interview them."

"Was there anything out of place when you arrived? Any strange smells? Anything different? Was the carbon monoxide monitor shrieking?"

"Apart from the strange man in the living room you mean? He was definitely out of place." Her voice rose, "And I want to know what he was doing in my mother's house."

"As do we, Doctor. Please can you give us the names and contact details for the home help. We will need to interview them. Which Meals on Wheels company did you use?" She handed over a notebook and the woman wrote down what she needed.

Shona could see a lot of interviews in her future.

Back in the cottage, Peter said, "Yon man's phone keeps ringing."

"Did you answer?"

"No. I didnae want to alert anyone to the death."

"Good point. I'll give the number a ring and see what they say."

She retired to the kitchen, where it was a bit less cluttered up with police and pressed the last missed call. The caller had made five attempts to contact their unidentified body.

"District Nursing Service. How can I help?"

So, it looked like their victim was a district nurse. "This is Detective Inspector Shona McKenzie from Police Scotland. You have been ringing this number trying to contact it."

"That wasn't me. Let me pass you on to my supervisor."

There was a delay and then, "Charge Nurse Lemongrass. Why are you ringing from Staff Nurse Sentinel's phone? Can you put him on as his next client is waiting. If he's a witness to anything, can you interview him later?"

"I'm sorry but he cannot come to the phone at the moment."

The phone went silent and then, "Why not. What's he done this time.' She cleared her throat. "How am I meant to find someone for his list today?"

This time. Interesting. He'd obviously done something before.

"I appreciate this is a lot to take in. Can you give us your address and we will come to see you." She listened to the response. "No, it cannot wait." More from the other end of the line and Shona responded, "My sergeant will be there within the hour and won't take much of your time."

She instructed Peter and sent him in the direction of the District Nursing Team with a picture of the dead man's face on his iPhone. "See if this is their missing district nurse, although I strongly suspect it is."

"Aye, Ma'am, I would have to agree."

Shona phoned Mary. "There are two bodies coming in your direction."

"So, you're adding another case to your portfolio? Two at once is a record, even for you."

"I'm not sure I am. I'll leave it to you to decide."

15

Back at the office, Shona busied herself making a map of all the victims and the places they had died. Then, she used red string to signify relationships. It sadly lacked in detail. She sat down and contemplated it, but the altered view did not help.

Peter barged through the door with news of a definitive on their dead man. As she suspected, they'd already worked out Sentinel was dead by the time Peter got there. They had also given him a name and address for Staff Nurse Malcolm Sentinel's next of kin. "It's his wife, Donna. He's got three bairns, all under the age of five."

This fact made Shona sick to her stomach. The thought of three fatherless kids was never going to make for a great day.

"Nina and Abigail. Go and speak to the wife. We need to break the news of her husband's death and figure out if he knew any of our other victims. Peter, can you get Charge Nurse Lemongrass in. I want to ask her some questions."

"She'll no' be happy. She complained the whole time I was there she was too busy for this."

"Ask her to come in the minute her shift is finished. That should focus her."

"And if she disnae want to come in?"

"We arrest her for hindering a police officer in the course of her duty."

"Aye, although we're using that a lot this time."

"That's because nobody in this bally case is keen to help the police with their enquiries. What happened to civic duty?"

Peter, thinking it was wisest not to answer, merely picked up the phone. He thought civic duty disappeared out the door years ago.

He was right, Sonia Lemongrass was not keen to help with their enquiries. "I've had a long day, and you drag me in here."

Given it was only 4 pm, Shona had a sneaking suspicion she'd suddenly found time to knock off early and come to the station. Funny what the thought of losing personal time could do for clearing a schedule. Even one where they were one staff nurse down.

They provided her with a coffee and Shona joined her in a cup, in an attempt to make things more relaxed. "I have to record this interview but would like to make it clear, you are a witness, not a suspect." Shona always wondered at those words as everyone was a suspect until proven otherwise, but she had to say them.

"Can you tell us a little bit about your staff nurse."

"Shouldn't you be asking his wife that?"

Why was every interview like pulling teeth with broken pliers? Was there anyone in the world who could answer a question without getting antsy? "We are asking his wife that. However, we would also like your perspective."

"Do I need a lawyer?"

"You are entitled to have a lawyer present but why on God's

good earth would you need one? I've told you, you're not under suspicion. I just want to get a clearer picture of the dead man." Shona's patience had left the building.

"He was a good nurse. Pleasant, the patients liked him. Did his job well."

"Thank you, that's helpful." She casually put her arms on the table, hands clasped and said, "So, why did you say what has he done *this time*?"

The woman paled. "Nothing. I didn't mean anything."

"I would suggest that's not the case. Please can you answer the question? When it comes to murder, hiding things is never the answer."

"I want my lawyer."

"Of course. Interview stopped at 4.15 pm as the witness requested a lawyer be present."

The lawyer hadn't even had time to arrive before the boss requested her presence in his office. "I believe you have Ex Lord Provost Brown's cousin in the cells."

"I knew it could only be a matter of time before Pa Broon was all over this." She took in his narrowed eyes and continued before he could lambast her. "If you're talking about Sonia Lemongrass, she's not in the cells. She's a witness and she's drinking coffee and eating chocolate digestives in the families' room."

"The Ex Lord Provost thinks your persecuting her."

"Persecuting! It's a few questions about one of her colleagues, not the Spanish inquisition."

"Rein in that legendary sarcasm of yours and be polite. Margaret McCluskey will be reporting everything back to her godfather."

Why anyone would be proud to say Pa Broon was their godfather was a complete mystery to Shona. "I'll be polite and pleasant." She hesitated and added, "I might need a warrant."

"What on earth for? The woman's a witness."

She explained about the question, what had their dead man done this time? "I'm not sure she is going to cough up the answer, especially with Margaret McCluskey on the case. I'm sure patient confidentiality will come into it."

"See what you can find out without a warrant. If needed, we'll get one."

She was left looking at his bald head, his usual way of dismissing her. Oh, well. At least he hadn't lambasted her this time and seemed to be supportive. Maybe he was mellowing.

Margaret McCluskey billowed into the station like a ship in full sail. She was her usual bombastic self. "This is outrageous. Preposterous. My client came in willingly to help you and you treat her like a criminal."

"Your client is drinking coffee and eating biscuits while thumbing through magazines on a comfortable sofa. I wouldn't call that treating her like a criminal."

"You detained her."

"No, I didn't. She is free to leave at any time. However, I do need to ask questions and you don't want me to think about charging her with hindering—"

"I would like to see my client."

"With the greatest of pleasure." Shona gritted her teeth and showed McCluskey to the relatives' room. This politeness lark was killing her.

Ten minutes, and one cup of hastily gulped coffee, later, she was back in the interview room."

"Thank you for coming in Mrs McCluskey. I'm sure my witness is reassured by your presence."

McCluskey glared at her. Shona could almost see the cogs

in the lawyer's head whirring as she tried to work out where all this was going. Politeness wasn't Shona's usual go to when faced with McCluskey or her brother.

"Please tell us everything you know about Malcolm Sentinel."

"I don't know much about him. He was married with children. Did his job well. The clients liked him."

"Did he have anything to do with Narrywells Hospital?"

"We all do. We need to liaise with them about patient discharge and care packages."

A lightbulb went off in Shona's head. "Did he do bank work up there?"

"Not that I'm aware of. He might do. You know as well as everyone that money is tight, and our wages aren't going as far."

You're telling me, thought Shona. The only thing she could say about her wages was that she never got time to spend them, and she and the team worked such long hours the overtime practically doubled their income. She picked up a pen and made a note to ask the wife about bank nursing.

"What was he doing at Elsie Dalhousie's cottage?"

The woman looked at her solicitor, who said, "That comes under patient confidentiality. My client doesn't have to answer."

"I know you're not the brightest lawyer in the bunch, but patient confidentiality dies with the patient. This is looking like a murder investigation, so your client does have to answer." Shona tapped her fingers on the table. "And if we could hurry it up, we'd all get to go home for our tea."

McCluskey looked like she'd sucked a particularly nasty lemon but instructed her client to answer."

"She had a large varicose ulcer on her leg, and he was dressing it."

Something puzzled Shona. Why was the dressing undisturbed and where was his nursing bag? She assumed he had one."

"Do your nurses carry equipment bags with them when they go on a call?"

"Of course. They'd be hard pushed to do their job without one."

"If you will excuse me for a moment, I just need to ask someone to check on something."

Margaret McCluskey said, "We haven't got time for this." She was speaking to Shona's retreating back.

Shona grabbed Nina and said, "Check Malcolm Sentinel's car, wherever it is. See if there are any medical supplies in there."

She returned to the interview room. "Apologies for the interruption. Mrs Lemongrass, can you please tell me what you meant when you said, 'What has he done this time'?"

The charge nurse looked at her lawyer again who said, "You should answer."

Good grief, the world really has gone topsy-turvy if the battleship McCluskey is being helpful. Shona wasn't sure she could take any more surprises.

The woman looked down and chewed on her lip. "There was a complaint made against him a few weeks ago. A woman said he stole her bracelet."

"And he was still visiting houses?" Shona said, her voice rising several decibels in astonishment.

His boss sat up straight and leaned forward slightly. "The woman has early onset Alzheimer's. Her daughter thought she probably misplaced it."

"Did anyone report it to us?"

She looked down again. "No."

"Is it being investigated by your department or the trust?"

Head still down, she said, "No." Then she looked up again and added, "The daughter didn't want it going any further."

Shona wondered why not. Did the daughter have anything to hide? Now she'd have to look into that as well. She sighed and said, "Thank you. You've been very helpful. You are free to go." She took in the woman's weary face and added, "I know you've had a tough day. I am sorry I had to add to it. I am grateful for all that nurses do."

The woman smiled. Thank you. It's been the day from hell." Her eyes filled with tears. "I hope I never have to repeat it."

"You and me both."

16

Moving, always moving. Making sure no one could find you. No one could guess where you would be next. One step ahead of authority. Thinking on your feet. Staying away from trouble – under the radar. Trust no one. Ever.

Look out for yourself. Make the most of every opportunity. This was the way the figure lived their life. No one knowing who they really were or what they were doing. This suited them now. It made life easier. Live your life on the fringes. Watch, wait, listen.

It had not always been this way. Their childhood seemed idyllic to the casual observer. Their mother would bake, and all the village children would sit in the garden soaking in the heat of the sun, eating pastries, their hands sticky with honey from their parents' hives. These would be washed down with warm goat's milk straight from the teat, to the urn, to the glass. They would play amongst the trees in their parents' orchard. Their father went to work each day, came home tired with a large smile on his face. Their mother tended their home and looked after the children. A childhood anyone would envy.

Then the world changed.

17

"I swear, every person we come across in this bally investigation has something to hide. "Why the heck does everyone need a lawyer for a few simple questions?"

Shona's stomach was telling her they should all be free to go home to their loved ones as well, but it wasn't going to happen. The bodies flew in thick and fast, no matter where they originated. She tapped her fingers on her desk. She wanted and needed Mary's take on the two bodies today, but there was no way on earth she was going to get it. Mary would have them tucked up in refrigerated drawers and she would be on her way home for *her* tea. They were the only sad sacs.

The team were keen on pizza and phoned an order in. They were promised them in thirty minutes, delivered to the front desk. Jason volunteered to hang around in reception and race them straight up.

"Roy. Any, update on Dave Carabiniere?"

"Looks like our Dave likes playing around, a bit of a wide boy to all intents and purposes. Also living high on the hog. Way above his pay grade."

Shona propped her chin on her hand. "Hence the second

job." Her eyes narrowed as she added, "You did come by all of this legally?"

"Yes, Ma'am, of course." The look in his eyes said otherwise but Shona let it slide. She'd take it up later. "I used social media. You'd be amazed about what you can find out on all those platforms."

"That is exactly why I'm not on them. No way am I letting everyone know my business."

"I'm wi' you, Shona, although my lassie has me on Facebook. I thought you were on there."

"My account's locked up tighter than an otter's pocket and I'm only friends with you lot and my family. Anyway, much as I'd love to discuss this, anything else about Dave?"

"I'll go and fetch printouts and we can all see the full extent of his shenanigans," Roy said.

By the time he reappeared the pizza was on the table, and they were tucking in. He grabbed a large slice and scarfed it down. Shona was reaching for a slice when her mobile rang. "McKenzie." She listened. "Pop him in an interview room."

"What, now? Another witness?" Nina asked.

"I wish. Nope. Auld Jock's here, wants a word with me." Jock was a man of the road, but he'd given up the homeless lifestyle for the sake of a puppy the station had given him. Every month they had a whip round and bought food for the dog.

"He could be a witness. He knows more about Dundee than me." That was hard as there was very little about Dundee that Peter did not know.

Shona swallowed a bite of pizza, then picked up four huge slices and slid them on to a plate. "I'll take them to him. He probably needs a feed."

Jock was waiting for her in an interview room with Fagin, the 'puppy', lying at his feet. He was no longer a puppy but a fully grown Weimaraner. Jock was slurping from a mug of tea and Fagin companionably slurping from a bowl of water. The dog leapt up when he saw her, whining with excitement. She just had time to throw the pizza on the table before Fagin launched himself at her and commenced washing her face with his tongue. She shoved him down and fondled his ears before saying, "Down." The dog obeyed immediately and put his head on his paws.

"What can I do for you, Jock? Are you just her here for a visit and a feed?" She shoved the plate over. "Here, this is for you?"

He pulled the plate closer and reached for a slice of pizza. "I need you to take Fagin for a few days."

"Why? What's up?" Her voice sharper than she intended, she added, "You know I'll help, but why the need?"

He swallowed and said, "My ma's no' well. I've to go and see her."

Shona was gobsmacked to infinity and beyond. She'd known Jock for years and didn't even know he had a mother.

"Your mother?" She gathered her tattered wits. "Where does she live?"

"Inverness."

"Please tell me you're not walking there." Jock hated being indoors, so this was a distinct possibility.

"No. I've got my bus pass, so I'm getting the bus." He rubbed the dog's head and belly and said, "You go wi' Shona, now. I'll see you soon."

The dog leapt up, gave Jock a big lick, and trotted happily over to Shona. She'd had him for a few days when he was a brand-new puppy and was his official on and off foster carer.

"I hope your Mum's okay. I'll be thinking of you."

"If you're a praying woman. A wee prayer would be welcome."

"You've got it. I'll get Peter to light a candle as well."

The team was delighted to see Fagin, a perennial favourite. He greeted each one of them and then lay down and closed his eyes. All this being friendly was exhausting work. Snores accompanied the rest of the meeting.

"Where were we?"

"Roy was updating us on his love life."

"I meant before I left. I see you took my absence seriously and did a lot of work." Sarcasm dripped from every syllable, but her smile softened the words. "Roy, take it away."

"It looks like Dave enjoys a flutter on the gee gees. He regularly attends Perth Racecourse."

"Did you know there used to be a racecourse in Dundee, at Longhaugh?" Peter snagged another slice of Pizza.

"Thanks for the fascinating insight, Peter, but we might want to stick to the case, not have a history lesson."

He grinned. "We wouldn't have had so far to go to investigate if it was still here."

"True that," Roy said. "That's not his only way of haemorrhaging money. "Turns out he's supporting two families." He sat back in his chair as he took in the stunned faces in front of him.

"Well, I'll be hornswoggled." Shona hadn't thought there was anything else that could surprise her today.

"Oor laddie's not as lily white as he paints himself."

Roy leaned forward again. "His wife had a baby six months ago." He paused for dramatic effect and added, "His girlfriend, four months ago."

Shona gathered any remnants of professionalism she had left, and said, "I'd say we have grounds for a warrant. Tomorrow, we'll be crawling all over his financial statements. Tonight, I'd like everyone's thoughts on the case so far."

"They batted ideas round and tossed theories into the air until everyone was too exhausted to formulate another word, never mind idea.

She rang Douglas to say she was on her way over with a

takeaway – she'd only managed to get three bites of pizza - and did anybody want anything. They'd already eaten but could she bring cakes in. She obliged and headed in his direction.

Rory and Alice were delighted to see her. They were even more delighted to see Fagin who was equally delighted to be reunited with his BFFs. Their Dachshund joined in. Rory, now fourteen, was as tall as her. Alice, aged nine, flung herself at Shona and hugged her tight. "When are you going to be my mummy?" She added, an anxious tinge to her voice, "Am I going to be a flower girl? Rosie was a flower girl at her big sister's wedding."

Shona had no clue who Rosie was but being the same as Rosie was obviously important to her future stepdaughter. "Of course, you are, Alice." Damn she would need to have that wedding talk. Not tonight though. Tonight, was for soaking up the atmosphere and relaxing with her future family. And other things, of course, but other things would have to wait until the kids were tucked up in their beds. She left the dog behind with Douglas. His mother would take care of him as well as the kids the next day. Shona had enough on her plate without a rambunctious dog.

18

The next morning brought more sunny skies and general joie de vivre. Until she walked into work, when misery descended like the Sword of Damocles. How was she ever going to solve this blasted case? There was no joined up writing in the slightest, just a bunch of dead women - and one man - with nothing to point to who had done the deed. Even coffee and bacon rolls weren't going to cut it on this one.

Her first task was to ring Mary.

"I haven't even had time to pull one of your victims out of the drawer yet." Mary sounded tetchy - not her usual style.

Her voice soothing, Shona said, "Absolutely. I knew that would be the case. When you have had a chance to do them, can you give me a ring with the results"

The pathologist sounded much more amenable. "Sorry, Shona. I'm up to my neck. I'll get on to them today."

"Thanks. You're the cat's whiskers."

Laughter came from the other end of the phone. "You owe me a drink."

"I owe you a bottle."

She strode towards the office, purpose radiating from every

fibre of her being, hoping if she appeared confident, confidence itself would follow. How she was going to solve this conundrum of a case was completely beyond her. She heard writers often thought their last book would crash their careers. She thought this case would crash hers.

She perched on the edge of Roy's desk. "Scrutinise Malcolm Sentinel, our latest victim. See if he has any links whatsoever to the hospitals we're investigating." She thought for a second and added, "or any links to any of the other victims." Standing up, she added, "I'm going to get warrants to look into Dave's finances and for the District Nursing Team to cough up the name of the woman with Alzheimer's as well as the name of her next of kin."

The Sherriff hummed and hawed but, in the end, rather than erring on the side of caution, decided to side with her. "Mr Carabiniere's finances I can understand but interviewing the poor old dear with memory issues sticks in my craw.

"I will be extremely respectful and work with the utmost professionalism. Her daughter will be there at all times and can stop the interview whenever she chooses. If the daughter says she is not fit to interview, it won't go ahead."

"I'll give you it, on one condition, you tread lightly."

Shona had her warrants. She asked Roy to look into Dave's finances and then invite him in for an interview."

"Aye, Aye, Captain. He turned back to his computer and whistled a cheery tune while he worked.

This drew censure from Peter. "Keep the noise down, I can't hear myself think. Your worse than my lad."

Roy slapped some headphones on and carried on, thankfully, without the whistling.

Shona retreated to her office to ruin another day in the life of Charge Nurse Lemongrass. She arranged to go and see her as she wasn't keen to provide the information without clapping eyes on the warrant. Much as Shona felt irritated that she had to schlep over there, she was impressed with the nurse's commitment to maintaining patient confidentiality.

The nurses office was tiny, so, there was only one occupant. Unfortunately, that occupant was not the person she sought. "Sonia says she is really sorry, but she was called to an emergency meeting." The woman took in Shona's downcast face. "I've to give you tea or coffee and she'll be back soon. There are some croissants left from our breakfast meeting as well if you would like one."

Shona said she rather would like a croissant and a coffee would be marvellous. She was deposited in a staff room which, rather surprisingly, had a view of the river Tay. They obviously took staff mental health seriously here. She watched the river sparkle in the sun; it soothed her brain and allowed her to think. She ran over every permutation of their case or cases. She still couldn't categorically say they were all related. She thought they were, but cold hard facts were all that was important in policing. Unfortunately, the cold hard facts were currently playing a game of hide and seek with her and, so far, were winning.

Sonia Lemongrass returned much more quickly than Shona envisaged. She wasn't sure if that was a relief or not. They were soon ensconced in the office with fresh coffee.

Sonia had aged considerably in the twenty-four hours since Shona last saw her. Saying she looked haggard would have been an understatement. "The meeting was about Malcolm's death. We aren't sure where this leaves the trust. We are also one man down in more ways than one."

"I can appreciate that must be difficult." She really could envisage that. She could always borrow a copper for a few hours – although she was sure she pissed off her contemporaries every time she did it - but they probably didn't have that luxury in the NHS. Staffing levels were already cut to the bone, and she supposed they couldn't borrow from the wards to cover the district. She'd rather have her own job any day.

Shona handed over the warrant.

The charge nurse had prepared for the meeting and handed over the name of both the patient and her daughter. "Please be gentle, she's in the early stages but still gets easily confused. She's a nice lady. You might want to speak to her daughter first."

"I'll bear that in mind. Thank you for your help." For once, Shona meant it. Why the heck did her job always seem to have her knee deep in interrogating people who, day in day out, slogged their guts out in service to others? People such as nurses, doctors, and nuns. She sometimes seriously wondered if it was all worth it.

She was about to leave when Sonia said, "We need to report medical equipment missing. Can we speak to you about it or do we need to go down to the police station."

"It's not usually our jurisdiction but as I'm here I can take the report." She thought she'd throw the poor woman a crumb; she looked like she was functioning on her last nerve. Yet again, Shona wondered how medical staff did this day after day and still stay polite, professional, and compassionate? Every last one of them deserved a medal.

The charge nurse opened a drawer and pulled out a sheet of paper. "It's all written down there. I've told the high heid yins in the hospital as well."

"Told who?" Shona was getting used to Scottish vernacular, but this was new for her.

"The folks in their ivory tower who are in charge. It's Scottish for High Head Ones."

"Makes, sense." She glanced at the sheet. There seemed to

be quite a bit missing and she'd no clue what most of it was. "What is all this?"

"Medicines, creams, dressings, syringes and needles for injections, bandages – she continued with an explanation that made Shona's eyes glaze over. However, the medicines and syringes part did have her ears pricked up.

"Where did all this go missing from? Surely, it has to be locked up tighter than the bank of England. If so, it sounds like an inside job. Are one of your nurses flogging it on the black market?"

"Of course, they're locked up." The nurse's tone was, quite rightly, sharp. "We run a tight ship. They were all stolen from Staff Nurse Sentinel's car." She stood up. "His car keys are also missing as it says on the list. Now, if you will excuse me, I've a patient to visit who is likely to end up in hospital if I don't go and give them their insulin."

An explosion went off in Shona's head. She'd asked Nina to check the contents of the dead nurse's car but never followed up on it. Now, it looked like someone was wandering the streets with a car boot's load of medicines. Not that it helped her in the slightest as how did this mythical person get the car keys and why would their murderer need to steal the drugs when they probably had access to all and every drug inside a hospital? This made no sense whatsoever.

19

Abigail seemed to be the least occupied of them all, so she took her to Invergowrie to visit the daughter, Mrs Prendergast, who just happened to be in and available."

They walked up a path that could do with some weedkiller and rattled on a door with peeling green paint. The woman who answered looked equally dishevelled. Shona flashed her ID card and introduced herself and Abigail.

The woman's eyes widened in fear. "It's not mum is it. I only left her with a respite carer for a. few hours." She burst into tears.

Shona hurried to reassure her. "No. Not at all. As far as we know your mum is fine. We just need to ask you a few questions regarding one of our cases."

The woman sobbed even harder. They followed her into a sitting room where she collapsed into an armchair, the back of which was covered in clothes. They gingerly stepped over a plethora of toys and sat on the sofa. Shona noticed a box of tissues on a beautiful antique sideboard and indicated to Abigail to fetch them. The sergeant did as she was bid and handed them to the woman.

"The woman pulled out several tissues and scrubbed her eyes with them. "I'm sorry. I'm just so exhausted with it all."

"Are you a full-time carer for your mother?"

"Yes. Yes, I am. This is the first time I've had to myself in weeks. And I've a family to care for as well."

"Can we get you a drink or something?" Shona's voice was gentle.

"There's diet coke in the fridge. One of those. You'll have one as well?"

Shona thought this wraith of a woman needed some of the 'fully loaded with sugar' coke. Abigail leapt up to find the drinks. She came back with three cans. Shona raised an eyebrow, but, with a slight shake of the head, Abigail handed them both a can. The hiss of escaping gas could be heard as each of them popped the tabs.

This seemed to calm the woman down. "We'll make this quick, so you can have a much-needed rest."

"Rest, I've a house to clean and washing to do. With five kids it's relentless."

This poor woman doesn't have her troubles to seek. "We want to ask about the nurse who may have stolen an item of jewellery from your mother."

"What! That was months ago. Why are the police bothering themselves with it now?" She slugged down some coke and said, "Anyway, I told you my mother probably made it up. Half the time she doesn't even know who she is, and the other half isn't much better."

"I thought your mother was in the early stages."

"If this is the early stages, I'm dreading the late stages."

"Did the missing item of jewellery ever turn up?"

"No, but she probably threw it in the bin, and it'll be on a council tip somewhere."

"Did you ever meet the nurse?"

"Several times. Mum had pressure sores, and they were

treating them." She looked Shona straight in the eye and said, "I'm doing my best, but she won't move. I can't force her."

"I'm sure you are," Shona said, her voice soothing. "What were your thoughts on the nurse?"

"He was great with Mum. They had a real bond, although on several occasions she thought he was my dad whose been dead for twenty years."

Shona thought the woman might have given him the jewellery rather than him stealing it. Why would he end up murdered though? "Was he usually alone with your mother?"

"Only a couple of times. I had to take my youngest to the hospital for an eye appointment. I left a key with the next-door neighbour."

"Thank you, Mrs Prendergast. You've been really helpful."

They took their leave and Shona said, "She needs an act of kindness. Let's buy the biggest bunch of flowers Tesco has, and we'll bring them back to her."

"Shona McKenzie, you're a big softie at heart."

"We're making a fortune in overtime out of the misery of poor souls like her."

"True that."

"Don't go telling anyone about this or we'll be investigating your murder."

Abigail grinned. "Wouldn't dream of it."

They didn't have the heart to question the mother. She would be an unreliable witness anyway, and nothing she said would stand up in court.

Shona, once again both questioned her career choice and thanked her lucky stars that all was well in her own life.

20

The change was subtle. A little, then a little more, as one day followed another. Their father's smile slipped a little more each day. Their parent's laughter faded. It was replaced by whispered conversations when they thought the children were asleep. Money was counted. Then counted again. Relatives called around and the children were excluded from the conversations. Their father disappeared. Days passed and then he returned, sick and in pain. Neighbours and friends brought food. Thick warming stews, filled with the best meat and the freshest vegetables. Soups so thick you could stand a spoon in them. Their mother looked old and careworn. The children knew something serious was wrong. But no one told them what. They shivered with terror that their father would die. Fear gripped at their heart as they realised how fragile happiness was.

Then, one day, their father smiled again. Their mother started baking, and life was good once more.

21

They bought cakes, as well as flowers, in Tesco's. Two boxes of them were handed in to the woman along with the flowers. She burst into tears again and said, "No one has been this kind to me in months."

"Could that be classed as bribing a witness?" Abigail asked, her brows furrowed.

"She's not a witness."

"She could have killed him because of the stolen bracelet."

"She doesn't have the time, the energy, or the means to do something that pre-meditated. I think she would have come to us if she'd been so bothered by it." She thought for a microsecond and then added, "If it worries you, I will get the money back from the Police Community Welfare Fund. That way we are blameless. I'll also record the fact we have done so and let the chief know."

They returned to the gulags with the remainder of the cakes, much to the delight of the troops who fell on them like vultures. Especially Peter as this was a rare treat for him on his new healthy lifestyle kick.

"Roy. Once you've wiped that dollop of cream off your nose,

where are we with Dave Carabiniere." She paused for a bite of cream cake. "Could he have a more difficult name to pronounce?"

"Everything's difficult to pronounce when your mouth's stuffed full of cake." At least that's what Shona thought Jason said. It was difficult to tell with his mouth full.

Roy grabbed a napkin and swiped at his nose before saying, "The man is practically destitute. How he's maintaining two families is beyond me."

"He's probably destitute because he's maintaining two families."

"Probably why he's throwin' money at the horse racing as well. He'll be hoping he makes it big. That's no' going to happen."

"I'm interested in whether he has any large amounts going into his bank accounts."

"Yep. Fairly large amounts – for a nurse that is. On a semi regular basis. But he haemorrhages it quicker than it arrives."

"What level are we talking. Thousands? Millions?

"Hang on, I'll show you. He hit print; the printer whined into life and churned out several sheets of paper.

Shona looked at them. "Five thousand. Two thousand. Three thousand. Not life changing but still more than doubling his combined wages at times." He took a sip of coke and said, "But there are also several deposits for a couple of hundred each time. It's a strange pattern."

"Are you thinking he might be killing people for money,' Nina asked. "A medical hitman for hire?"

"I'm not ruling anything out. Although they're not huge amounts. You'd expect a hitman would get paid more. Get him in for a chat. Roy and Jason, you can fetch him. I don't want him disappearing into the wind."

The pair trotted off and Shona updated everyone else on

their chat with Mrs Prendergast, omitting the part about the flowers. This was no one's business but hers.

"Do you think he's getting that money from the Alexeyevs?" Iain asked, his voice glum. The poor lad was feeling a bit out of sorts as there weren't many crime scenes for him to process in this case.

"I'm sure of it." Shona decided to throw him a bone to perk him up a bit. "Have you any results on the crime scene?" She didn't need to elaborate as to which one.

It had the desired results. "The place was spick and span – her daughter obviously has it covered. As you know, no blood found except the television. We're still waiting on the lab to get a definitive on whether it belonged to either of our victims." He paused to draw breath.

Shona took advantage of the break in speech. Iain could wax lyrical about forensics for hours. "Fingerprints?"

"Gazillions of partials mostly smeared and a few that I could lift. I'll get prints from the victims and Dr Dalhousie to rule them out. Also, anyone else who might go into the house, so we can rule them out."

"Good luck with that one. Could be anyone up to and including the telly repair man."

"It'll keep me occupied." He did look a lot perkier now he had something to get his teeth into.

"Good chap. I've no doubt you'll solve the crime by teatime."

"You should get a job as a stand-up comic, Ma'am."

"Ha, flaming, ha. Jump to it then."

He did as instructed and disappeared.

"Nina, I've a little job for you."

Nina took the instructions and said, "Nice one. Ma'am. I like the colour of your thinking."

She went to update the chief on the case and give him the

heads up re the flowers and the cakes. She took him some tea and a chocolate eclair that she'd saved especially for him.

He eyed up the proffered offering, a suspicious glint in his eye. "What have you done this time that means you have to bribe me?"

Damn. He was getting wise to her move. "Nothing, Sir." She told him about the flowers and cakes. "I'm letting you know in case anyone says I was bribing a witness or possible suspect."

He thought about it for so long, beads of sweat started to form on Shona's forehead. She wondered if he was working out if this was the straw that would finally give him reason to sack her? Surely not in the middle of an investigation. Eventually he said, "You're fine. She's so far removed from the murders nothing will come of it. And that's what the welfare fund is there for. I'll make a note and back you up." He smiled. "Sometimes, I'm proud of you. What a lovely thing to do."

Shona let out a breath she didn't even know she was holding. Astonished didn't even begin to cover it. "Thank you, Sir."

He smiled again. Shona left, her legs weak. This case had her completely discombobulated in every which way.

22

An hour later Shona found herself sitting in an interview room opposite Dave Carabiniere. Not surprisingly, Margaret McCluskey, was also in attendance. This time it was a wise move as he wasn't going to like what Shona had to say.

She slowly straightened the papers in front of her and then also straightened her pen for maximum effect.

"Are you going to ask a question or are we just going to sit here and look at each other for a couple of hours?" McCluskey's face took on a sterner glare than usual which gave her the general demeanour of a harried camel.

Shona sat up straighter in her chair and tucked a stray lock of hair back behind her ear. "I'm working out where I should start. Anyway, as your being paid about four-hundred pounds per hour to be here, I'm not sure why you're so bothered."

"Preposterous."

"So you keep saying. Do you know any other words?' She took in the lawyer's puce face and said, before McCluskey could respond, "Dave... I can call you Dave, can't I?"

The man nodded, despite suspicion clouding his eyes.

"Thank you. For the audio recording, Mr Carabiniere nodded his consent. Please tell me about your family."

McCluskey stepped in, "What's that got to do with anything? He's a witness and his personal life is nothing to do with Police Scotland."

"If he doesn't answer my questions, I'll promote him to a person of interest."

"What?"

"You can't..."

Both Dave and McCluskey spoke at once. Margaret threw her client a look that could fell a highland cow; he slumped in his chair. The battleship herself, continued, "Are you arresting my client?"

"Not yet, but I will if I am not satisfied with the answers to my questions."

"Is he free to leave?"

"At any time." She waited until McCluskey started to rise and said, "Then I'll arrest him."

"For what crime?"

"Murder." The lawyer opened her mouth to speak but Shona cut her off. "We currently have motive, and as he works at the hospital, we also have the means. I am not arresting him for now, but I need answers. The more fully he answers them, the better for him."

McCluskey's lips puckered but she turned to her client and said, "Answer the detective's questions."

Dave managed to muster up an expression that looked both wary and resigned. *He should take up acting.* "I can't remember the question." Not surprising since Shona had accused him of murder since she asked it.

"Tell me about your family?"

"I've a wife, a two-year-old daughter and a six-month-old baby."

"And where do they live?"

"Gowrie Park." His brows drew together as he attempted to figure out where this was going.

Shona leaned back in her chair and said, her tone casual, "Now, tell me about your other family."

His face turned fifty shades of pale as his mouth opened and closed without a sound coming out.

"Why are you asking my client such stupid questions." McCluskey's rage had her large bosoms swinging from side to side, an impressive feat considering they were ensconced in a grey suit so tight it could be considered a straightjacket. Shona was glad she was on the other side of the table, or they might knock her out. It was a fascinating sight, if a trifle dangerous.

Shona pushed one of the bundles of papers across. "If both you and your client would like to read these, they will enlighten you." The battleship took one look and said, "I need to speak to my client."

"Of course. Would you both like a drink as we could be here for some time?"

Shona made a hot, fresh pot of coffee and rummaged around for two non-chipped mugs. She also put some custard creams on a plate. She needed them nice and relaxed for the next little bomb she would lob after they'd discussed the matter of supporting two families. Dave and McCluskey would never know what hit them. She added a few chocolate digestives for good measure. McCluskey needed more than a custard cream to let down her guard.

23

"I take it you are both now au fait with the situation?"

"My client will answer your questions?"

"Thank you, Margaret." Shona's teeth were aching with all this politeness.

"Now, as I was saying. Please can you tell me about your other family."

He fiddled with his wedding ring and looked everywhere but at Shona.

"Today would be good. We'll be drawing our pensions if you don't get a move on."

More ring twiddling, then he said, "Things aren't good between me and the missus. She's obsessed with the baby and never has any time for us."

How Shona stopped herself throttling the man, she would never know. Instead, she slammed her fist on the table and said, her voice so cold it could crack glass, "How dare you blame your wife. You obviously got your bit on the side pregnant at the same time as your wife. This was going on long before your wife gave birth."

"She's not my bit on the side, I love her."

"How long has this been going on?" She threw him a scathing look and added, "Don't even think of lying to me."

"Eighteen months."

"Are you married to them both."

"Are you accusing my client of bigamy?"

"No. I asked him if he was a bigamist. There's a difference."

"Of course not. How would I manage that you dozy cow?" His voice got higher. "It's illegal in Scotland. You should know that."

Shona leaned forward and said, "Yes. And punishable by a prison sentence. I'm already crawling over your business like wasps on honey. Call me names again and I'll be watching you so closely you won't be able to take a shower without me knowing about it."

They were interrupted by Nina, who handed in a sheet of paper.

"It turns out you were telling the truth. Who knew you could be so honest. Your girlfriend confirms it."

His face grew even paler if that were possible. "You spoke to her."

"We did indeed." She waited for him to take that in and asked, "How can you afford to support two families?"

"I'm on a good wage."

"Two good wages. Which you spend before the first week of the month is finished." She shoved the second pile of papers towards McCluskey.

She read them and opened her mouth. "Where did you get this information? You cannot look into my financial affairs without a ..." She eyed the warrant that was now heading across the desk towards her.

"I take it you want to talk to your client again."

It turned out she did. Same old, same old.

After another twenty minutes of hurry up and wait, Shona was back in the interview room. This time there wasn't a custard cream or a cup of coffee in sight. Nor was Shona quite so patient. That particular emotion had worn thin about thirty minutes ago and was growing thinner by the second.

"Are you ready to tell me about your finances?"

"Why are you so interested in my client's finances? He's a witness and you've had him incarcerated here for hours."

"Incarcerated? Hardly. He's spent more time speaking to you than me which is why he's been here so long." She took a deep breath before continuing. "And I wouldn't call eating biscuits and drinking coffee, hard time."

"Harrumph." She threw Shona her best glare. It was almost impressive. "And the finances?"

Shona was running on her last shredded nerve. "If you would let your client speak, I might be able to answer that. For heaven's sake, we'll be here until midnight. If I was paid silly amounts of money per hour, like you, I might be happy with that, but I'm not."

Silence fell as the lawyer sat back in her chair and sulked.

"Now. Your finances. It seems you're more broke than Bob Cratchit."

"Who? What are you going on about?"

Not a Christmas Carol fan then. "Never mind. Your pay packet seems to disappear faster than snow in an oven. But that's not what I'm interested in. It's the large deposits that seem to drop into your account regularly."

He opened his mouth, but Shona forestalled him. "Between pay packets."

He shuffled around and looked at his lawyer."

She tried a half-hearted, "He's a witness."

"I know that. And as I explained, I'm currently wondering if he's a bit more than that. This is his chance to prove he's not." She leaned forward. "If he'd only answer my blasted questions. Now, Mr Carabiniere, where is that money coming from?"

Shona's tone was such that he said, "I can't tell you. They'll kill me."

"Who'll kill you?" Her heart sank as she believed she already knew the answer.

He hesitated before blurting out, "Stephan and Igor."

"Just to be clear, we are talking about Stephan and Igor Alexeyev?"

His voice so low Shona could hardly hear him, he said, "Yes."

"Can you say that louder for the recording."

He obliged.

"Why were they giving you all that money? What were you doing in return?"

"That's got nothing to do with your investigation." McCluskey had obviously awoken from her stupor."

"It does if they were paying him to kill people."

"You can't prove that."

Sadly, she was right. Damn. "So, it would help your case," *and mine*, "if you told us what you were doing for them."

"A bit of this and a bit of that." Some of Dave's cockiness had returned. He wouldn't remain cocky for long if Shona had anything to do with it.

"Would you like to be more specific?"

"No. It's between me and them."

As their witness refused to answer any more questions, she ended the interview there. It was time to check out bigger fish.

"Thank you for your time, Mr Carabiniere. We will speak to the Alexeyevs and ask them what this mysterious business is."

Dave turned a hundred shades of pale this time, when it dawned on him what this would mean for his future.

She handed him a yellow highlighter. "Highlight the transactions from the Alexeyevs and then you are free to go."

He did as he was asked and bolted from the room as though the hounds of hell were snapping at his ankles. The Alexeyevs soon would be, by which time he'd be begging for the hounds of hell, a much better option than Stephan and Igor if you double crossed them, something Dave now realised.

Sometimes Shona hated her job. Other times, like right this minute, she felt it was the best job in the world.

24

"Why are the Alexeyev's always all over my cases like lice, only ten times as irritating?"

"Because they're all over everything in Dundee like lice, Ma'am." The sad part was, Peter was right. They seemed to have a finger in every single pie Dundee had ever heard of. They were up to their Slavic necks in nefarious goings on but seemed to wriggle out of it like a monster Russian eel. This creature, like Alexeyev 1 and 2, was snake-like and slimy. Described them pretty well thought Shona.

"Does Dave realise, now he's dropped oor Ruskies in it he'll be at the top of their hit list?"

"Probably not. For someone with such a high-powered job he's not got much common sense." She looked around at the assembled cast of characters, aka, her team. "Who wants to go and bring in the Kalashnikov brothers?"

Stunned silence and frantic shaking of heads ensued. Then, Jason said, "Can we take guns?"

Roy smirked and sat up straighter. He took on the demeanour of an excited puppy.

"No, you flaming well can't. But you've just volunteered and laughing boy here will go with you." She pointed at Roy.

Roy swallowed and said, "You're going to need more than us to bring in that pair."

"Agreed. Nina, Abigail, and Iain. You're going too. Make it clear they are witnesses."

If there was a competition for the most downcast copper in Scotland this lot would take the first five places.

"Suck it up and stop acting like a bunch of toddlers. Nina, change your shoes." The last thing they needed was her falling off her three-inch Balenciaga's and out of commission for weeks. She had form in this department.

As they disappeared out of the door, Peter asked. "What do we do?"

"We, my friend, are going to have a strategy meeting in the canteen over a spot of lunch."

"I like the cut of your jib, Ma'am."

"I'm rather fond of it myself. She smiled, stood up, and strode off. "Hurry up or the steak and kidney pudding will be finished."

He stood up and bolted after her. She maintained a pace that would keep him well exercised.

Apparently the Alexeyevs came fairly quietly. For them. It still involved a struggle which resulted in Jason gaining a black eye. Everyone else appeared to be in one piece – some sort of minor miracle.

"Arrested for assault again?" Shona asked. "I wonder how long it will take them to wriggle out of it this time?'

"Right after Angus Runcie puts in a complaint about police brutality and the despicable behaviour of every single officer in Police Scotland," Nina said.

"Yep. Let's go interview them. Peter you're with me. Jason, we're fresh out of steak so shove some ice on that eye. The rest of you, grab food before you're putting in complaints about slavery and servitude." She'd heard the rumbles from their stomach loud and clear and starving the team wasn't her number one priority.

The stampede showed how hungry they were. "Bring Jason back a plate," she yelled, hoping they could hear her over the rumbling of stomachs and the thumping of feet.

The Alexeyevs had to cool their heels in the families' room with freshly brewed coffee until they were interviewed. Shona only hoped they didn't throw it at the newly painted walls. They'd had a complaint from a witness the room was depressing, so the chief had dug deep and paid for a couple of cans of paint. She wasn't sure who painted it, just hoped it was maintenance rather than a couple of coppers who were in the bad books. She left the brothers glowering, especially Igor who had raised the art to a whole new level. That and brooding. Since Igor appeared she found herself thinking longingly of Gregor, the Alexeyev who was currently doing twenty-five to life at His Majesty's pleasure. Then she returned Mary's phone call.

"Have you got news for me?"

"Good afternoon to you, too, Shona."

"Sorry, I'm faced with interviewing the Chuckle Brothers, so I'm not in the best of moods."

"That'd do it. How did Stephan and Igor come to your attention this time?"

"They come to my attention by doing nothing more than existing but this time they are witnesses."

"You must be desperate to attempt to have that pair in your corner."

"You don't know the half of it. You rang me."

"I did. I've managed to do Elsie Dalhousie's post-mortem. She was injected with something but I'm not sure what. Yet. I'll send specimens to labs worldwide to see if we get a hit on anything."

"There was a district nurse in the room, the injection could have been legal."

"You're right. But you and I both know it's more than a coincidence the nurse is also occupying one of my drawers."

"Coincidence doesn't wash in court. I need to prove it beyond all reasonable doubt."

"And that's why they pay you such big money and me a pittance. I am merely a tiny cog in the huge machine that is Police Scotland. Off you go and prove, whilst I go and undertake a post-mortem on Malcolm Sentinel."

The Alexeyev brothers' mood had deteriorated even further by the time they got around to interviewing them. They'd asked for Angus Runcie to be there, and he barrelled up the corridor minutes before the interview started. "I want to speak to my clients."

"Of course. Would you like some coffee?"

"Your usual sarcastic self, I see. Why do you always have to be so rude?"

Her eyes opened wide in an attempt to appear innocent."

"I'm shocked at your opinion of me. I was being polite. Now, would you like some coffee whilst you speak to your clients?"

His brow furrowed as he tried to work out where she was going with this. "Black with two sugars."

"Coming right up. Shona's café is open." The Alexeyevs asked for a top up and she agreed. All this politeness malarky didn't half slow things down but she could do with a coffee herself. Double strength, let's get wired caffeine was required to deal with the Bobbsey Twins.

Once they were all suitably caffeinated, Shona started the interviews as they had to interrogate each of them separately. Double the angst. "Interview with Stephan Alexeyev. DI Shona McKenzie and DS Peter Johnston in attendance."

She leaned back in her chair. "Stephan, are you aware you are not under suspicion but are being interviewed as a witness?"

"You must call me Mr Alexeyev."

"Much as I would love to oblige, there are two of you, so I need to use your first name to differentiate."

"You are rude woman."

"What have I said, this time, that could be construed as rude? I've been politeness itself since you got here." She sat up straighter. This charade needed to come to an end. Neither Alexeyev 1 nor Alexeyev 2 understood subtlety, so pussy-footing around and being polite were just delaying the inevitable.

"Have you got a man called Dave Carabiniere, working for you?"

"I do not know all employees. My assistant will know this."

"Cut the crap, Stephan, you complained to my boss that I'd arrested him, so you know damn well he works for you."

Stephan did a bit more glowering, and Shona stared him straight in the eye despite this. Quite bravely she thought.

"He is a security guard at Cat's Eyes."

"Why is your club always slap bang in the middle of all my investigations?"

"You persecute us. We run respectable business and you are always trying to shut us down."

"A respectable business? If I had any coffee left, I'd be choking on it right now."

Runcie chirped up. "Are you accusing my client of any criminal activity?"

Shona had wondered how long it would be before he was defending his slimy client. "You can watch and listen to the replay of this video as many times as you want. You'll find I did nothing of the sort. I asked why their nightclub has come up in my investigation. Again."

Runcie said, "I am taking a note of every word." He sat up straighter in his chair and picked up a pen.

"I'm sure you are, as are the video and the audio recordings." She turned her attention back to Stephan who was doing some smirking as he waited for the witty exchange between the police and his lawyer to end. She was about to wipe the smirk off his face faster than it arrived. "Apparently, you're paying him handsomely as a security guard."

"Paying staff well is not crime."

"No. But I'm interested in why you are paying him so often."

"I do not know what you are talking about."

"Maybe this will refresh your memory." She handed copies of the bank statement over to both Runcie and Stephan. Much of it was redacted, so the relevant information clearly stood out. "You will see several of the transactions are highlighted. According to Dave Carabiniere, those payments came from you."

No one spoke as Runcie and Stephan perused the statements. Then, "I need to talk to my client in private."

"Why am I not surprised. "You've got ten minutes."

Shona needed to answer a call of nature anyway, so she was grateful for the pause in proceedings.

In her absence the pair had obviously cooked up a story. She expected nothing less.

"My client does not deal with the books in his place of business. He has staff that deal with that side of things."

"He must authorise extra payments." She leaned forward. "Stephan, I have one of my 'staff' applying for a warrant right now. If you don't tell me what those payments are for our forensic accountants will be crawling all over your accounts for months."

This jogged his memory. "These were overtime payments."

"That's a heck of a lot of overtime. Thousands every month."

"We like to reward our staff."

"Awww, aren't you positive little angels."

Runcie sat bolt upright. "There's no need to be sarcastic."

"There's every reason to be sarcastic. It's the only language your client understands."

"We're halting this interview here."

"Absolutely my pleasure. That warrant should be here any minute. Now, on the little matter of assault to actual injury—"

"I will discuss the payments with my accountant." Stephan pulled out his phone, dialled, and spoke Russian, and when he hung up said, "She will be here in one hour."

"So, you do think women are capable of more than flashing their boobs in a bar."

"Inspector, stop insulting my client." Runcie stood and buttoned his jacket. "We will be back in an hour."

"Not so fast, sunshine. Your client's not going anywhere until I speak to my officers about the assault."

"You haven't arrested him?"

"Thank you for the reminder. Stephan Alexeyev, you are under arrest for assault to actual bodily harm on DC Jason Roberts. You do not have to say anything other than giving your name, address, date and place of birth and nationality. Anything you do say can be used against you in a court of law." She stared Runcie straight in the eye. "At the moment, I'm leaving the pair of you in here rather than throwing your client in a cell. I'll see you both in an hour."

In the spirit of her newfound politeness and goodwill to all men, she sent them coffee. This time there was a singular lack of biscuits. Someone had eaten them all.

25

One hour and thirty-four seconds later, Shona found herself sitting in the interview room once more. Even she was sick of looking at the same four walls and thought longingly of a crime scene. Any crime scene. Then she told herself to get a grip and think of something else, anything else, before the crime scene became a self-fulfilling prophecy. Her brain immediately switched to wedding plans, so she bullied it back to crime scenes – and their witness.

The cast of characters now included a young woman whose blonde hair hid most of her face. She was chewing on a strand of it. How the heck did this child get involved with the Alexeyevs?

She didn't have to wonder for long as Stephan said, "This is my sister, Ekaterina Alexeyev."

"Your sister?" Dumbfounded didn't even begin to cover it. How on earth could this frightened wraith be related to the Alexeyevs, let alone work for them?"

"How old are you?"

The lawyer leapt in with both size twelves. "What's that got to do with you?"

"Because she looks about ten. I'm wondering about the child labour laws."

The girl looked up and shoved her hair behind her ears. "I am twenty-three. Her accent was less noticeable than her brothers and her command of the English language greater. Her voice was as weak as the rest of her.

"Why is she here?"

"She is our accountant."

Good God in heaven, Shona couldn't take many more of these surprises. A forensic accountant would wipe the floor with her.

"She will tell you what the payments were for. She knows our money."

We'll be here forever. Shona sat back in her chair and sighed.

The woman opened a folder and her demeanour changed the minute she started talking. She outlined clearly and succinctly what payments went to Dave and exactly what he did for those payments, dates, times, and tax taken off. Everything down to the last penny. She waxed lyrical about money coming in and money going out and the cost and expenditure of running a club such as Cats Eyes. This woman was an accounting genius. Shona had no doubt she'd just been told a pack of lies, but before she could open her mouth the woman slid a sheet of paper over the table towards her. It was all there in black and white. Without evidence to the contrary the police didn't have a reason to charge either Dodgy Dave or the Alexeyevs.

Nor could she charge them with assault as no one was sure which Alexeyev smacked Jason in the eye, and no one was sure it wasn't an accident.

"Thank you for your co-operation. The assault charge has been dropped and you are free to go."

"So, you arrested my clients on false charges?"

"Quit while you're ahead, Angus, before I think of something else to charge them for."

"It's Mr Runcie."

"Bye Mr. Runcie. Have a nice day now."

He flounced out of the room, a spectacular sight in someone so tall. Shona slouched out after him. When it came to confidence, she was all mouth and no trousers. Her confidence had fled somewhere around the first suggestion this was a case she should investigate.

She asked Peter to join her in her office and showed him the breakdown of the Alexeyevs' monetary dealings with Dave Carabiniere.

"Do you believe it?"

"Not a word but, as there is nothing to suggest it's a load of old Horlicks, there's nothing we can arrest either of them for."

"So, oor Dave's in the clear."

"Not quite yet. Where are all the couple of hundred quid deposits coming from?"

"Do we need a forensic accountant?

"I rather think we do. Hence the reason I asked you in here. Any suggestions?"

"Yep. You need Andy Gillespie from Glasgow." He sat for a minute and said, "They might no' be keen to lend him out. They're a right dodgy lot in Glasgow; They could tell you a tale or two about hiding money."

"You can't say that. I'm sure the people of Glasgow are a lovely bunch."

He grinned. "You should hear what they say about us."

"I'd rather not know. Can you ask around and see if they'll send him hot footing in our direction?'

He disappeared to do just that, and she picked up the phone to ask the Procurator Fiscal for Advice."

26

Little did they know this time of newfound happiness would not last. One day their father was there. The next he was gone. Swallowed by his illness, then swallowed by the grave in which he was buried. They stood huddled on a mountainside, sobbing as their father was lowered into a dark hole, not realising this one fact would change their life forever. One child, teetering on the brink of adulthood, made a pact that day. A pact with themselves that they would bring a halt to such suffering. No one should go through what their father had endured.

On returning home they slipped away from the wake. In the bedroom, shared by all the children, they started the computer, opened a search page, and typed the first word that would change the course of their life. The search was thorough, and continued until a sibling burst through the door, sobbing and needing comfort. The search engine closed, they provided that comfort.

The search had moved them one step closer to their ultimate goal. When all their siblings were asleep, they would open the computer again and take the next step into the future.

27

Douglas was delighted to hear from her. "Are you ready to talk wedding plans yet?"

"I'm knee deep in the strangest case yet, and you want me to talk about wedding dresses and flowers."

"It's a bit difficult to do that without a date." His voice had cooled by several degrees.

"Quite frankly, Douglas, I've better things to worry me right now. I need advice. Advice that might help me solve these blasted murders."

"That I can do." The smile reappeared in his voice, much to Shona's delight. That voice flamed her insides whatever they were discussing. Which seemed extremely peculiar considering they were discussing murder. Still, one couldn't control hormones and hers were screaming at her in every which way and more.

She shoved her feelings to one side and gathered her wits. "I have a strange request and I'm not sure if we can actually do it."

"If you tell me, I'll see what I can *actually do* to help you.

You'd be astonished at some of the decisions I've had to make during my time as procurator fiscal."

"After the time I've had of it since arriving in Dundee, nothing would surprise me."

"Your request?"

"Could we ask every ward in the hospitals in Dundee, Fife, and Angus to let me know if anyone dies suddenly right before they were expecting to go home."

There was silence from the other end of the phone. Shona tried a tentative, "Douglas?"

"I'm stunned. I'm trying to formulate a response."

"I know it's a bit off the wall."

"Off the wall? It's off the planet. I'll think about it and let you know tomorrow."

"Are you and the kids free for pizza tonight? I think I could wangle a night off."

"My mother would be happy to have them tonight. How about a little you and me time?"

Heat swept through her body. Her voice husky she said, "What time?

The team were stalled, as was the investigation, so she sent them home, much to their astonishment. "It's only five o'clock," Nina said.

"Remind me, is this the time we're meant to knock off?" Roy chipped in. "It happens so rarely, I've forgotten."

Shona smiled. "Remember, it's all that overtime that is paying for your designer clothes."

"Dinnae be so cheeky to the DI, Roy." Peter was halfway out the door before he'd finished the sentence.

The others followed post-haste. They weren't taking any chances the boss would change her mind.

The us time didn't start off so well as they argued about a wedding date, He wanted to discuss it. She wanted to relax on her rare night off, not discuss the finer details of a wedding.

"I'm getting the impression you don't want to get married."

"Stop sulking. It's not a good look for a grown man. I do want to get married; I just don't want to spend endless hours discussing it.

"Why? I thought all women loved weddings."

"You're on dangerous ground speaking like that. Quite frankly, I'd say it was sexist." She glowered at him. "I'm not the type of woman who's been planning her wedding since childhood. Also, I've had to go through all the endless organisational details once already. It's exhausting."

"So have I. That doesn't mean I don't want to do it with you."

They were interrupted by the takeaway arriving. Dinner started out quietly but by the time they'd finished the samosas and onion bhajis, they'd agreed a truce. The minute this case was over, they'd spend a day discussing the wedding. The remainder of the us time turned out to be fabulous.

She didn't put the key in the lock of her own front door until 1 am. Shakespeare told her mistress vociferously that this was not an acceptable time to return as she was currently starving to death. Shona tried to stroke her, but Shakespeare was having none of it, showing her backside and a disapproving tail. Shona opened a tin of salmon something or other and deposited it in a dish. "There you go you wee fraud. I left you with a full dish of dried food this morning and it's all gone." Shakespeare fell on her dinner and totally ignored her mistress."

Shona trudged to bed wondering how she managed to upset both her fiancé and her cat in the space of a few hours. Way to go, Shona.

She fell into bed wondering why she was so reluctant to arrange the wedding. Then exhaustion took over and the wondering stopped.

28

Shona awoke to the cat cuddled into her side – she'd obviously been forgiven – and the entire pipes and drums banging in her head. She stumbled out of bed and headed for the bathroom, where she swallowed a couple of aspirin. The headache was the result of a restless night rather than overindulgence in whisky. She'd had zero in the way of alcohol due to the strict laws on drinking and driving in Scotland, and she couldn't afford to lose her licence. She slugged down some water, threw on running gear, and headed out of the door. A swift five miles would blow the cobwebs away. Her steps took her towards the seafront where the water sparkled in the early morning sunlight. She moved her sunglasses from her head to cover her eyes as her feet beat out an even rhythm on the uneven pavement. Scotland was a truly magical country, and she thanked her lucky stars she had moved here, regardless of the circumstances under which the move occurred. She no longer gave her ex-husband even a passing thought.

. . .

One shower, two slices of toast, and a car journey later she walked into the main office. Not a soul to be seen. They'd obviously taken her, "Relax, you deserve it," exhortation seriously. She hadn't meant to this extent, but she only had herself to blame. She started a pot of coffee, filled the kettle, and dropped six teabags into a huge teapot.

Peter was the first to arrive and he fell on the tea like he'd just staggered through a desert. "The town's gridlocked. There's been a major Road Traffic Incident which has shut one of the main roads. All the other roads are so jammed with cars, they're like a car park."

"So, we'll see them when we see them?"

"Aye. I'm only here because my mate let me go up a pedestrian only street."

"Do I really want to know this? You didn't knock over a member of the unsuspecting public did you?"

"It's being kept free of pedestrians and used for emergency vehicles."

As they sipped their tea, Roy strolled in. He forestalled Shona by saying, "I couldn't even get the car out of my driveway, so I walked here."

Shona poured him a cup of tea and handed it over. "I wondered how you managed to get around the traffic issues."

Shona's mobile rang. It was Mary. Never good news at this time of the morning; although it could be if she'd identified what was being used to kill their victims. "Morning, Mary. Have you got an answer for me?"

"You may think I'm God but I'm fresh out of miracles."

"Oh, well worth a try. What can I do for you?"

"I've another one in my morgue that fits the pattern. Came in last night from Narrywells."

"You have got to be kidding me."

"I wish I was. I'm not happy about it either."

"What's the name and which ward?"

"Mary Lewandowski. She rattled off the name of the ward.

"Thanks, I'll go and investigate with the few team members I have. If I can actually get there."

"I got here okay. I've also got an update on Malcolm Sentinel. Another one injected with an unknown substance."

"What the heck is going on?"

"That, Shona, is your problem. I merely afford them the dignity of a professional post-mortem that may help you in your enquiries."

Unfortunately, Shona knew that. What she didn't know was how to even start solving it, never mind catching a killer.

She set Roy to on finding out as much as she could about Mary Lewandowski, whilst she and Peter grabbed a police car and hotfooted it to the hospital. She wanted to see that room before another patient took up residence. She needed a crime scene."

As they arrived on the ward the cleaning crew were walking out the door of the room in which their victim had died.

"Damn and blast."

Blimey, the DI must be rattled, speaking like that, thought Peter.

"Maybe we should have rung in advance and asked them to leave the room until we got here."

"You think?" Shona was berating herself for this very fact. Deciding self-recrimination wasn't going to get them anywhere, she moved on to interviewing the staff.

The student nurse who found her was young, anxious, and miserable, which did not make for the best witness. The charge nurse, reading the situation, asked if she could sit in on the interview. Shona, who wasn't usually keen on two witnesses being interviewed at once, agreed. They'd get nothing out of young Morag Duncan if she didn't have someone she knew in the room. Shona wondered if she really had a future in nursing.

"Thank you for agreeing to speak to us, Morag. We are only asking questions; you are not under suspicion for anything."

"It wasn't me. She was fine when I did her obs." The girl shook so hard the chair rattled.

"No one thinks it was you, Morag." This wee lassie would have difficulty killing a conversation far less a patient. "How did you find her?"

"I went in to say cheerio before I went for the night. I'd been looking after her for the day."

The conscientious type. Exactly what we need. "Can you tell us more?"

"I thought she was asleep. I was about to leave when I noticed the cap was off her cannula."

The charge nurse must have taken in Shona's face because she said. "We put intravenous drugs in it." She looked at Shona again and explained. "Straight into the vein."

"Was she receiving intravenous drugs?" Shona hoped she'd got the word right. There were many reasons she hadn't gone into medicine and the long and complicated names was one of them.

The charge nurse, or charge nurse if she wanted to be correct, continued to answer. "No. If someone has one that's working, we leave it in until they go home. It makes it easier if they take a turn for the worse, we have intravenous access."

Shona turned back to the student nurse. "What did you do when you noticed the open cannula?"

"I went over to shut it. It's an infection risk if it's left open." She looked at the charge nurse who gave a reassuring smile. "That's when I noticed she wasn't breathing. I yelled for help." The young woman's voice trembled, leaving Shona wondering why she'd even turned up for work that morning.

The charge nurse stepped in again. "We started CPR and a crash team arrived, but she was gone."

"What was she admitted for?"

"Pancreatitis. She was over the worst and going home today." She looked down and smoothed her dress. When she looked up, she said, "This seems to be happening all over the hospital. Is someone doing this deliberately?"

"That's what we are trying to find out. Thanks for your help in our ongoing investigation. Please may I have a copy of your staff rota?"

"Of course. I'll email it to you within the hour. Do you think it was someone on the ward who did this? I would guarantee none of my staff are involved."

"We will need to rule them out." What she was thinking was, it could be any member of medical staff in the whole blasted hospital. Talk about a nightmare.

"Can I have a chat with you in private before I go?" Shona asked the charge nurse.

The student scuttled off and left them to it.

"Do you think that young Morag has anything to do with this?"

"Not a chance. That wee lassie is on her first ward and has only done two weeks; she wouldn't even know where to start pushing intravenous medication. Also, she's no access to any medicine whatsoever, unless she buys it from WH Smith's in the foyer. I don't think Aspirin or paracetamol are much of a risk." The woman looked stern. "Did you not see her? She could barely string a word together. This is the first dead body she's seen."

"I agree it's unlikely, but it's my job to ask." Shona wondered why she'd jumped to the intravenous drug angle so quickly. Then she realised that was the scenario suggested by the student. This case had her rattled to the nth degree; she wasn't thinking straight.

The charge nurse didn't look convinced. "Was there anything else you wanted to ask? I've a ward to run and we're flat out. There's a patient in that room already."

"How did you find out about the death?"

"When nurse Duncan screamed holy murder. I came running and instigated the arrest procedure."

"Did you notice anything out of the ordinary?"

The charge nurse's look said she thought Shona was completely addled. "I was in the middle of trying to resuscitate someone, not looking at the surroundings."

"Fair point." *She didn't have to be so rude about it though.* She decided not to say so as this woman could be looking after her one day.

"Are there any new staff on your ward." She thought and added, "In any capacity."

"No. Well, apart from the student nurses and student doctors that is. They're always moving around."

"Prior to the alarm, did you notice anyone on the ward that shouldn't have been there?"

"It was visiting time. There were people everywhere."

"Don't you have a two visitor limit? That's what it says at the door."

"Nobody pays a blind bit of notice to that. Anyway, I've not got time to be watching comings and goings."

What a shambles. Anybody could stroll in and kill half the ward without anyone noticing. That got her thinking. Whoever their murderer was, they had more confidence than enough. They were obviously sure no one would be paying notice to them or what they were doing. No one would question them. How did this fact help their case? The killer obviously had a reason to be strolling around the ward at all times of the day and night. But what of the two who shuffled off this mortal coil in Liff. She made a mental note to buy some more aspirin on her way out and decided to move the conversation on. "Can I speak to the doctor in charge of Mrs. Lewandowski's care?"

"He's off at a conference today. I could get a message for him to ring you."

"If you could. That would be helpful. What about the doctor who certified her dead?"

"He's on the ward. Do you want a chat?"

"I most certainly do."

The chat threw up the square root of nothing new. Mary was recovering, the death was more than unexpected, and the young Indian doctor had no clue what to put on the death certificate. Therefore, he requested a post-mortem. This was getting old. The same mantra for every victim – suspicious death, no clue what caused it. Different ward to the others. How could anyone, even if they were medical personnel, go to all the wards and not be noticed?

As they drove back, she asked Peter, "Have you got any thoughts?" She slammed on her brakes, narrowly missing a puppy, who had darted on to the road. The child walking it sheepishly pulled it back on to the pavement and cuddled it.

Peter braced himself, stopped the action of popping a mint in his mouth, and said, "It's a good job you never hit that. It would be all over *The Courier.*

"My question, Peter."

"My thoughts aren't worth a penny. For the first time since I started in the police, I'm questioning my career choice. There's literally nothing in this case I can get my head around or sink my teeth into."

"You and me both." She pulled a mint from the proffered packet. Hand halfway to her mouth she added, "It would be bad enough if we were only worrying about hospitals but how do we cover every single patient who's discharged from hospital. This is nuts."

"Aye, it is." They both sucked mints, lost in their own thoughts.

29

Hard work and perseverance meant the next stage of the life plan proceeded well. Not that it was easy; poor to start with, the death of the breadwinner meant they, as the oldest, had to bring in money. So, work they did, and handed over every cent to their mother to ensure the family's survival. At the same time, they stayed in school and worked even harder. Education was the only way out of this endless cycle of poverty. Neighbours helped, but they did not have their own worries to seek. Money was tight for everyone.

Work. Study. Work. Study. No time for anything else. No time to be a child. Thrown into an adult world too quickly they consoled themselves with the fact they would all be out of this one day.

School ended and university started. Even with a scholarship it was hard. So much harder, and still they had to work. Exhaustion became the norm, but the mantra was repeated over and over and over. Work. Study. Work. Study. One day this will end. One day this will be worth it. Keep going. Don't quit. Rewards are closer than you think. The next seven years stretched before them in an endless chasm of fatigue and misery. It seemed it would never end.

Still, they kept going. Quitting was not an option.

30

When they returned, they were a full compliment.

"Good of you to join us. I thought you'd all resigned left me to it."

"Trust me, Ma'am, I'd rather have been here. Sitting in a car in the blazing sun is not my idea of a good time." Nina looked a little dishevelled, not her usual elegant self.

"Have you all had plenty of fluid since you got in?" Most of the team off with heatstroke wasn't going to help their case in any way whatsoever. "And I mean water."

"Yep, gallons of the stuff, and I need to pee." Jason dashed off.

"Too much information. Did you not have air conditioning on in your cars?"

"Have you seen the price of petrol, Ma'am?" Abigail wiped her brow with a tissue.

"Good point. Moving swiftly onwards, Roy, anything on Mary Lewandowski?"

"Not a thing. She obviously didn't do anything newsworthy. She doesn't even have a social media presence."

"Or she, quite rightly, kept herself to herself. Sensible

woman re the social media." She clapped her hands. "Right, you lot, I'm going to send more rotas to the printer in here. Back to crosschecking. Roy, there must be something on the internet that mentions Mary, so dig deeper. Hop to it." She stood up. "I'm off to speak to Mary."

They all looked at her and she burst out laughing. "Mary the pathologist. Not our victim. I haven't turned into a psychic." Then she added, "Yet." The laughter followed her up the corridor, cheering her up considerably. She'd take it where she could get it.

The trip to the mortuary was more to bat ideas with the pathologist than anything else. Mary said she could spare half an hour while she had a lunch break, then she'd have to get back to it. Shona grabbed two meal deals and a couple of cakes from the supermarket as a thank you.

"I'm completely flummoxed by this, Mary. Its' driving me nuts not knowing where to go next."

"It's driving me equally nuts as I hate not knowing."

"No joy on whether a poison was used?"

"Nope."

"You don't think it might be coincidence and they all died of natural causes?" Shona thought this was the daftest idea in the case so far, but she had to try it on for size.

Mary halted in the act of taking a bite of roast beef on rye, too surprised to continue. "Are you having a laugh?" Her brows rose so high they met her hairline. "Up until the two from Liff I might have said a tentative possibly, but I'll stake my wages for the rest of the year on the fact, if they were murdered then, so were the rest." She waved her sandwich in the air and a few crumbs landed on her chest. She brushed them away and said, "Talking of the pair from Liff, they both had puncture wounds, so I'm guessing they didn't shuffle off this mortal coil voluntarily.

They chewed in silence for a moment. Shona swallowed the last bite of her cheese and pickle sandwich and wiped her hands on a piece of blue roll that doubled as a napkin. "First clue in an otherwise baffling case." She sighed. "Who, in a hospital would have access to all the wards and no one would pay them any attention?"

"Good question. Let me think." She had a couple of bites of cake while, Shona waited patiently and attacked her cake. "There are a lot of them. So, doctors, nurses, physios, phlebotomists, occupational therapists, ministers of the church, priests—"

"Stop and let me write all this down. I'm losing the will." She tapped the notes app on her phone and said, What's a phleb watsit?"

"Someone who takes blood."

Shona perked up at this. "So, they'd know their way around a cannula." She thought she was getting quite good at this medical lingo. She still didn't want a medical career though. Everyone in the hospital, and the community nursing team, were more exhausted than the police. She didn't think that was possible.

"They might know their way around a cannula, but they don't usually use them. It's strictly needle and syringe."

"Something to bear in mind though. Anyone else?"

"All the people who support the staff in their endeavours to keep the good people of Dundee alive and well – porters, cleaners, catering staff, dieticians, ward clerks, medical records maintenance staff. To be honest the list is endless."

"The dieticians and catering staff might be worth looking into. Thanks."

Mary stood up, wiped her hands on the blue roll and threw it in the bin. "I've a body waiting my attention. Good luck."

Shona needed all the luck in the world, and then some.

Where did they even start with the information she'd just been given? This was a beggar's muddle if she'd ever seen one. She didn't have much time to think about it as there was a message waiting for her from the chief's secretary. Could she please go and see him.

She didn't stop to get anyone coffee this time. She'd have to face the chief's wrath cold turkey.

"Inspector, did I not tell you to remain polite and to stop antagonising every single person that walked through the doors of this station?"

'You did, Sir, and I have complied fully. I've been so polite my jaws ache."

"If that's the case, why have I had Angus Runcie on the phone saying otherwise?"

"He's a sensitive wee soul. How come it's taken so long for him to complain anyway?"

"This has to stop, or I will be looking for a new inspector."

"But, Sir, I—"

"Stop arguing with me. Now, get on with your job without angering half the city." As a parting shot, he added, "And if George Brown contacts me, I'm definitely sacking you."

She left, wondering if she could find their murderer and do some sort of deal that would involve the chief's demise. And the Alexeyevs, Runcie and McCluskey. She needed a large glass of Talisker, or at the very least caffeine. She slammed the coffee pot down so hard the contents slopped out and Peter, who was making tea, jumped.

"What's got up your humph?"

"The chief."

"Ah. Been told off again?"

She ignored him, took a sip of coffee, and sighed. How was

she meant to interview the likes of Stephan and Runcie, speaking like a choirboy? She only got an answer when she used tactics that skirted on the edge.

She drained her coffee and picked up the jug for a refill. "Sod the lot of them."

Peter felt it prudent to remain silent.

The phone in her office rang so she dashed to answer it.

"DI McKenzie."

"This is Charge Nurse Anderson from Narrywells."

"What can I do for you?"

"I'm not sure if this is relevant." The line went silent.

"Are you still there?" The phones in the station could be dodgy so Shona couldn't be sure they weren't cut off.

"Yes. Yes. It's probably nothing."

"Best you tell me. If it's not important, no problem. If it is important Police Scotland will be eternally grateful." She secretly hoped it would be something of import but had her doubts.

"My staff nurse says something had been bothering her, but she couldn't remember what." She stopped and Shona gave her space to gather her thoughts and continue, although the finger drumming indicated her impatience. "It suddenly came to her today. When she found Mrs Treacher, she was lying on her back, the blankets were folded at the bottom of the bed, and the sheet was pulled tight up to her chin and smoothed tight."

Shona wasn't sure that helped them in the slightest. "Why would that bother her?"

"Because it's unheard of. After a night's sleep most of the beds are rumpled with none of the coverings tucked in anywhere."

Okay. She'd run with it. "Why would you say it's significant?"

"Because I think whoever killed her, pulled up the sheets and tucked her in after he, or she, did it."

Interesting theory. "Thank you, Charge Nurse Anderson. Please keep us informed if there is anything else you, or your staff, think of." Hanging up, she was in two minds about its importance but decided to investigate anyway. Let's face it, she'd no other thread to pull so she might as well pull this one and see what unravelled.

Half an hour later, having made several phone calls it had unravelled precisely nothing. Not one relevant staff member was available to speak to her. She requested they be asked to ring her as soon as possible. One was on holiday in Mexico, so a no go. One was on night duty, so no one was willing to wake him up. She was promised the others would be contacted and asked to ring her immediately.

While she was waiting Douglas strolled into her office clutching the lead of an excitable Fagan. The minute he saw her the dog leapt in her direction almost pulling Douglas off his feet and, quite literally, knocking her off hers. She managed a firm, "Sit," and the dog obliged gazing at her adoringly. After being helped to her feet by a laughing procurator fiscal, she gave the dog a treat and told him to lie down, before asking, "Have you made a decision on my request?"

"It's good to see you too." He took in her glare and said, "My answer is, yes."

Shona threw herself at her fiancé and hugged him. "You are pretty awesome; do you know that?"

"I've long suspected it." His smile lit up his whole face before he turned serious. "I've met with the CEO's of all the hospitals in the area. They're keener than us to clear this up, as patients are refusing to be admitted. People are going to end up dying due to fear of hospitals."

"It's grim. I wouldn't want to be admitted to hospital at the moment if I was honest." A lightbulb went off in her brain. "Can we also have permission to take photographs in any possible crime scene? I mean the ones where the suspicious deaths have happened but we're not sure if it's suspicious or not. Will I need a warrant?"

"To answer your question first. A warrant would be tricky, but I think you have grounds for one. I'll make it happen somehow. He snapped his fingers and Fagin jumped up. "I wouldn't want to be admitted to a hospital around here at the moment either. What is the world coming to when you're not safe in the NHS?" He stroked Fagin's ears which elicited a low whine of ecstasy. "I'd better take this reprobate for a walk." Fagin was easily pleased.

"How come you've got him anyway?"

"Mum has things to do and people to see. Things that don't involve walking a lively dog for hours on end."

He took advantage of the fact no one was around, and they weren't at a crime scene, to kiss her. Fagin lay down and covered his eyes with his paw. Jock had obviously been teaching him tricks. When the pair left, she had a hollow feeling in the pit of her stomach. The minute she was finished this case, they really must arrange that wedding. Fagin could be a ring bearer.

Douglas had no sooner left than the phone rang – a Health Care Assistant who had discovered one of the dead women.

"Thanks for getting in touch." Shona was going to do this by phone, but she made a snap decision to ask her to come in. She wanted all these interviews on video, so she could replay them and look for patterns.

The woman's voice vibrated with anxiety, rising higher with every word. "I didn't do anything. She was dead when I went in her room."

Shona rushed to reassure her. "No. No. We don't think you've done anything. You're not under suspicion, I just need to ask you a few questions to help us get a better picture. Would you mind coming into the station?"

She could hear the woman exhale and bravado return. "I'm busy and I've a wean to pick up from school."

"Bring your child and one of my officers will give him or her a tour of the police station. That should give them bragging rights with their friends." That sealed the deal and she agreed to come in after school. Shona could have sent a couple of heavies to bring her in, but the woman was doing her best to help them and antagonising a witness was not only poor form but would get her sacked. Despite all the difficulties she loved her job and didn't want to push the boss any further.

Four-thirty found her giving a child juice and some chocolate, and Abigail agreeing to show Rabbie around the station. "We'll have a grand time."

The lad looked at Shona with adoration and smiled a gap-toothed smile. This got her thinking about her impending motherhood yet again. How on earth would she cope with this job and children?

Five minutes later, Shona, and Rabbie's mother, were in an interview room. She'd also asked for some juice and Shona obliged.

The preliminaries over, Shona didn't even have a chance to ask one question before Rhianna started "I was so worried. I thought you thought I'd done it. I'll answer any questions. Anything to help. Please, ask me anything." She was almost wagging her tail in an excited puppy-dog manner, now that she was off the hook for murder.

Shona supposed all the staff in the hospital were probably terrified they were going to become a suspect and be arrested for something they knew they didn't do. Except one. Their murderer was probably so confident, they thought they could never get caught. If it was a member of staff that is, but it had to be. All these thoughts flashed through her brain before she said, "Rhianna, when you went into the room and found Mrs McTaggart dead, how did she look?"

There was silence. Shona could see every emotion dance over her face, wondering where this was going. "What's that got to do with anything?"

"If it wasn't important, I wouldn't be asking. I know it sounds strange, but I need you to think about it and answer my question as fully as you can."

"She was white. It was obvious she was dead."

Shona needed to re-evaluate her interview questions. "Can you talk me through everything from walking into the room until the crash team arrived."

I went in at 6 am to do her obs…" She took in Shona's blank look and said, "Her pulse and blood pressure. I said good morning and switched on the low light. That was when I knew something wasn't right. She was white and her face looked like wax. It was obvious she wasn't breathing as her chest wasn't moving up and down. I took her pulse, shouted for help, and pulled the emergency cord."

If she could see her patient's chest, then it looked like Sarah McTaggart was lying on her back. "Do you remember how she was lying in bed?"

Rhianna looked up at the ceiling, her eyes half closed. Eventually she looked back at Shona and said, "On her back. She looked so peaceful."

"Do you remember how the covers were arranged?"

More ceiling searching and then, "She only had a sheet on, and it was pulled right up and tucked under her chin." She thought again and her brows furrowed. "Now I think about it, it was odd. It was tucked in all around her. Like a shroud. I had to pull it out to check her pulse."

Bingo, she had her pattern. Or at least the start of one. She also had another idea.

"Thank you. Let's find Rabbie and see if he enjoyed his tour of the police station."

It turned out Rabbie did and now wanted to be a policeman instead of a fireman. Shona wondered what he would want to be next week. She jolly well hoped it wasn't still a policeman thirteen years later. He was in for a sore disappointment if it was.

31

Her idea involved more phone calls to the hospital. She wanted the names and roles of every single person who had attended all the crash calls. If there was a name that came up repeatedly, then they could be killing the patients in the first instance for the thrill of the resuscitation attempt. The hero, or heroine, rushing to the rescue and playing the hero. At the back of her mind, she had the feeling it was somewhat unlikely, but she had to follow every possible lead no matter how improbable it might be.

It was officially knocking off time, so she went to see the team. She'd no sooner set foot in the office, than her phone rang; she did another dash to answer it. This was growing old. It was one of the charge nurses from the hospital.

"Another suspicious death?" Her pulse quickened. She might get to see the crime scene this time.

"No. I wanted to let you know that Dave Carabiniere has been admitted to my ward."

What? She wasn't expecting that. "Did he ask you to ring us?"

"No." There was silence and then her voice continued,

tentatively, "In fact he told us not to tell you. However, it looks like he's been beaten and dumped at the front door of A&E. I'm reporting a crime."

"Isn't that breaking patient confidentiality, informing us about his admission?" She hesitated for the space of a heartbeat and added, "And his diagnosis.

"Not if I feel a crime is being committed."

What this meant, she wasn't sure, but she intended to find out.

Peter volunteered to come with her as he was the only member of the team who didn't have plans that night, other than watching Emmerdale and Coronation Street.

"I didn't have you down as a soap opera fan."

"Oh, aye. Never miss an episode. The wife will record them for me, and I'll eat my tea while I watch them."

It just goes to show you never really know anyone. How long had she worked with Peter, and this little fact had escaped her?

Dodgy Dave was not in a good way. The bits of his body that could be seen were varying hues of purple with his usual peely wally skin tone peeping out in the odd space between. Both arms were in plaster and one eye was so swollen Shona wondered if he'd ever open it again.

"Who did this to you?"

"Who called you lot? I told them not to." He slurred his words; they were difficult to understand.

Shona took a stab at responding. "Someone reported a crime, so we're here to investigate it. We need a wee chat."

"Not easy." He tried a new sentence on for size. "Not now." It was marginally clearer.

"I promise we'll make it quick. Who did this to you?"

"Fell downstairs."

"I can see a bruise shaped like a size nine footprint on your side. That gown's not exactly covering your modesty."

As he attempted to cover himself up a groan escaped from his lips. His breathing quickened but that also brought a yelp of pain.

"Fell."

"And dumped yourself at the door of the hospital? I don't think so. Do you want to know what I do think? The Alexeyevs are right up to their thick Slavic necks in this."

Fear flashed in his eyes, or at least the one they could see. "No."

Peter looked at Shona and she gave an almost unnoticeable nod. He said, "Come on now, Dave, man tae man, do you no' want to put them away for a few years?"

"It was not them." His was his clearest sentence yet.

"See, I think your lying and I'm no' sure my DI believes you either."

Shona had had enough. "It's obvious this was done by human hands." She paused. "And feet. Now, if you don't help us, we'll think you're lying about everything you've told us." She looked straight into his one good eye. "Including the murders."

That loosened his tongue but not enough. "Didn't see them. Maybe moneylenders."

"Did you borrow that money form the Alexeyevs?"

"No." He then refused to say another word, regardless of what they asked him. The staff nurse gave them short shrift and threw them out.

"Dodgy Dave's lying through his teeth."

"Aye, Ma'am, but we can't prove it."

"And Tweedledum and Tweedledee get away with it again. Safe home."

"Sometimes you can be right English." His grin took the sting from the words.

"Aye." Laughing, they parted company and headed for their respective cars and home.

32

The hard work paid off and graduation day came. The sun shone brightly, and their mother and siblings were there to cheer them on. Pride radiated from their mother's face; the careworn look changed if only momentarily. She looked younger, happier, more content.

The weight lifted off their shoulders, knowing that life would now be easier in one sense. Only one job to do, albeit a hard one. Long days, long nights but the possibility of progression. A steady wage now coming in, life would be easier for everyone. That wage may not be huge but there would be regular increases. Also, one of their siblings had joined the Army and the other the Air Force, so the money worries had eased. Life was once more comfortable for the family.

Still the work was hard, but they were happy to be doing some good in the world. The hours were gruelling but that did not bother them, they were used to little sleep; it was as though they had been training for this role for the last seven years. People respected and looked up to them. They met their partner and fell in love. This was how life should be. Idyllic. Beautiful. Perfect. They now had it all.

33

Shona regretted her request to be notified day and night at precisely 2.13 a.m. when she was awoken from a sound sleep by a ringing phone. She sat up, fumbled around on the bedtable, and grabbed it. "McKenzie."

She felt a claw scratch at her leg; Shakespeare registering her disapproval at being disturbed. "Oww. No not you," she said into the phone. "What's up?" She threw back the quilt, staggered out of bed, and headed to the kitchen. As she listened, she hit the on button on the Tassimo machine. "You've to go to Narrywells, Ma'am," a sleepy sounding desk sergeant said. "There's a suspicious death requires your attention. They said to hurry as they need to move the body ASAP."

"Tell them I'm on my way. Also, tell them not to touch anything." She brushed her teeth and hair and threw on some clothes; she'd just have to join the great unwashed for the next few hours. True to her word, she was on her way within five minutes clutching a travel mug filled to the brim with the nectar of life itself.

She met Peter and Iain at the hospital. The rest of the team were still asleep. Too many people cluttering the place up would just cause havoc in such a small space and she wanted to let the other patient's sleep. It would be an unusual crime scene in that, it wasn't really a crime scene. It was a suspicious death in a hospital.

Peter moaned fit to bust all the way to the ward but stopped the minute they walked through the door. Having been a patient himself not so long ago, he knew how noisy a hospital ward could be and the almost impossible task of trying to sleep through it.

She needn't have worried about telling them not to touch anything. The patient's room looked like a herd of heiland coos had stampeded through it.

"What's with all the mess?" she asked, her voice low.

"It's always like this after a resuscitation attempt."

Good grief, how would she make sense of this. What she wanted was to see them before the crash team arrived but unless she moved her entire life into the hospital, that wasn't going to happen. There went that plan. Maybe not such a good idea after all. She was still going to follow it through though as you never know what an immediate investigation might throw up. Also, the staff would be much more able to remember all that happened. Before they stepped through the door, she asked Iain to take photographs. He looked far happier than any sane man had a right to at 3.30 am. He'd no sooner got the camera ready and put one step through the door, than a nurse screamed up to them, saying, "You can't take photos in there." Her voice was much higher than a night shift would dictate.

"Shona whipped a piece of paper out of her pocket and handed it over. "If you check the warrant, it says we can take photos."

"Fine. Just be quick. We've another patient coming in who needs the bed. We've got to prepare Mrs. Entwistle's body for going to the mortuary." She looked relieved. As long as she wasn't on the hook for any impropriety, she was happy to let them do what they wanted.

Ian was efficient, speedy, and in his element. At last, he had something to get his teeth into. There wasn't much in the way of photographs to be taken. Shona wondered if they were allowed to do fingerprints. Was this a crime scene and could they treat it like one? This was a whole new bailiwick for her. She was used to going in all guns blazing and investigating the heck out of a scene. All this tiptoeing around had her shackled up ways of Wednesday. She was in half a mind to ring Douglas and ask him about treating it as a crime scene. She pulled out her phone before common sense prevailed and she shoved it back in her pocket for several sensible reasons. Firstly, this was taking advantage of her personal relationship with the procurator fiscal. Secondly, she'd probably wake the kids and she wasn't keen on dragging them into this whole sorry mess. Thirdly, he was not going to make a decision in the middle of the night. Lastly, he would probably join forces with the boss to get her sacked thinking she'd finally flipped. She resolved to do it first thing in the morning. She asked Peter to take a general look around the ward to see if there was anything that appeared suspicious.

"How am I meant to know. I don't know anything about hospital wards."

"You were a patient in one, so you know a damn lot more than me."

Once the photographs were completed, Shona stepped into the room. She didn't know if she was relieved or saddened. Once the resuscitation attempt was completed, the staff had left the body as it was, in accordance with the directive from the procurator fiscal. How they'd remembered was a mystery to her; then she realised they were probably as keen to get to the end of all of this as she was. More so, in fact.

The woman could be roughly in her late fifties, early sixties, although it was difficult to tell these days. Hands were what Shona usually used as a gauge, so she knew she was somewhere in the ballpark. Mrs Entwistle had neatly trimmed fingernails and hair that, despite the obvious bed hair, was also neatly trimmed. She obviously took care of herself. There was nothing to suggest why she had died. Nothing out of the ordinary apart from the fact she was dead. She searched the room but couldn't tell what was out of the ordinary in amongst the normal accoutrements of someone who had been a patient for some time, and the detritus of a failed resuscitation attempt. As a reader herself, she was interested to see the woman had been reading *A Thousand Splendid Suns* by Khaled Hosseini. The bookmark showed she was almost finished. Shona felt sad that Mrs Entwistle would never know the end. It brought the death into stark reality and personalised someone who could otherwise just be seen as yet another victim.

The nurse who found their potential victim agreed to have a coffee break to answer their questions. Shona was grateful for both the chat and the coffee, her caffeine hit from her early morning brew having long gone. She felt like Methuselah on a bad day.

In response to Shona asking what she'd found, she said, "When I looked through the window of her room on a routine check, something didn't feel right, so I went in to take a closer look. She was dead. That was obvious but I took her pulse anyway. I called the crash team. The doctor certified her and then called you."

"What did the room look like? Was there anything out of the ordinary."

"Nothing, but to be honest I was too busy worrying about Mrs Entwistle to take in much of the surroundings."

This may seem a strange question, but I have to ask. Can you remember what the bedcovers were like?"

She thought for a minute and said, "Now you come to

mention it. She only had the sheet on and that was tucked in and pulled right up to her chin."

"Thank you. Final question, what's the name of the doctor who certified her dead, and can I speak to them?"

"Dr Somers. I'll ask her to come to the ward. She might be a while as the whole hospital seems to be crazy busy right now."

So much for no one wanting to be admitted. Shona would hate to think what it would be like if there wasn't the hesitancy re admission. Then the name she'd been given penetrated the early morning brain fog.

"*Natasha* Somers?"

"Yes."

They had the first name that came up twice in respect of any of these deaths. Did they have their killer? She didn't want to think that lovely young woman would be their murderer, but she knew the nicest of people could turn out to have a dark side. "If she's free, can I speak to her?"

The nurse came back and reported that Dr Somers would be about twenty minutes. She asked if Shona wanted to speak to anyone else.

"I'll need to speak to all the night staff. Were any patients nearby awake?"

"Mr Bagaley was awake and asking for a cup of tea. You'll not get much sense out of him though as he's got special needs. Lovely chap but his IQ is somewhere south of sixty. There's only one more member of staff on – Alex Leander, my HCA. I'll send him in, but I'd be grateful if you'd be quick as we're flat out."

"Before you go, think carefully are you sure you didn't notice anything or anyone out of the ordinary?"

"No. Definitely not."

"If anything comes to mind, here's my number." She handed over one of the flash business cards they were now all forced to carry. It felt a bit unnecessary to Shona, given the budget cuts but who was she to argue with the top brass.

Alex knew even less than the staff nurse as he was down the other end of the ward. The first he knew about anything was when the emergency alarm went off. She handed out another business card with the same exhortation, call me if anything comes to mind. She wasn't confident she'd hear from either of them but at least they could get hold of her if the need arose.

While she waited, she grabbed the staff nurse and asked where any needles and syringes would be disposed of and could they see it. She grabbed Iain and asked him to come with them. Once they clapped eyes on it, she asked Iain to get it into evidence.

"I'm not sure I've a big enough bag as it wasn't officially a crime scene as yet."

"Get uniform to blue light one over."

Natasha was there in under thirty minutes, looking as harried as she had the previous time, with dark circles under her eyes and obviously having difficulty putting one weary foot in front of the other.

"Thank you for coming to speak to me again."

"It does seem to be like a particularly nasty habit. No offence meant but speaking to the police is not in my top ten favourite ways to spend my time."

"Speaking to doctors in the middle of the night isn't at the top of my list either, but here we are."

The Doctor attempted a smile and said, "If the questions are the same as last time, then I'll save you time. No, I didn't notice anything unusual. No, I don't know what the cause of death was. Yes, I sent her for an autopsy. No, I don't know what might have killed her."

"That's those ones done and dusted then. Were you surprised when she died?"

"I didn't really know her. I was just the doctor on call."

"What was she admitted for in the first place?"

"She had part of her foot amputated for gangrene but was recovering at warp speed and looking forward to going home. According to her notes that is. As I say, not one of my patients."

"Why were you called? Surely it should have been her own doctor?"

"Her own doctor was pushing out the zzzz's in his own bed in Invergowrie. I, on the other hand, was snatching a well-earned ten-minute nap slung on top of the covers in the on-call room."

"I'm still puzzled as to why cancer patients and orthopaedic patients were being looked after by the same doctor."

"They weren't. They were certified dead by the same doctor. There's a difference. I'm on call. I'm called. I certify them dead."

Shona gave the doctor a pass on the sharp tone as she was sleep deprived and busy. "Do you know anything about the other women who died under similar circumstances?"

"What other women?"

Shona's first response to this was to tell her she was taking the mick as the hospital was awash with gossip about the dead women. Then she decided prudence was the best option and told her the names of the women. "Has this jogged your memory?"

"Not in the slightest. I don't recognise anyone on that list."

She hoped the doctor was telling the truth as she was going to investigate her responses every which way and back again.

"Are you sure?"

"Do you think I have anything to do with those murders?" Natasha looked ready to fly the coop.

"You know we have to check everything."

"Okay." She looked less than convince2525255

"It's important that you tell us everything. No matter how inconsequential it is."

The doctor's phone rang. She answered and said, "On it.

Now." Hanging up she said, "I've got to go. If I think of anything that would help, I'll let you know. I hope I don't see you too soon."

Shona thought there was every chance they'd be seeing each other down the nick directly. In fact, the minute the doctor had some sleep and wasn't a walking zombie.

Shona had a couple of more questions for the staff nurse before she, Peter and Iain headed for the hospital staff canteen and a spot of breakfast. The harried nurse said she could spare two minutes and no more as the patients were waking up and they barely had a minute between them never mind two.

"Are Mrs Entwistle's next of kin coming in?"

"Not until later." Her eyes darted all round as she took in what was happening on the ward. "Much later."

"Do they not usually want to see the body?"

"Yes. But Mr Entwistle chose not to. He's coming in later to get the death certificate and her effects."

"Can we please have her address?"

"I'm not allowed to give that infor—"

"Remember this?" Shona showed her the warrant again.

The staff nurse hurried to the office with Shona hot at her heels. She wrote the address down and handed it to Shona, saying, "I've really got to go now."

Shona really had to go as well. A full Scottish breakfast and a large coffee were calling her name in the staff canteen.

"Do you no' think it's weird yon woman's husband didn't want to come in and see her body?"

"I think it's extremely weird, hence the reason, Iain and I will be visiting him. You, my friend will be going back to the station to make sure the troops have their nose to the grindstone."

Peter looked both exhausted and singularly happy about

the suggestion. He, like many of them, was too old for this middle of the night malarky, but Shona wanted his take on things as his knowledge of crime scenes was unsurpassed. His take moved the case forward not one inch. "I'm fair flummoxed with all this. It's no' as if you can look at the body and know exactly what went down."

"It's tough when we don't even know if it's a crime scene. We can't do all the usual forensic checks."

Then the only sound that could be heard was that of chewing, swallowing, slurping. From their table that is. Shona listened carefully to the conversations at the tables around them. There was nothing useful to be gained. Like them the staff were baffled. And scared. They were all terrified it could happen on their ward and they could be blamed.

Shona's car pointed its nose towards Clepington Road, whilst the state-of-the-art infotainment system blasted out Tchaikovsky. She was convinced the system cost as much as the car and wanted to make good use of it. The rush hour traffic was crippling so it took her forty minutes to do a ten-minute journey, a situation never guaranteed to boost her mood. She drummed her fingers on the steering wheel and considered using her horn, then decided that was not the best move for an officer of the law and it wasn't the fault of the poor sods in front of her. They were just trying to get to their job much like her. As her mood fell her adrenaline levels rose in direct proportions. Shona had never been famed for her patience, but this case had knocked all her patience into the middle of next week. She wanted something she could gnaw on. Something tangible. This case was so intangible it was more otherworldly than real. The journey at least gave her time to think about the case but that got her antsy, pushed out yet more adrenaline, and made her jittery. That in turn gave her a headache.

She'd need every single jolt of that adrenaline in the not-too-distant future and have to put it to good use.

34

Iain met her outside the next of kin's closie, as tenement blocks were known in the fair city of Dundee, and they trudged up three flights of stairs to a top floor flat. Shona was glad all that running kept her fit as there seemed to be a fair few flats in Dundee and their witnesses or victims all seemed to be on the top floor. In the absence of a doorbell, she rattled the letterbox. No one answered, so she rattled it even harder. Eventually it was opened by a man wearing nothing but a grubby vest and boxer-shorts. His hair was long and greasy, his beard equally long and greasy. Behind him there were bags piled up. He glared at them with a look that suggested this was not a man who was grieving.

"What the fu—"

The smell of alcohol radiating from his breath as he spoke nearly knocked Shona off her feet. Flashing her ID card she said Detective Inspector McKenzie. I'd like a word with you about your wife's d—"

"I'm no speaking to the polis." He slammed the door in her face.

Shona said, "Call for backup. Ask them to bring an official car, the type with a blue light on the top. I've a feeling we're going to need it." She sighed again, in fact make it a couple.

Iain complied.

Shona rattled the letterbox again and when there was no response banged with her fist. She didn't know what was going on, but she wasn't leaving without finding out.

Then, the door flew open, the man grabbed Shona by the shirt and pulled her in through the door. Shock and the huge kitchen knife that gleamed in his hand convinced her not to put up much of a fight. Just before the door slammed, she heard Iain shout, "They've got the DI. Send assistance immediately."

Then she and her captor were alone.

"What did you go and do that for? I only wanted to speak to you about your wife. Now you're on a false imprisonment charge. We could put it down to grief and you'll get away with it if you let me go now."

"Shut the fu—"

"I know your wife's death must be devastating and grief makes us do things we wouldn't normally do." Shona's calm voice belied the hammering in her heart which threatened to burst out of her chest.

"What are you on about? I'm glad the stupid cow's gone. She'd walked out on me anyway. The only thing she did right was die before the divorce came through." He ran one hand through his greasy hair. The other still clutched Shona's shirt. "It means I'll get her insurance money."

He shoved Shona through a door into the sitting room, which was packed floor to ceiling with boxes. From what she could see, there were televisions, phones, tablets, microwaves, and every other electronic device that had every been invented. She had no doubt they'd fallen off the back of a lorry; this bloke was a fence. How could a simple chat with a supposedly grieving relative turn into a hostage situation. The chief was going to freak.

"Sit down." The couch was as greasy as the man and Shona didn't really want to sit down. The knife waving about in front of her face convinced her otherwise. Trousers were replaceable her looks, or life, less so.

"You know you'll get less time for holding me against my will than you will for murder, right?"

"Do women always speak as much? You're worse than my wife." He grinned. At least Shona thought it was a grin – it looked more like a grimace. "No' that she's my wife anymore. I should say dead wife."

"Not much cop in the wife department then?"

He looked at her askance, but the hand holding the knife relaxed a bit.

"Bloody useless. Always nagging. Didnae give me my conjugal rights if you know what I mean." He winked.

Shona's heart sank. Just when she thought it couldn't get any worse it turned out she was stuck in a top floor flat with a randy drunk holding a knife, who thought sex was his God given right. She had a feeling this was not going to end well for her. All the training at the police academy was focussed on a hostage situation where the officer wasn't the hostage. Her leg started to jerk but she forced it to stop by pressing down hard on her thigh. She just needed to keep him talking for long enough that the others would do something.

"Tell me about her."

"It was great at first and then she started whining and whinging. I was never good enough. Get a job. Change your life. Stop smoking. Stop drinking. Stop thieving." He pulled a packet of cigarettes from his pocket, opened it with his free hand and pulled out a cigarette. "On, and on, and on. Best day of my life when she walked out the door."

"You are best shot of her. Sounds like my fiancé. Moans I'm always at work. Carps on about a wedding date. Turns up at all times of the day and night. Never gives me a minute's peace." She missed out the part that he was the procurator fiscal, and the day and night usually involved a dead body and official business. Building a rapport was more important than sticking to the exact truth.

"So, you know what I went through?" He grabbed a lighter from the table and lit the cigarette taking a deep drag and exhaling slowly.

The smell told Shona it wasn't tobacco, it was blow. Just when she thought things might be picking up, they took a nose-dive. Let's add drug fuelled maniac to the previous list of crap that life had dealt her in the past hour.

The flicker of the emergency vehicle strobe lights bathed the room in a multicoloured hue. Shona ignored them and tuned out the accompanying noise.

"Have you got any whisky? I could do with one and you look like you could too." She hoped he'd put the knife down and she could maybe overcome him. Mind you, he might be a drunk and a user, but he had some serious muscles. She didn't think he got them in a gym; probably lifted a home gym and did a spot of weightlifting somewhere in this flat. Either that or he was legally employed as a builder.

"Good idea." Unfortunately, for her plan, there was already a bottle opened at the side of the chair. He poured generous measures into a couple of mugs. That just happened to be standing by. Damn, what level of bacteria were they sporting? Shona worked on the assumption the alcohol would kill anything off. He swallowed it down in one and glowered at Shona. "Are ye not drinking?"

Shona had seen the label, and this was the cheapest gut-rot he could buy. Even with minimum unit pricing this could not have cost more than twelve quid. "She took a swig and let most of it slosh back into the mug. She'd learnt this little trick at university when she didn't want to take part in drinking games. She was more a sip and savour girl than a slug and get sloshed.

"Do ye want more?" The man's words were beginning to slur.

"In a minute. I don't want to drink all your best whisky." She appealed to his vanity.

He slugged down another generous measure and then another. His eyes started to droop, and the knife fell to his side.

Shona watched him carefully. The minute his eyes closed, she took advantage, leapt up, and bolted for the door. She yanked it open. The man jumped up and stumbled after her. She ran like the devil was in hot pursuit, which she actually felt he was. She leapt down the stairs, missing some and praying she wouldn't miss her footing. As she approached the door of the close she started yelling, "It's Shona. Don't shoot. It's me but he's behind me."

A yell came from behind her, and she ran harder. She burst out through the door and was whisked into a waiting ambulance. The team, fully armed, stepped forward waiting for the abductor. He didn't appear.

"I'm going in," Peter said.

"Be careful, he's got a knife," Shona yelled after him.

She'd have been better saving her breath to cool her porridge, neither he, nor the rest of her team, paid a blind bit of notice. They were out two minutes later.

Nina pelted up to the ambulance crew. "You lot are needed in there. He's gone beard over backside down the stairs and is spark out. I checked his pulse, he's alive."

Shona, who'd been given the all clear by the paramedics before the rushed off, said, "Roy, go in and cuff him. The rest of you, go in and catalogue all the electrical gear he's got stashed in there." Don't touch it as it will need to be dusted for prints. "I'd wager my pay on the fact it's as hot as hell."

Exhaustion set in as the adrenaline washed away. She sat down on the stretcher in the ambulance, lay back against the wall and closed her eyes.

35

Then, in an instant, everything changed. Tanks rolled in. Soldiers patrolled the streets. Family, friends, and neighbours were forced from their homes at gunpoint. If they argued, they were shot. They watched as blood flowed in the street. Did what they could to help but it was useless. They could not stem the endless tide of inhumanity which had taken over their country. People, who had known each other all their lives, turned one against the other – every man, or woman, for themselves. They fought over every scarce scrap of food and deaths occurred over nothing more than the last loaf of bread. Their fellow countrymen died of starvation, in a country once rich in resources. Still, they tried to help - worked morning until night to provide care for their fellow countrymen and food for their family. Compassion for humanity flowed through their veins, pumping out with every hopeful heartbeat. One day, this would be over, and their beautiful country would return.

Then, their partner and two of their siblings were raped, beaten, and shot, for nothing more than the soldiers' sport. Pain tore through them. How could this happen in the twenty-first century? That day, something snapped.

36

Back at the station, the chief insisted she went home for a couple of hours and had a rest. He said the paperwork could wait. As could her being interviewed as a victim. For once she didn't argue, although, she wasn't that keen on being described as a victim. She instructed Peter and Iain to do the same and set the others a task.

"I want you to get warrants to search the houses of all the dead women. Inform their relatives and ask them to be present."

"They'll flip," Nina said.

Abigail chipped in, "And I wouldn't blame them." She brushed crumbs from her jacket. "Why are we searching their houses when they've not been accused of any crime?"

"I want to see if they had anything in common. We're looking for diaries. Notebooks. Letters. Literally anything that might mention names."

"Are you thinking secret society?" Roy asked, excitement shining from his eyes. He and Jason high fived.

"I'm thinking connections but after some of our cases I wouldn't dismiss cults or societies out of hand." She rubbed her eyes and blinked to keep the utter exhaustion at bay. "Ask the relatives in the first instance. Save the warrants as a last resort. Explain we are merely looking for anything which will help us solve their relative's death."

"Won't they think it's a bit strange given the deaths happened in a hospital?" Abigail's eyes were twin pools of concern.

"As we are all over this like measles, they have probably worked out this is now a murder investigation and their nearest and dearest are a part of it. Reassure them neither they, nor their relatives are under suspicion." She stood up realising she'd just lied through her teeth. Everyone was under suspicion until proven otherwise.

"Nina, as the senior sergeant here, you're in charge until I return. Get this lot moving or I'll be back before they get going."

She left them to it, after asking a copper to take her home in a squad car and pick her up again in three hours. In her current state, driving would be, not only foolish, but dangerous. The same car dropped Peter and Iain off. Even the fiercely independent Peter didn't have the energy to argue.

Three hours later she was back at the coal mines and writing a statement about the hostage situation. She was also awaiting an interview regarding the former and the accident and subsequent injury of the only other person involved in most of it. The chief had lost all care and concern over the matter and had entered the righteous indignation stage of the process.

"Why does every single case you are involved in end in drama?"

"To be fair, Sir, I couldn't have foreseen this."

"You're off the case until your interview—"

"What? Sir no, I—"

"If you'd let me finish, I was saying, I have arranged your interview for one hour's time. Leave the building, go to the nearest café, and don't step foot back in here until I phone you. Do, I make myself clear?"

"Yes, Sir. Thank you."

"One final thing, Inspector, don't ever interrupt me again."

"Sorry, Sir." This time she meant it.

As the hospital breakfast had long faded from memory, she occupied herself getting outside a spot of lunch and topping up her caffeine levels. Before she knew it, she was in an interview room explaining herself to a couple of po-faced civilian suits. She forced herself to remain calm and polite, otherwise they'd recommend a long and tedious investigation that could last for weeks. The gist of it would be, she had such a temper she shoved the unconscious man down the stairs. The only thing she had going for her was that the screams happened after she'd hurtled through the front door of the flats. They said they were satisfied for now and she could return to duty. However, they still had to interview Iain and the team.

Peter and Iain were also back in the fold; the others were conspicuous by their absence.

"How come you get an hour off and we were straight into it?"

"Straight into it? What have you done in the last couple of hours?"

"Done all the paperwork for our visit to the hospital." His face shone with virtue."

"Me too," Iain said, before she had a chance to question his work ethic.

"Well, aren't you a couple of little angels. Have either of you had lunch yet?"

"No. We were too scared the chief would come in and find us missing. He's no' in a very good mood."

"Off you pop to the canteen then. I'll get my side of the paperwork squared away and catch up with Nina."

They scurried off before she could change her mind.

Nina had left a note on Shona's desk. She and Roy were searching a house in Fife; Abigail and Jason doing similar in Dundee. They'd borrowed a couple of uniform to assist. Shona decided to catch up with her own paperwork before ringing her. The state of play could wait another hour.

37

An hour later found the three musketeers – Shona, Peter, and Iain – searching Sarah McTaggart's house. Her son had agreed to the request and was currently helping them. Shona wasn't sure about the idea of the son stepping in, but she searched with him, and Peter and Iain paired up. That way, she could be sure nothing would be hidden, and the search would be quicker as the house had six bedrooms, three sitting rooms, a gym, study, dining room, library and enough bathrooms it could be classed as a hotel. Not that she was too worried about the son hiding anything as he was not only fully compliant but sure there were shenanigans going on. He wanted answers.

"My mum was on her way home. There's no way she should be dead. Who dies days after a bloody appendicectomy? Nobody, that's who."

"It does seem a bit unusual. Did the hospital give you any answers?"

"No, and they didn't give us her body either. We haven't even been able to have the funeral. At this rate, my brother will have to go back to Australia before we've had it."

Shona made soothing noises as she pulled open yet another

drawer in the study. She also resolved to have a word with Mary, and the chief, about releasing the body. "That must be difficult for you."

"You think?" He pulled a drawer open, picked a notebook up, rifled through it and handed it to Shona. They both wore gloves; not that they were going to dust for fingerprints, but the chain of evidence needed to be maintained just in case. Shona dropped the notebook in an evidence bag and, in turn, into a larger bag she carried. Not having a full forensics team in situ was not only unusual, but inconvenient.

"What do you think happened?" By this time Shona was looking in the bookshelves for anything out of the ordinary. They were jam-packed with cookbooks, at least thirty of which were written by Sarah herself. Not surprising considering Sarah made a living as a television chef. A good living if this house was anything to go by. Shona had noticed the headlines in *The Courier* about the chef dying but hadn't really paid much attention. Having no interest in cooking or the newspapers, it passed her by, so she didn't directly tie it in to her case. She wondered why Peter hadn't told her.

"Someone on that ward murdered her."

"Do you have any specific reason to believe that?"

"Other than she shouldn't be dead? No."

"Was there any member of staff who you think acted a bit oddly or your mother complained about?"

"Not at all. She was complimentary about everyone from the consultant to the cleaners. Not that I ever saw either of them, of course. Just nursing staff who were all attentive."

Shona stopped her search and wiped her brow with her arm. It was stifling in here. "Did any of them seem too attentive?"

"I was more focussed on my mother than the nursing staff, although one of them was a stunner." A smile lit up his face, the first Shona had seen, and she couldn't help but smile back.

Shona reached an antique rosewood writing bureau which was locked up tighter than an otter's pocket – not only the top but the drawers and cupboards at the bottom. "Any idea where the keys are kept?"

"Not a clue."

They added keys, or one individual key, into their search. This much security could only mean one thing – evidence.

It was time to change tack.

"Is your father on the scene?"

"South Africa. They divorced years go and we've barely seen him since. I let him know but he's too busy with a wife and six kids out there to come back." He didn't sound too bothered by it.

"Was it acrimonious?"

"My father was also a chef and jealous as all get out; she'd made it to the big time and he hadn't. He used the divorce money to open a restaurant in South Africa, where he was from originally. It's gone like gangbusters and is now an international chain. So, he's happy as a clam." He slammed a cupboard door shut and Shona winced. This was definitely the real McCoy in the way of antiques and treating it like that wasn't the wisest of moves. "If you're thinking he had anything to do with this, you're barking up the wrong baobab."

Shona assumed that was a tree indigenous to South Africa. Unlikely her ex had killed her for the money then. Still, you never knew. In fact, who did get all the money from her death? The house must be worth over half a million and the antiques filling every nook and cranny would add on another million at least. Could be more.

"Has her will been read yet? Who inherits all of this?"

"No. We were hoping we could do it after the funeral, but we might need to bring it forward while my brother's here. Why are you asking all this? Do you think one of us had her bumped off because we benefited from her death?" He paused and stared at her. "Let me make it easy for you. My seven siblings and I all have high paying jobs and not a one of us wants for anything. Except a mother now."

Shona would reserve judgement on that and resolved to look into the finances of all eight of the siblings. She also resolved to look at the wills of all the women who had died; there might be a common denominator.

"I am sure you understand we have to look at everything."

He acquiesced but they carried on in silence.

The search quick and methodical, they left carrying several notebooks and numerous letters. Shona signed a receipt for everything in the evidence bag, saying they would return them ASAP. She reassured him they would do everything in their power to find out anything about his mother's death. She gained permission to return when she'd worked out a way of getting into the bureau.

They repeated this another couple of times. The niece of one of the victims was happy to oblige, the daughter of the other just wanted to put the whole sorry mess behind them and get on with life. They wanted a funeral, the will to be tied up and their family to start grieving. Neither knew any of the other women nor did they know what was in the will. The one thing they were completely sure of was, their relative was murdered by someone in the hospital. No specific reason, just gut feeling and the rumours flying around. By this point Shona had what felt like a squadron of two-year-olds banging away in her head, and enough evidence to keep them going until Christmas.

38

The others had an equal amount of evidence. They'd gone to Malcolm Sentinel's house, despite a gut feeling he was an innocent bystander who got caught up in this ongoing nightmare. Still, they couldn't be too sure and gut feelings didn't stand up in court. Going through all the evidence was mind numbing, intense and sheer hard slog. Every word was cross checked and cross checked again by everyone. They looked for patterns, names or anything which could be considered unusual.

"Some of these women are a bit racy," Peter said, his face bright red. "This is no' good for my heart."

"Stop talking rubbish." The laughter in Shona's voice took the sharpness from her tone. "When did you turn into a choirboy. You've probably seen more than most in your time on the force."

"Aye, maybe, but I'm too old for this now." He turned a page and fanned himself. "Heavens, I didnae know such things went on in Dundee."

"Me neither." Even Roy, the original wild child of the team, was looking askance at the pink leather diary he held in his hands. He dropped it on the table and said, "Such things shouldn't be allowed."

"Roy, you spend all day wallowing in this sort of thing on the internet." Shona took in his face and added, "For official reasons of course."

"That's different. These are women just like my mum."

Nina said, "I've got one that's extremely sexually explicit as well."

By this point even Shona was looking somewhat scandalised. "Anyone else."

The others all shook their heads. "Mine's positively boring compared to those," Abigail said. "This place is much more exciting than Skye."

"By the sounds of it, it's more exciting than Oxford. That takes some doing considering the shenanigans the students get up to, especially during freshers' week." She threw down the notebook she was looking at and said, "Jason and Iain, go and photocopy the three explicit notebooks twice. We'll split into teams and compare all three at once to see if there are any themes."

"You mean I've to read that again?"

"Man up, Peter. Pull your big boy pants on and set to it."

For the next hour the only sound to be heard was the slurping of coffee, the crunching of biscuits and the turning of pages. In the end they'd gained an extensive education and the knowledge that all three women belonged to an organisation called, Horny Housewives of Dundee.

Shona sat back in her chair and cradled her coffee cup. "Who knew Dundee was such a hotbed of sin and debauchery?"

"Who knew a bunch of old women would be into such things." Roy looked like he'd sucked a lemon.

"Roy. That's quite enough." Her look could kill an elephant

at a nine-mile distance. "I can see another equality and diversity course in your future."

This was enough to drag him back in line. He'd done one when she first took the team over and swore he never wanted to do another as he'd gone through the wringer the first time.

"Sorry."

She turned her attention to the whole team. "Does anyone know anything about the Horny Housewives?"

To a man and woman, they looked at their feet and shook their heads. Who knew her team were such a bunch of prudes. Especially the men, who jumped at every chance to visit Cats Eyes, a lap dancing club, yet were scandalised at the thought of older women doing much the same thing. Double standards didn't even begin to cover it.

"Roy, go and do a search on the interweb. I want to know everything this group gets up to. And I mean everything."

He blushed from his head to his toes and mumbled.

Shona ignored whatever complaint he was making. "Just do it and stop being such a wuss. You're one of Dundee's finest detectives, not a ballerina." He scuttled off and she yelled at his retreating back, "Get me the name and address of someone I can interview."

"What will *we* do, Ma'am?" Jason asked.

"We," she said, picking up her mug, "will be refilling the coffee and then reading every other piece of paper we have in evidence to look for more patterns."

The team groaned in unison, united in their hatred of the current task. Shona loved a coherent team, something which was rarer than a mountain climbing haggis.

Checking, and double checking took what seemed to feel like forever. It was slow, painstaking, and turned their eyes to sandpaper. Eyes were rubbed and notebooks filled up at a crawl. Several carafes of coffee and pots of tea later they'd discovered the square root of nothing. There appeared to be only three housewives in the secret society. The remainder of the women, and Malcolm, had nothing in common, according to the diaries, notebooks, and letters they had scoured in such detail. Shona put down her pen and wandered off to find Roy.

His eyes were also red, and if all the sweet papers strewn on the ground around him were anything to go by, it would seem his search was sponsored by Mars.

"How's it going, Sherlock?"

"I'm not easily shocked, but the things I've seen on the Internet today would make the most hardened prossie blush."

"Anything about our housewives with the strange hobby?"

"Not yet but I haven't given up."

"How on earth did they find out about this oh so secret society?"

"If my mother is anything to go by, then they'll be passing things on by word of mouth." Then he realised what he had just said and hurriedly added, "Not that I mean my mum is anything to do with our housewives. I mean she and her cronies tell each other about any groups they join and encourage their friends to join as well."

Shona laughed as she took in his beetroot face. "I knew what you meant, Roy. I've met your mother, and she's a paragon of virtue." Then, a grin on her face, she said, "Apart from the fact she spoiled you rotten, that is."

Roy winked and turned back to his computer, effectively ending their conversation. Shona shrugged and headed off. She'd grown used to being totally ignored at the end of every conversation she ever had. A couple of years ago she would have bitten his head off, but the lad had grown on her, and he didn't half come in useful when it came to computing skills. She'd come to realise the team would be a lot worse off without him. Even if he had let her down when it came to the housewives. If it was word of mouth that was spreading good cheer and goodness knows what else, to middle-aged women in

Dundee, then they were up the creek without the proverbial paddle. Not a housewife in Dundee was going to fess up about being part of a group that involved the type of sexual shenanigans that Shona had never even heard of. Usually, she would ask her gran about any societies, clubs, or groups. There was no way on God's good earth she was even mentioning this to her grandmother. That's if she was even in Scotland. She being the adventurous type could be anywhere in the world. Still, wherever she was, Shona was not broaching this particular topic regardless of how long it took her to solve the case.

She was still puzzled. She couldn't believe that this organisation existed only in Dundee. She had a feeling there would be branches in every major town and city and the whole of the British Isles. So, why could they not find anything about it on the interweb. If they had tripped across it in the course of their investigation, then she would bet her aforementioned granny on the fact the other forces had done so as well. She hurried back to her office and started a Scotland wide e-mail to her contemporaries asking if it was a group that had ever troubled their investigations in the past.

By the time she returned to her office, having done nothing more than top up her coffee, the emails had started to come in. The first three denied all knowledge but the fourth, from Barry, had her reaching for the phone.

"I thought I'd be hearing from you, Shona, but I didn't think it would be this quickly."

If you had an investigation like the one I'm currently wading through you'd understand why I'm ringing you without passing go."

"So, how did you come across our housewives?"

"I've three victims; all of them appeared to be members."

There was a low whistle from the other end of the phone. "Three? Blimey, you certainly like to go for overkill in Dundee."

"How did you fall across them?"

"We'd a young lad read his grandmother's diary for some reason, and he came storming in here roaring about the fact we should be investigating the group and shutting them down."

"Did you shut them down?"

"Shut them down? We couldn't even find out what they did. We did go and have a word with the grandmother, who told us we should mind our own beeswax and she'd be having a strong word with her grandson. Anyway, what middle-aged women get up to in their own time is up to them and nothing whatsoever to do with police Scotland."

"I like the colour of her thinking. I would have to agree with her; however, with three dead housewives, I need to find out if their group affiliation is anything whatsoever to do with their deaths."

"Good luck with that one."

39

Rage boiled within them as they put in motion the steps which would change their life forever. Change it more than even this monstrous regime had done. Money changed hands. Large amounts of money. New identities were bought. Transport was sought, found, and paid for, then, just as everything was about to move forward, more money requested. No, demanded. More scrabbling around. More money found. Desperate people, pushing money into the hands of the greedy and evil. The ones becoming rich off the misery of others. The journey started. First on foot over terrain no sane man or woman would ever go near. Grinding heat wore them down, yet still they put one foot in front of the other their new lives dancing tantalisingly in front of them. This vision was the only thing that kept them going. Desperation reeked from their very pores along with the sweat which turned rancid as it dried and grew stale. They were crammed into boats until they were full. Then more were crammed in. They had been promised safe passage. They had been promised comfort. They had been promised food. The only true thing out of what they had been promised was that they were receiving passage. How this could be classed as safe was beyond human comprehension. Food was scarce, and beyond edible. Still, they stuffed it in, starvation overcoming their fear of illness. Yet, illness came. fellow travellers died lying in a pool of their own vomit and faeces. Excrement washed the decks of the ship. Those who avoided what seemed to be inevitable illness did their best to keep areas sickness free. Those who died were thrown overboard with nothing but a silent prayer to assist that passage to heaven. Surely, they would go to heaven as they'd entered hell here on earth.

How long that passage lasted, no one knew. Time passed in a hellish quest for survival. They did what they could to help others but when the chips were down their own family came first. They cared for their mother and siblings. Scrabbled for scraps of food that would keep them alive until they touched shore once more. At last, that shore could be seen. They had been told someone would be waiting to welcome them and take them to safety. They had been told a home was waiting for them. They had been told life would be different. Yet more lies. The rage grew stronger.

40

The team came back to it bright eyed, and bushy tailed the next day. “Roy, I want you to scour the Internet to find out anything whatsoever about this organisation. go as deep as you want and anywhere you want. I'll sanction it and we'll get a warrant. I want you all over the social media of those three women like a rash. Is there any way you are able to get into secret Facebook groups?”

“Blimey, Ma’am, you don't ask for much do you? I'm not sure I'm up for miracles this morning but I'll do my best.”

“I have the greatest of faith in you. Don't let me down or you'll be directing traffic for the rest of your natural.”

Roy said, “You'd like that wouldn't you? But I still think you'd miss me.”

“Don't test me. The rest of us will be scouring every syllable of every piece of paper we have in evidence for those three women. Look for anything that will give us a clue as to the where abouts and raison d'etre of the Horny Housewives.”

“Jings, Shona, I'm no’ sure I can go through all that again. I never knew the woman of Dundee go up to such things.”

The others looked equally as miserable at the thought.

"You'll just have to put on your big boys' and girls' pants and get on with it. People are dying and all you're worried about is what's written in a few diaries from three bored women."

"Somehow or other, I don't think they were bored," Jason said to gales of laughter.

"Very witty. Now, heads down, eyes on paper, focus. I want to see your notebooks smoking."

Groans ensued but they complied accompanied by the sound of silence.

An hour later Shona leaned back in her chair and rubbed her back. The others did the same. "My eyes are bleeding and my brain is screaming for respite from this muck. Time for a coffee break. I think we'd be justified in scarfing down a bacon roll. Jason and Iain you're off to the canteen." She handed them thirty pounds and they trotted off quite happily, the thought of sustenance adding a lightness to their step.

She freed Roy from his shackles to join them as they munched on their impromptu breakfast before reconvening and comparing notes. Shona wiped the bacon grease from her mouth and hands and lobbed the napkin at the waste bin. "What's the skinny?"

Everyone looked at everyone else with no one saying anything.

"Today would be good."

Abigail stepped into the breach. "If there's anything in there, then it's written in code. I can't make head nor tail of most of it."

"Me neither," Nina added.

The rest nodded their heads in agreement.

"Roy, please tell me you've got something. Don't you dare let me down."

"I wish I could. I might be onto something, but I want to a

deep dive before I pin my colours to the mast. Can you give me another hour?"

Shona sighed and said, "All this hurry up and wait is driving me nuts. I suppose I'll have to. Give me a yell when you've got something." She told the others to examine the documents for any hint of a hidden code.

"Soldier boy, you must have done something about coding when you did your stint in the Territorial Army," Nina said. "You need to come in useful for something."

"I'm useful for lots of things, but deciphering codes isn't one of them. I was in the infantry not the intelligence corps."

Shona stood up. "Stop with the bickering and get your noses to the grindstone. I want you all working so hard steam comes out of your ears. I'm off to make some phone calls."

Nina grabbed the empty coffee pot and followed her out. As they walked up the corridor she said, "If my mouth were any drier, I'd be declaring drought conditions."

"You've drunk enough coffee to float the RRS Discovery. I'm surprised you're not bouncing off the ceiling with all that caffeine."

Nina's laugh ricocheted off the walls. "You've a cheek to speak. Anyway, I'm used to caffeine hits as Christophe makes real Greek coffee for me. Mind you, he uses a Turkish coffee pot to make it in which blew my mind, as I always thought the Greeks and Turks were at odds with each other."

"What is it with my team? I don't think there's a stereotype ever been written you don't love and cling to. Anyway, who's Christophe?"

"My new boyfriend. He's Greek and has a huge—"

"Nina, I'm warning you, the next word out of your mouth had better be clean."

"Tattoo of Aphrodite on his back. You really need to sanitise your mind, Shona McKenzie."

"With you as a friend, I'd say that's nigh on impossible." She filled up her coffee cup and left Nina standing in the kitchen with a grin the size of Scotland on her face.

"You love me really," she yelled at her boss's retreating back.

Shona phoned Mary to get an update on the status of the identity of the medication that may have been used to kill the woman. She still had nothing. She was apologetic and reassured Shona that they were pulling out all the stops to get an identification. She'd ring the minute she had one. Whilst Shona was sure this was the case, it didn't help her move the investigation forward. she drummed her fingers on the desk then leaned back and closed her eyes. The chief just happened to wander into her office at that point.

"I'm glad you've got time for a nap, McKenzie."

She sat bolt upright. "I'm sorry, Sir, I was trying to think."

"Most of us do that with our eyes open." He sat down and leaned back in the chair, crossing one leg over the other. "I'd like an update on the case. I've got George Brown on the phone. He wants to know what you're doing to solve these murders."

"What's Pa Broon after this time?"

"Inspector, how many times do I have to warn you? Sometimes, I think you're the brightest person in Police Scotland; other times I think you're as thick as a haggis pudding." He frowned.

"Sorry, Sir. I'm just a little confused as to why the esteemed Ex-Lord Provost is so interested in my case."

"Sonya Lemongrass is wondering what you're doing to solve the murder of her staff nurse"

"Since when do Police Scotland run their investigations according to the whims of Pa..." she took in the look on the boss's face unchanged tack. "Ex Lord Provost Brown's family?"

The chief leaned forward and put his beautifully suited arms on her desk. He looked weary. "Could you just give me the update and stop questioning everything I say to you?" His mouth turned up at the corner slightly and Shona could swear he was attempting to smile. "You would think you would have learned by now that George Brown is up to his Harris Tweed clad armpits in anything that happens in Dundee."

"Have the Alexeyevs been in touch at all?"

"Shona, just give me an answer." his voice had moved from weary to sharp, so Shona thought she'd pushed her luck far enough. She gave him a succinct overview, blushing as she mentioned the latest little twist in their case.

The chief took it in his stride. Shona was impressed. Very little seemed to rattle him. "Well, you do seem to push the boundaries when it comes to investigations. Only you, Shona, only you." This time he really did smile. "I have got to hear what this is all about, so keep me posted."

Shona, eyes wide with astonishment, said, "Of course, Sir." She wasn't sure she could formulate any other response. She also wasn't sure what surprised her the most - the chief smiling or him wanting to know about the housewives' gig. This job never ceased to amaze her. Neither did the chief.

She picked up the phone to ring Charge Nurse Lemongrass when it startled her by ringing. The minute she heard the desk sergeant's voice she knew it would not be good news. "You're wanted up at Narrywells, Ma'am. There's a crime scene requires your attention."

"A crime scene? You mean a proper crime scene with evidence we can actually collect?" her voice contained a frisson of excitement. At last, something they could get their teeth into and investigate properly.

"Aye, Ma'am. it would seem so. It was the POLSA who asked for you."

Shona leapt to her feet. She grabbed Peter, Abigail, and Iain, and left the others slaving over their current task. The team she'd chosen to go with her were as happy as a pig in muck. If moaning was an Olympic sport the remainder of the team would win gold.

41

An entire ward being a crime scene had to be a Police Scotland first. It was certainly a first for her. Two young coppers stood at the door looking more miserable than anyone had a right to be. However, she thought they had every right given they were being harangued by someone who professed to be a doctor.

"I've told you; I need to go inside to do my rounds. There are patients waiting for treatment and others waiting to be discharged."

The copper remained polite, but his voice was tinged with irritation. "And I've told you numerous times you cannot go inside the ward unless I've been informed you are needed for an emergency."

Shona stepped forward and into the argument. She flashed her ID card for the benefit of both the doctor and the policemen on duty. "DI Shona McKenzie." She smiled at her colleague. "Thank you, PC..." She peered at his badge, "Jones, you're doing an excellent job." The wattage on her smile dimmed by about 3000 watts when she turned to the doctor.

"I need to get in there. you're stopping me doing my job." He had the demeanour of a petulant child.

"And you're stopping me doing mine. The only difference between you and I is that I can arrest you for stopping me doing mine. It's called hindering the police in the course of their duty. Now, run along and leave us to do our job." she smiled and threw him a bone. "We'll move along swiftly if we don't have to stop and chat to every doctor who wants to come through the door. Give your phone number to PC Jones here and she will phone you the minute we've opened the ward up again. If you are called for an emergency, we'll let you in in a heartbeat."

He walked off muttering. From what Shona could gather he was damning the police to a particularly nasty corner of hell. She shrugged her shoulders and pushed through the door, having better things to worry her than the hurt feelings of the general population of Narrywells hospital. She stepped into chaos. Whereas the ward was usually busy but peaceful, it now appeared to be the inner sanctum of bedlam. Sergeant Muir, the POLSA, had crime scene tape around one section of the ward. In front of that were several coppers who were fast losing their temper as they argued with staff.

"How am I meant to run a ward when the place is heaving with the flaming police?" one nurse, who looked to be about seventeen, said. "I have patients who need to go for tests. There are others who need x-rays. And none of the patients have had any lunch."

"I've explained over and over this is a crime scene and it's no one in and no one out. Do you think those poor sods lying in that room give a toss about you running your ward?"

Although Shona secretly agreed with PC Winnows, she couldn't let her get away with talking to the general public like that. "That's quite enough. Keep a civil tongue in your head." she turned to the nurse and said, "I know you're stressed, and it must be grim, but please do not speak to my officers like that. They're doing their job just like you."

The nurse burst into tears. Through sobs she said, "I'm sorry. It was just seeing..." The sobs grew stronger.

Before Shona had a chance to open her mouth, a woman, her hair sprayed to within an inch of its stiff life, strode up to them with a no nonsense look in her eye. "What's the meaning of this? How dare you harass my staff."

Shona recognised the overpowering Stella Barrington-Smythe, CEO of the hospital. "Harass your staff," Shona said, indignation apparent in every clipped syllable. "I've barely opened my mouth since I arrived."

"We need you off this ward immediately. How are my staff meant to carry out their duties when the place is cluttered up with extraneous people?"

Shona had reached the end of a very short fuse. She stepped forward, tried to keep her voice calm, but failed miserably and said, "Your ward is also my crime scene. Given someone has died in there, someone I still have not clapped eyes on incidentally, you'd think you'd be a bit more accommodating. My team also have a job to do, and they'd be able to do it a damn sight quicker if your staff got on with their own job and let mine do theirs."

"We need to get patients out of here to have tests. The ward has come to a grinding halt and people could die waiting for you lot to sort this out."

"We need to interview every single person on the ward before they leave it." Barrington-Smythe opened her mouth to speak but Shona lifted a hand to stop her. "I'll see what I can do." Her voice softened. "I appreciate everything cannot stop in terms of treatment for the remaining patients. Now, if you will excuse me, I really need to go and visit the crime scene." She swivelled and walked away, her ramrod straight back leaving no room for argument. All this polite chit chat meant she hadn't done a minute's investigation since she stepped inside the hospital. It might be necessary for her to oil the wheels of investigatory progress, but it was a giant pain in the assets.

She walked into the room where the victim, Caris Pleasant, was and stopped dead, her jaw almost hitting her chest. No one had prepared her for the fact there were two victims. Not only that, but she knew one of them. She'd never in her life clapped eyes on the patient in the bed, but the woman sprawled on the floor was the young student nurse she had interviewed only a few days ago. She searched her brain for the name. Ah, yes, Morag Duncan. Misery clutched at Shona's stomach and for once in her life she felt physically sick at a crime scene. This poor girl had done nothing to deserve a death such as this. All she was doing was her job and should have been safe doing so. This explained the attitude of the staff; they were in shock. Her head swam and she left to find a glass of water before returning.

"Are you okay, Ma'am? You're no' looking so good," Peter asked when she returned to the room.

"Yes." Her face told a different story. "Well, to be honest, no. I interviewed this young lass a few days ago. She's a brand-new student nurse."

Peter. A devout Catholic, crossed himself. "May God have mercy on her soul."

"I'm hoping God will guide us to find whatever utter basket case is doing this as, quite frankly, I'm fresh out of any other ideas."

"I'll light a candle on my way home."

"Light several." She was ready to take any help she could get.

Whilst this ecclesiastical exchange was going on, Shona, fully suited and booted as befitted a crime scene, knelt carefully next to the body of the nurse. Apart from what looked to Shona to be a huge bump on her head, the young woman appeared peaceful. She wondered if any of the others had a similar bump and resolved to ask Mary. She felt around the head of the woman in the bed; she appeared to be bump free. The body remained completely undisturbed – no attempt at resuscitation - as this was very definitely a murder investigation. It didn't take the brains of a surgeon to work that one out, given the body of a student nurse was currently taking up space on the side room floor. Nurses, especially one so young, did not tend to die in harness, not with another corpse in close proximity.

Shona sighed. A crime scene it may be, but she wasn't sure what it would elicit in the way of clues. Still, they would do their damnedest to get the scene to speak to them. Not one speck of dust would remain unturned and not one surface remain free from meticulous investigation in the hunt for something, anything, that would lead them to their killer.

She stepped from the room, waved Iain over, and ushered him *into* the room.

Furious gazes from staff members, aimed in her direction, almost scorched her suit. She returned her own steely eyed gaze, swivelled, and entered her crime scene. No matter how sorry she felt for the staff, she had a job to do, and they would get on with theirs much more quickly if she did hers.

42

And then there were two. Their siblings died on a frozen British beach, their bodies ravaged by disease and malnutrition. Wading through the icy sea water proved to be too much for their weakened bodies. Then rain lashed the beach as dismal grey skies loured above them in a land so different from their own sun-drenched country. Yet again, they wondered why they had undertaken this perilous journey. Then they remembered the evil they had flown from. They raged at a God in which they no longer believed. From one godforsaken country to the next, surely no God would allow such misery and heartache.

They held their mother in a tight embrace as she sobbed and wailed, mourning the death of her children. They could see the light fade from her eyes as all hope drained from her body. "They will be here to help us soon. They promised this. For this we paid."

Still the keening continued, piercing a heart that had long since hardened against humanity.

"I will protect you. No harm will come to you." Even they did not believe the words, but words were the only thing that could be offered in this hellhole that was their new life. This life should have been one of safety, security, and hope. An escape from their old life. yet, they had only moved from one hellish situation to another. If this was all that life had to offer perhaps, they would have been better dying on that boat.

They waited for the promised help which they knew in their heart of hearts would never come. Their heart, once so tender and compassionate, hardened just a little bit more. the only compassion remaining was for their mother, the woman grieving beside them. They would do anything it took to make sure her remaining days on this earth were ones of comfort. How this would happen they did not yet know, but it would. Right now, all they could do was try to protect her from the rain which lashed down and soaked them through every item of clothing they wore. They sat and waited, clutching their last remaining possessions - two small rucksacks containing all their worldly goods. How did life come to this? As the rain lashed down, sadness turned to anger, anger to hatred, and the hatred solidified in their heart. It spawned a burning rage and murderous thoughts of stamping out evil.

43

"Iain, I want every single inch of this room dusted for prints." She looked around and added, "Including the bathroom." She wiped a stray bead of sweat from her face with the back of her arm. It was hot as Hades in here; there was a good chance their sweat would contaminate the crime scene. The patients certainly wouldn't die of hypothermia; heat exhaustion, on the other hand was a distinct possibility.

Iain set to with bottles of fluid, powder, and a look of satisfaction. This case, with its lack of crime scenes, had everyone's teeth on edge and, despite the sorry circumstances, they couldn't help feeling glad they had something to actually investigate.

He, worked in his usual efficient way, neatly and methodically doing things that Shona knew would help to move the case forward; this despite her ignorance in knowing the precise details of his work. She had done several days training on forensics when she worked in Oxford, but those days were long gone. She preferred to leave it all to Iain who knew exactly what he was doing. Once finished, he said, "It's all yours, Ma'am."

"Did anything catch your eye?"

"Apart from the fact our corpse seems to be tucked up nice and cosy in her bed?"

"Yep. Tight as a kipper. We seem to have a murderer who likes to keep things neat."

Iain shook his head. "Most murderers cut and run; not many of them hang about to make sure their corpse," he paused, looked at both the bodies and continued, "is looking bonnie."

"Are you having a laugh? Every single one of our murders since I started on the force have been beautifully displayed."

"You make a persuasive argument, Ma'am. Mind you, this is a hospital with a lot of people around you'd think our killer would want to hot foot it in the direction of freedom as soon as possible."

"You'd think. Although, I'm assuming they would be wandering the corridors of the hospital legally. Then, they would not need to leave the premises."

"Hiding in plain sight. I like it, Ma'am. Well reasoned."

Whilst this exchange was going on Shona moved around the room examining every single item and both bodies. Something niggled at the back of her mind. She did another tour of the room and gravitated back to the bedside cabinet. Something on there was jogging her memory. She picked up the book and flicked through it. Then it dawned, one of the other victims had been reading the same book. *A Thousand Splendid Suns* by Khaled Hosseini was certainly popular amongst the patients in Narrywells. Coincidence? Possibly, but she wasn't taking any chances. That book had been out for years and wasn't exactly on sale in the hospital newsagent shop. Shona strode from the room and grabbed Abigail. "I need you to go back to the gulags and ring around the relatives of our victims. Ask them if a copy of," she rattled off the name of the book, "was in the effects returned to them by the hospital."

Abigail threw her a quizzical look but bounded off, nonetheless.

In a departure from the usual hospital procedure their victims' relatives had been asked to wait at home for the police to arrive rather than coming in to see the deceased. Shona waited until the bodies had been removed from the ward before opening the crime scene. At the front of the queue to enter the ward were a horde of cleaners. One, who looked vaguely familiar to Shona, smiled as he passed. She smiled back; it was nice to see someone happy in their work. Especially in the midst of all this misery.

Shona had two sets of grieving relatives to visit. Ordinarily she would divide them up between the team, but she wanted to visit the student nurse's parents herself. In fact, she was going to break the news of her death as the hospital had not informed them. The house was small but beautiful outside and inside. Shona took a deep breath before ringing the doorbell which, she noted, was a video doorbell. She wondered what was going through the residents' minds as they viewed two complete strangers on whichever device it was linked to. Whatever they were imagining it would never live up to the horrors that were about to be unleashed in their lives.

The dead nurse's parents were both elderly and devastated. The mother informed Shona they could not have children and finding out she was pregnant in her fifties came as quite the shock. Morag was loved, cherished, and adored by everyone who knew her. No one would want to harm her. Their bewildered look told Shona all she needed to know. Having gently questioned the couple, she left with the sneaking suspicion this poor young girl was collateral damage. No eighteen-year-old could manage to stir up enough hatred that some perverted killer would murder several other victims to cover up her death. Still, she owed it to her to investigate her death as thoroughly as all the others.

. . .

The son of their other victim, Mrs Caris Pleasant, lived on the top floor of the multis at the bottom of the hill. Shona, whose Dundonian had come on in leaps and bounds since her arrival in the city, had figured out multis were high-rise flats. Unfortunately, in this instance, they were high-rise flats without a working lift and the man they had come to visit lived on the top story. Shona thanked her lucky stars for every run she'd ever done in her life. Peter on the other hand was cursing every demon in his known universe for the hand that fate had dealt him. "I'm too auld for these sorts of shenanigans. Could you no' have taken one of the youngsters?"

"You've been exercising for months since you had that heart attack, so stop whinging. Your cardiac surgeon will be delighted I'm dragging you up these stairs." Inwardly she celebrated the fact Peter actually made it to the top floor. Pre heart attack this would not have been possible. She might gently chastise him, but Peter was the bedrock of her department. She shuddered to think what she would ever do without him. She would also miss him on a personal level.

The man who opened the door was tall, neatly dressed and, from his jerking limbs, had a mild case of cerebral palsy. As Shona flashed her ID card and introduced herself and Peter, she couldn't help wondering what possessed the council to house someone with cerebral palsy on the top floor of a high rise flat.

The sitting room he ushered them into was pristine and contained an equally pristine young woman who was breastfeeding a baby; it looked to be about ten months.

"How can I help you, officers?"

Shona, who had been expecting a speech deformity, was surprised by the clarity of his speech. She gave herself a mental slap for making assumptions. "Are you Sean Pleasant?"

"Yes. Are you here about the break ins that have been happening in these flats?"

"I'm afraid not." She broke the news of his mother's death.

Sean broke down, the young woman rose to comfort him and the baby, obviously sensing the tension in the air, screamed. It settled when it's mother once more offered her breast.

"Who'd want to kill her? She never had much. She just did her job, loved her grandson and went to a writing group."

Shona's brain fired every synapse at once at the words writing group. She'd had a text from Roy which shed some light on one part of their puzzling, murderous jigsaw. Despite some inner misgivings she was going to follow this thread to its horrifying conclusion. Horrifying for Sean that is.

"I'm sorry I have to ask this but it's important. Do you know if..." She couldn't believe she was about to utter the words which came next. She took a big deep breath and continued, "your mother's writing group was called Horny Housewives of Dundee?"

Sean's face could not have mustered up a more convincing example of shock if he had tried.

Peter looked equally stunned. "Ma'am—"

Shona held up her hand and said, "I'm sorry. I know it's an unusual question but please know it is important. I wouldn't be asking it otherwise.

"I have no clue what it was called but I'm telling you it wouldn't be that. I loved my mother, but she was a right old prude. She barely recovered from the fact I was 'shacked up' with Heidi." He indicated the woman sitting on the sofa and now attempting to wind the tiny bundle of joy. "They were her words. It wasn't till Briony came along that she relented."

"Did your mother live alone?"

"Yes." His eyebrows drew together in a quizzical look.

"Do you have a key to her house? If so, would you mind if we took it and had a look inside?"

Heidi stood up, placed the baby in a travel cot, and said, "I'll fetch it for you." She hurried from the room.

Sean gave his consent to the search. Shona asked him several questions and requested he come down to the station later in the day. He agreed, and they left with Shona slipping the key into her pocket.

As they settled back into the car, Peter asked, "What was that all about?"

"According to Roy, Horny Housewives of Dundee is a writers' group where the members focus on erotica."

"Just when you thought you knew everything. I bet they're no' members of the Scottish Association of Writers."

"The who? How do you know these things? Are you a writer in your spare time?"

"Nah, I prefer reading the newspaper. My lass is a member. She's studying Creative Writing at uni."

"All we need to do now is pin this lot down, regardless of who they are attached to, and ask them some questions." Her face lit up. "Would your daughter know anything about them?"

Peter crossed himself and said, "I'm not having that conversation with my bairn." Indignation hung on every clipped syllable.

Shona's voice was equally clipped. "Then I'll do it." Her voice softened. "Can you ask her to come in for a chat. I promise I'll be gentle."

"Aye." The fact he'd lapsed back into Scottish showed he'd softened on the subject as well."

Shona parked in the gulags, otherwise known as Police HQ, car park. "At a time suitable to her."

44

At a time suitable to her turned out to be thirty minutes later. She had a break from lectures at the university and was hanging out in the union bar when daddy dearest phoned her. She promptly swallowed the last dregs of her wine, grabbed her coat, and hot-footed it in Shona's direction.

Shona rustled up some tea and chocolate digestives and they made themselves comfortable in an interview room.

After a couple of minutes small talk, Peters daughter asked, “So, what's so important that my dad couldn't ask me?”

Shona fiddled with her engagement ring, took a deep breath, and said, “It's a bit of an awkward question to be honest.”

“I'm a uni student. There's nothing I haven't heard before. Spit it out.”

“Have you heard of the Horny Housewives of Dundee?” A spray of coffee covered her as Morag choked on her coffee. Shona jumped up, helped the lassie and grabbed some tissues to mop up. Once they were done and dusted, she said, “I thought you uni students were unshockable.”

“I wasn't expecting those words to come out of *your* mouth.”

Her face was returning to pale pink rather than beetroot red. “You're my father's boss, for freaks sake.”

“So, I take it you've never heard of them?”

“I never said that. Of course, I've heard of them. Everyone on my course has heard of them.”

How the heck do a bunch of uni students know everything about a group the police can't seem to find anything out about? “Would you like to enlighten me?”

“They're a writing group dedicated to writing erotica.”

“Are you a member?”

Morag's eyes were round Os of astonishment. “Are you having a laugh? No way. They're a bunch of old prunes. I wouldn't be seen dead in a group like that.”

Shona didn't feel it was her place to remonstrate with the young woman for her ageism. “Have you any idea where we could find them?”

“Yep. They meet in one of the little rooms off the library in the University.”

How on earth were the police not able to find this lot, when they could literally walk to the meeting and have a word with them? She thanked Morag and let her go. She had a sneaking suspicion the farthest she would go would be to her dad's office to ask him for money. She had to replenish that drink she left behind somehow.

On returning to her office, she phoned the university. As luck would have it the group were meeting that very afternoon. She strolled into the main office and asked for a volunteer to join her in visiting the writing group. Stunned silence was her only response. “Since when did you lot turn into a bunch of prudes? You're police officers, so man and woman up.”

More silence ensued, until Peter grabbed his courage by the horns and said, “I'm not sure my heart could take it, Ma'am.”

Shona, thinking of what Mrs Johnson would say if she delivered her husband home in a box, tended to agree with him. "You're off the hook." She looked around at the rest of them. "You're all a bunch of wusses." She stared at them as they squirmed and looked away. Then, Nina stepped in and said, "I'll come with you. It will probably be a right laugh."

"A right laugh. You had better be joking. We need to interrogate them; no giggles allowed."

This was a cue for mass hysteria, and she watched the tension drain from them. She let them laugh for a couple of minutes then said, her voice stern, "That's quite enough. Back to work."

A couple more giggles and some hiccups and peace once more reigned.

Shona wandered to the briefing room, coffee in hand, snapped several pictures of the investigation boards and returned to her office. Whilst the good citizens of Dundee would think she would carry all the names of the deceased in her head, this wasn't quite how it worked. She needed all the names to do yet another search on what these women had in common. Putting her password into the computer, she bent to her task. She would not let this defeat her.

45

From the hellhole of a freezing beach to hellhole in the back of a freezing lorry, the hatred burned brighter and grew ever hotter.

How was it possible for humans to be treated this way? Where was the humanity? Where was the care for a fellow human?

They shifted, easing cramped muscles. Crammed in with hundreds of others there was little room for stretching. Their mother moaned and they pulled her close whispering soothing words in her ear. She settled again. They stifled a scream against the searing pain in their arm. They had not moved in what seemed like hours. They were convinced, no, they knew, there were now corpses amongst the living. Desperate people who died seeking a better life. No one would go through this horror unless the horror left behind was worse. Terrified children sobbed. One such child, now an orphan, snuggled into his side with her thumb in her mouth. They thanked a God they no longer believed in she had managed to fall into a fitful sleep. Sleep alluded them; they did not think they would ever sleep again.

. . .

Eventually, the rattling of the lorry stopped, and the engine died. They hoped this signalled the end of the journey and not another stop. Stops where they were not allowed out. This meant the putrid stench of human excrement hung heavy in what little air there was, almost choking the occupants. Perhaps, those who were now deceased had a merciful release.

The occupants stumbled from the lorry barely able to stand and rubbing limbs burning from the long journey. They blinked in the sunshine bewilderment written on every line of every weary face. The building they stood in front of looked derelict. Boards stood where once there was glass. They took it in not saying a word. Speaking only brought beatings. Keep quiet. Say nothing. Obey. Once they were settled things would improve.

They were shown to a room which held nothing more than two beds, a cupboard, A table with two chipped mugs and plates, and a gas burner. On the bed sat grubby sheets and blankets. As they now had a child in tow, sharing would be required. No one cared.

Another hellhole.

46

The rain had eased, and the sun had put on its best party frock, so Shona and Nina decided to walk to the university. Nina did a lot of moaning about not taking a car.

"If you wore sensible shoes and not Jimmy Choo's with a six-inch heel, you'd have no trouble walking this teensy weensey little distance."

Nina threw back her head and laughed. "I wouldn't be seen dead in anything less."

"So, stop whinging."

They strolled in companionable silence until they reached the university where they came up against bureaucracy at its finest. Judicious use of police ID and Shona's forceful tone of voice soon convinced Attila the Hun at reception they should be allowed to carry out their duty. She marched them up dreary corridors to the relevant room, threw them a dirty look, turned on her heel and left them to it.

"Why does every person we meet make me feel like slapping cuffs on them? What happened to helping the police? What happened to civic duty?"

"Everyone has their rights now, Ma'am."

"And don't we know it." The door creaked as she shoved it open meaning the entire room stared at them as they traipsed through it.

"You must be in the wrong place," a diminutive woman, sporting white hair, twin set and pearls, said.

"Detective Inspector Shona McKenzie," She flashed her ID card and waved a hand towards Nina, "and Detective Sergeant Nina Chakrabarti."

A collective dropping of jaws ensued. Eventually, one of them managed to muster up the ability to speak. "You must still be in the wrong place. This is a writing group; we don't exactly get up to anything that police would be interested in."

Shona grabbed a chair and plonked herself down in it. Nina followed.

Shona leaned forward. "I know it seems unusual, ladies, however your writing group has come up as part of our inquiries."

More collective jaw-dropping. If there were an Olympic sport for it these ladies would take gold in a heartbeat, thought Shona.

Shona, girded her loins, took a deep breath, and said, "I believe your group is called Horny Housewives of Dundee?"

There was that synchronised jaw-dropping again. Shona believed she'd never seen anyone bristle before, however, one woman who had a lot of flesh to bristle, managed it. "How dare you come in here and say things like that."

Shona 's patience came to a grinding halt. Her gaze steely, she stared at them. "Right, I've had enough of this. It would appear that at least three of your members are dead under suspicious circumstances." She leaned forward and put her arms on the desk. "Playing games isn't on my docket, so, one, or all of you, needs to start answering our questions and doing so honestly."

This time there were a few quivering lips and some tear-filled eyes. Not a dropped jaw to be seen.

"Now, who's in charge of this group?"

A woman, who looked to be about ninety, put up her hand, and said, "Me."

"Thank you. Can you confirm the name of your group?"

"Writers Together." Her eyes told Shona the woman was lying through her dazzling false teeth. They could double as a stage light.

"Not the name you've registered at the university. The one every writing student in Dundee knows."

The woman mumbled something, a red flush starting at her neck and creeping up her cheeks.

Shona, realising her usual scare tactics wouldn't work with this particular witness, said, "Could you please speak up as I can't hear you, Mrs...?"

"Santorini. My name is Rose Santorini." She found a sudden interest in the woman to Shona's right.

"Thank you. And the real name of the group is...?"

The woman, looked at her feet and said, her voice still low but at a level Shona could just catch, said, "The Horny Housewives of Dundee."

Hearing a sound from Nina's direction, Shona stole a glance at her and then a full-on look that said, 'Laugh and you're dead.'

Nina took the hint and bit her lip.

"Thank you. We have no interest in what you ladies get up to in your spare time, and we're not here to judge." She kicked Nina under the table. "We are only interested in the deaths of your friends."

"But they all died in hospital," a woman sporting a bright red top and matching lipstick said. "Nothing to concern the police."

Shona was willing to put the woman's belligerent tone

down to nerves. Once. "They obviously do concern the police otherwise we wouldn't be here. Now, I'd be grateful if you could all help us by answering questions, rather than interrogating every one of our questions." Her smile took the sting from her words. "Thank you for helping us."

She and Nina had prepared some questions in advance. Nina took over the questioning while Shona tuned her ears to every nuance of every word uttered. If there was something to be found here, she would find it.

Nina opened the beige folder she had placed in front of her and looked at the sheet it contained. She looked up. "Could we please check some names with you." As she read out the names, the various expressions of shock, horror, and dismay around the room gave Shona the answer before they opened their mouths. This was way past the jaw-dropping stage.

Rose, her voice trembling, said, "We can't give you that information, it's confidential."

Shona, her voice growing a little sharper, leaned forward and said, "We are currently investigating the murders of several women, many, if not all, of whom, were members of this group."

"Murder..."

"You don't think we..."

"Are you accusing us of..."

"No one said anything about murder..."

"How dare you...

Nina put her hands over her ears.

Shona, who fully expected the Tower of Babel to appear, said, in a tone that brooked no nonsense, "Ladies. Please." Babel continued, so she said, her tone rising. "Enough." She didn't think her usual table banging would go down well with the blue rinse brigade, even if they were writing outside the usual literary box. And she'd bet her granny on the fact at least one of these ladies was related to the not so esteemed Ex Lord Provost. This disaster had his name written all over it.

The uproar died down as they all stared at her.

"No one is accusing you of anything. We are merely trying to establish what is going on." Shona clasped her hands together so hard the knuckles turned white. *Do not antagonise these women. Do not antagonise these women.* The chant kept going and kept her on the straight and narrow. "Sgt Chakrabarti, please continue."

"Were these women members of your group?

Rose, straightened hair that had so much hairspray it couldn't have moved if it tried and said, "Yes. They were. Now, can we get on with our writing?"

"Not quite yet, we've more questions to ask you." Make that several she thought.

Shona, a thought zipping through her brain, and exploding into variegated fireworks, leaned forward and said, "May I clarify something?"

Nina nodded despite the quizzical look stealing over her face.

Shona rattled off the names of all the other women in the investigation. "Were these ladies members?"

They all looked at each other, various degrees of horror etched on their heavily made-up faces. This told Shona everything she wanted to know. "I take it the answer is, yes?"

Belligerence replaced by, a high pitched squeak, Rose said, "Y..Y...Yes."

Shona sat upright, and said, her tone now full on no nonsense, "I need a full list of all your members." She looked Rose straight in the eye and said, "Immediately."

Rose aged in front of Shona's eyes. "Do you mean locally or nationally."

It was Shona's turn for a spot of jaw dropping. She dragged

it up far enough to splutter. "You mean there are more of these groups?"

Rose had recovered her equilibrium. "Yes. There are seventy-two groups in Scotland."

Shona couldn't muster up a cogent word. She threw a pleading look in Nina's direction.

Her sergeant, pulled herself together enough to say, "What are the other groups called?"

"The same name, dear. We started the organisation."

Rose's voice was far too cheery for Shona's liking. "How many members are there?" Then she realised she had better be specific. "Locally and nationally."

The woman, pausing for neither thought nor breath, said, "293 locally and 5,621 nationally. Although the recent deaths will have brought these down slightly."

Shona slumped back in her chair before gathering her equilibrium and dragging her unwilling body upright. "I think we need to continue this conversation at the station."

"What are you accusing me of. I had nothing to do with those deaths. They all died in hospital you stupid girl." She clutched her single strand pearls. "The police weren't this incompetent in my dear father's day, God rest his soul. He'll be turning in his grave."

"I'm not arresting you for anything but continue to speak to me like that and I will think of something."

"You can't speak to me like—"

"I just did. Now, I would like you at the station in one hour. I will be interviewing you as a witness." She pulled out her business card and wrote a time on it. "Just so there is no misunderstanding."

She stood up and said, "Bring a member list with you on a USB drive. There will be a warrant for you to view at the station for us to look at those names."

47

As they hurried down the Perth Road, Shona sent a message to the Sherriff. There would be a warrant waiting for her when she got back. She'd thought about ringing, but she wasn't sure she could cope with broadcasting the name of the group to the unsuspecting public. Seriously, she had the weirdest job in the world. She knew she'd be getting a phone from the Sherriff later asking for all the details. She'd never live this down. As if her reputation as the Grim Reaper wasn't enough to cope with. When she got back to the station, she reported to the Chief's Office to update him on the situation. Her face adopted the appearance of a well boiled beetroot as she recounted the whole sorry tale.

The Chief shook his head. "Only you. Shona. Why is nothing ever simple with you around?"

For once, she didn't even have the energy to think of bumping him off. "It wouldn't surprise me if you get a call from Pa...," she took in his face and changed tack, "Ex-Lord provost George Brown."

"Is there a reason for this?"

"I'm sure he must know a Mrs Rose Santorini. She's probably his aunt or something.

"How do I know you've upset the woman?"

"I was polite up to a point but might have got a teensy bit defensive towards the end." As he opened his mouth to speak, she butted in, "In my defence..." She rattled off her conversation with the woman. "I think I was fairly polite given the circumstances."

The Chief stared at her.

Shona kept quiet and clasped her hands together to stop them fidgeting.

After what seemed like a century, he spoke. "I'm sure you feel you were justified. Rein it in in future."

The mild tone shocked Shona as she had expected a blasting.

"Of course, Sir." She left feeling he might just live to see another day. Perhaps he wasn't so bad after all. Perhaps they were both growing soft.

Rose Santorini appeared at the station precisely one hour later. She, of course, had the battleship McCluskey in tow. Shona knew either her or her brother would be involved in this. She also knew Pa Broon would be on the blower to the Chief before this interview was over. If he hadn't already of course.

The usual polite introductions and reassurances about being a witness and nothing more, out of the way, Shona began. "Did you bring the USB stick with you?"

Rose looked at McCluskey, who nodded. She then slid the USB stick over the desk without protest. "My son copied them on here for you."

McCluskey piped up, "I would remind you the contents of this are confidential."

"Thank you for the reminder of how to do my job. How kind of you."

"Don't you—"

"For heaven's sake woman, I was being polite. Let me do my flaming job." She ignored McCluskey, whose face had taken on the hue of an unripe turnip, and turned to Rose. "I would like to ask you a few questions if that is all right with you?"

Rose, looking like she'd pricked her finger on a bush of the same name, said, "Of course. Anything I can do to help the police in their duties." Her tone suggested she meant, 'they need all the help they can get'.

Shona, deciding to ignore the tone asked, "How well do you know the women in the group?"

"I know some of them more than others. Of course, I know the writing of most of them. They each have a unique voice."

Shona, no prude, still wondered how they could tell the unique voice from the brief sections she had read.

Shona chose her next words with caution. Investigating a bunch of pensioners, whose life revolved around erotica was not something she came across in the course of her duties; she was treading new ground. Carefully. "Did any of the stories you read indicate the writer might have issues?"

"What sort of issues?"

Before Shona could answer McCluskey bellowed, "You can't ask that." Her ginormous bosum heaved and quivered in the manner of Hattie Jacques in one of her more melodramatic moments.

"I'd say that's one of my less contentious questions. Given the circumstances it was fairly mild."

"My client does not have to answer that. The content of her colleagues' stories are confidential."

"Not in a murder investigation. Would you like me to get a warrant for them to hand over every single story they have ever written?" *Please God, say no. If we all have to sit through hundreds of thousands of pages of erotic fantasies, the Mutiny on the Bounty will pale in significance to the Mutiny in Dundee Police.*

She let out a breath she didn't know she was holding when Rose said, "That won't be necessary." She paused before continuing. "Of all the ones I have read or listened to, there was nothing."

Shona nearly lost it at the thought of these elderly women reading out their work aloud. Then she shook her head and told herself to get a grip. *Why shouldn't they? They are as entitled as anyone else to be writing such things and it has nothing to do with me what sorts of fantasies they harbour.* Except that someone was targeting them, and she needed to find out why. Who on earth, or at least in Dundee and Angus, could take such exception to a bunch of women writing stories regardless of their subject matter? It made no sense whatsoever and no sense meant no clue as to what was going on. This was not a feeling Shona liked at all.

She felt like she needed a long lie down in a dark room; instead, she grabbed some extra strength rocket fuel and turned to the first task on her to-do list. She picked up the phone and sighed as she dialled Lemongrass's number. The woman was not a happy camper and wanted to know about progress. Shona made some soothing noises, assured her they were doing everything humanly possible to solve the murder and updated her on progress so far. All without breaking any confidentiality. Sometimes she felt like a magician. Hanging up she then went to find Abigail.

"Hey, Ma'am, what's up? Are we any further forward?"

"I'd tell you we'd solved the case, but I would be lying. Where are we at with the books? Did any more of them have *A Thousand Splendid Suns* in their effects?"

"Two of them did. I've not managed to track down the other relatives as yet."

"What the actual heck? If it's a clue, then it's a pretty strange one. Unless they are also all members of a reading group. Could you chase that up?"

"On it." She picked up the phone.

Shona, back in her own office, picked up the phone to ring Rose Santorini.

"What do you want now? I've told you everything."

"Are your members all reading *A Thousand Splendid Suns* as some sort of group read in?

"Of course not. Our members mainly read romance. Also we're a writing group not a reading group."

Shona, thinking romance was a euphemism for mommy porn, said, "Thank you for your help, as always. Police Scotland appreciates it." She needed a strong whisky to get her through all this politeness and being nice malarky. *How do those nurses manage it day in day out. I can barely manage an hour.*

With an even louder sigh, she pulled the Horny Housewives membership list forward, opened HOLMES and started checking the names against the database.

By the time the others clattered through the door looking for fluid and sustenance her back was breaking from hunching over a computer and her stomach complaining it hadn't had food for at least a year. She appeased it with a sandwich from the canteen and asked Roy to join her in her office once he'd scarfed his down.

"Have you got an update on the results of the analysis of the various crime scenes?"

"Today, too early."

Shona nodded in agreement.

"Elsie Dalhousie's cottage. The blood on the television was hers. The only fingerprints belong to Elsie. Clean as a whistle otherwise. If her daughter is cleaning that cottage, I want to hire her."

Considering Jason's mum did everything for him, Shona wasn't sure what he'd need a cleaner for, but she wouldn't mind employing the woman herself. Not that she was ever home long enough to make a mess.

"Mind you, it's a wee bit strange our other victim's prints aren't all over the place like botulin."

"Probably wore gloves. Everyone's being super careful these days. Anything from the other scenes?"

"Only today's. About a gazillion prints. Probably belong to the nurses and doctors."

"And every other member of the health care profession, all who have a good reason to be there."

"Yep." He shrugged and added, "Don't forget the visitors and ministers."

Shona groaned. Jason's tone was far too insouciant for her liking. "Needles and haystacks spring to mind." Where on earth would they start to unravel all of this? There were literally thousands of people to eliminate. Considering it looked likely their killer had a good reason to be there, was eliminating prints even worth it? She groaned again.

"You all right, Ma'am."

"I'm fine." She rubbed her temples. "Work on getting the results from today's crime scene and keep me posted." She leaned forward and added, "Throw the word expedited around and attach my name to it."

He trotted off with the look of a dog with a bone; the only member of staff who was happy in their work. The rest had the demeanour of a certain Disney donkey on a bad day.

She felt like banging her head off the table. Instead, she arranged to visit Caris Pleasant's flat. Her son said his wife would meet them there; he was currently confined to barracks due to the council's inability to fix the lift.

They didn't take long to arrive at their destination as their victim, in direct comparison to her son's home, lived in the luxurious flats down at Riverside. She thanked every lucky star she had that the woman's flat was on the ground floor as more stories was more than one inspector could bear. She, and Roy, who had begged for a break from the shackles of his computer, searched the place from ceiling to floor. There wasn't a sheet of paper to be found but they liberated a laptop and USB stick as per the warrant she had acquired before heading in the direction of the flat. You'd think Caris would have it locked up somewhere safe in case a visitor fell over it but, no, it was in plain sight on the kitchen table. She wasn't sure why they were taking it into evidence but there might be something on it which gave them even the tiniest clue as to what connected the group to their killer. There had to be something that linked the hospitals and the Horny Housewives group, and they needed to find out what it was. Fast.

As they were leaving, Shona had another thought. "Let's do one more sweep."

"What? Why?"

"Does it not bother you the laptop and pen drive were in full view?" A click was heard as the key turned followed by the creak of a door opening. "She was in hospital. You'd think she'd have at least popped them into a case and stowed them somewhere."

Roy, who'd reached the limits of his patience, huffed and puffed but followed her. "We've searched everything already."

"If I wanted whine I'd have gone to an off licence."

Roy laughed. "Where and how, Ma'am?"

"Look for hidden spaces."

"A mystery within a mystery. Got you."

An hour later they were exhausted, thirsty and no further forward.

"A waste of time then. So much for my bright idea."

"We could try the fridge." Roy headed towards the kitchen.

"For heaven's sake, all you'll find in the fridge is rancid milk and mouldy cheese. Documents would be ruined with the moisture."

"But flash drives wouldn't."

"You what?"

Roy wasn't paying her any notice as he rustled around in the fridge. He pulled out several containers and looked inside them. "Nope. How about the freezer."

"Are you having a laugh?"

"For once in my life, no." He rummaged around and pulled something out. "Yep. I knew it." He held up a flash drive so tiny, Shona wondered how he'd managed to find it. "Well, my horn is well and truly swoggled." She opened an evidence bag and Roy dropped it in. "Will it be any good? Will we be able to read it?"

"We most certainly will." He tapped his nose with his finger. "There are ways and means."

"With you involved, I have no doubt there are. Lead the way, Macduff."

"You know that's not the right—"

"Everyone's a critic."

48

Day after long weary day, the clouds gathered, and the rain came down in grey sheets one could barely push through. Horizontal rain driven by wind that laughed at you before tearing you in half.

Their mother's cough rattled windowpanes more cracks than glass.

They dreamt of sun and olive trees, family and love. They woke to hell.

Each day they forced one foot in front of the other on slick cobbled roads, rather than sweet, sweet grass. Worn shoes sloshed in water and chaffed heels to a bloody pulp. Their qualifications void here, they looked for any work they could get. The thought of home now seemed comforting, familiar. Should they look at returning? Should they hand themselves into the authorities? Would they then be sent back?

There was no let up or no comfort in hell. There was no welcome in this godforsaken country they now called home. Which was worse this life or the one they wished to escape? It was hard to tell.

49

Roy set to with forensic analysis like the hounds of hell were nipping at his heels, thinking that would be preferable than the DI nipping at his heels. Now he had something to do he was as happy as a kid in a sweet shop. Shona, on the other hand actually felt like she was in hell; cross reference hell to be precise. She could almost feel the discontent of the rest of the team radiating through the walls. Except for Roy, who was forensically analysing Caris Pleasant's laptop and resurrecting flash drives; she knew he would be in seventh heaven. The department fell into silence as the enormity of the task overtook them. Silence except for the frantic tapping of keyboards as names were typed into HOLMES and any possible evidence scribbled down.

Two agonising hours later, Shona stretched, rubbed her back, and stood up to go in search of caffeine, and the team, in that order.

They all sat back as she entered the main office, an expectant look on each and every face. Misery replaced expectant when she said, "Tell your nearest and dearest you'll be receiving more overtime pay."

To a man and woman, they adopted similar looks of expectation. "Can we grab some grub?" This from Peter, a man who thought better with his stomach full.

"Go for it but back in the briefing room the minute the last mouthful hits your stomach.

She followed the stampede, knowing there was a plate of fish and chips with her name on it. Terminal exhaustion she was used to; starving to death was a step too far. She'd run home tonight and back to the station again in the morning to offset the effects.

It was astonishing how much they managed to shovel down in the twenty minutes they were in the canteen. Doreen did not let them down and piled their plates high; at this rate the canteen would go bankrupt.

When they returned, Adanna Okifor was sitting in the squad room swigging back a cup of coffee. A stunningly handsome male uniformed officer sat next to her, companionably swigging on his own coffee.

"Why are you pair having a meeting in my team's office?"

The pair grinned showing off perfect pearly whites. "Shona, nice to see you too. I've come for an update." She waved a laconic hand at the man next to her. "Meet my cousin, Malik, also known as PC Okifor."

"I take it you're the person who gives free rein to this one to come and go as she pleases?"

Malik's smile was the size of Scotland, the type that made Shona feel all warm and fuzzy. "That's me."

"Won't your sergeant be wondering where you are?"

"My sergeant sent me in your direction and says I'm on loan."

Shona frowned, suspicion clouding her eyes. "Why is he trying to get rid of you?"

"I need more input on HOLMES."

"Mmm. Well, finish up the beverage and hop to it." She pointed at Jason. "He'll help you."

Jason's eyebrows drew together but he remained shtum. He quite liked his career and arguing with the boss wasn't the best way to keep it. Malik pulled up a chair and the pair bent to their task.

Adanna and her coffee followed Shona to her office. The reporter promptly made herself at home in the spare chair. Even lounging she looked exquisite, the bright colours of her clothing perfect with the colour of her skin. She took a sip of her coffee and grinned, showing off perfect white teeth.

In contrast, Shona felt she looked like the Wreck of the Hesperus, with teeth so furred they could double as AstroTurf. She swallowed a mouthful of her own coffee and then opened her mouth and breathed in and out hard and fast.

"Beverage a bit hot then?"

"And some." She swiped a tissue and wiped her eyes. "To what do I owe the pleasure?" Shona's pathological hatred of reporters had warmed since Adanna replaced the previous incumbent. This led to a much more harmonious working relationship.

"My boss says I need to start reporting these murders."

"My boss says we've to keep quiet." She slammed her coffee mug down and stood up. "Although, I think it's time we did a press release. Bear with me."

"And what makes you think you know more than me on the matter, Inspector?"

"Not at all, Sir. I am concerned the press will get hold of it anyway and it might be better if we control the narrative." She looked him in the eye practically daring him to argue. "You know what they are like. They may give away more than we would choose to."

The chief folded his arms, sat back and glared at her.

"Very well. Set up a press conference for tomorrow morning." He stood up and carefully removed his jacket from the hanger. "10 a.m. sharp."

Shona broke the news to Adanna she would have to wait until the next morning and returned to inputting names into HOLMES. Two hours later she released her team from their shackles and sent them in the direction of their loved ones. She folded her weary body into the car and pointed its bonnet in the direction of Broughty Ferry, her cat and a glass of Talisker. She had definitely earned that drink. In fact she strongly felt she deserved two.

Shakespeare was not in the best of moods when she returned; her look stated death by starvation was imminent. Shona, who was used to obeying the whims of a recalcitrant cat, opened a tin of salmon Whiskas and scooped the whole can into the cat dish. "Eat it. You're getting nothing else." Shakespeare, obviously too near starvation to care what she ate, stuck her tail in the air and her head into the cat bowl.

Shona took a large glass of Talisker to bed, glad she didn't have a dog to walk. She thought about ringing Douglas, but sheer exhaustion took over. She fell asleep, teeth still unbrushed.

Until the world once more dragged her out of slumber in a frantic cacophony of banging.

She threw the duvet back and staggered from her bed. Shakespeare swiped her with a paw that brooked no argument. The cat was not amused with the early morning callout given the lateness of the previous night's bedtime.

"Stop whining. You think you've got problems." She hurtled

towards the door. "All right. All right. I hear you." She pulled it open to be faced with Jason.

"What the heck? Can you use a phone like a normal person?"

"Tried. You never answered on either."

"She staggered into the kitchen, Jason in hot pursuit. The Tassimo machine was pressed into service. "What's up?" she said rubbing eyes that felt drier than a prohibition pub.

Jason grabbed a mug and shoved it under the machine as the coffee started to trickle. "Suspicious death in—"

"Don't tell me. Narrywells."

"Nope. King Albert Hospital."

"In Kirkaldy?"

"The very place."

Shona groaned and said, "Rummage around, find some travel mugs and make copious amounts of coffee." She grabbed the recently brewed cup and headed towards a shower, thinking longingly of a couple of painkillers which she would liberate from the medicine cabinet. *I'm seriously getting far too old for whisky, late nights, and early mornings. I need to go back to clean living and running.* Then, realising none of that was happening anytime soon, she turned herself to the task in hand. A copper's life was not an easy one but, despite all evidence to the contrary, she would not change it for the world.

Twenty minutes later she was in a squad car, siren blaring, blue light flashing and coffee in hand. Thankfully, the wail of the siren prevented any meaningful conversation, so she was able to sip at her beverage and watch the world go by at warp speed. They needed the siren to get over the Tay Bridge which resembled the inner circle of hell even at this early hour. She longed for the renovations to be finished. She idly wondered why they were bothering with the siren and lights given their murderer would be long melted into the crowd. She was utterly convinced this was one of the medical staff but couldn't prove it beyond all reasonable doubt and couldn't pin down who it was. She sat up straighter in her seat. "We're going to catch this despicable basket and throw the book at him."

"Or her." Jason took a bend in the road like he was at Silverstone.

Shona, caught mid sip, managed to splash coffee on her jacket. "Damn. I've got a press conference later." She rummaged around in the glove compartment and found a stray napkin which she employed in mopping up the mess. Squinting at it she thought it didn't look too bad. It would pass muster.

They screamed up to the hospital entrance, switched everything off and left the car where it lay. It was pretty obvious from the word Police, and the Gaelic Poileas, it had every right to be there. Then they made a dash through torrential rain into the covered walkway up to the hospital. Shona shook her long her to get most of the water off. "All it ever seems to do is rain here. If this is the sunniest city in Scotland, God help the rest of Scotland."

Jason thought keeping quiet might be the best course of action. Dundee actually got more sun than the rest of Scotland put together, but this wasn't the time to be arguing with the boss about the weather. In fact, no time was the best time to be arguing with the boss about anything.

Once again chaos ensued in front of the crime scene tape, although the occupants of the space seemed a little less frantic than at Narrywells. Maybe there was a little less pressure here than at the regional hospital up the road. Shona was just glad the main hospital at Edinburgh wasn't involved as that was a right pig to get to, involving a roundabout that no sane person would tackle - with or without a police car.

She sought out the nurse in charge of the ward, a young

man called Balfour McPherson. There was certainly no mistaking he was Scottish.

His accent was pure weegie, which Shona had learned was a colloquialism for Glaswegian; she had gained enough mastery of Scottish dialect to figure out he was asking what he could do to help them.

"We'll dae onything we can. Jist ask."

"Much as I love the way you speak it might be easier in terms of my investigation and you getting your ward back, if you speak a little more English." She might snap at Peter for his use of Scottish vernacular, but she had no jurisdiction over their current witness. Politeness might help move things along at a faster pace.

"Aye, I can do that. You'll be wanting to interview all the staff and patients?"

"We will. How many staff and patients are we talking about?"

"Two on night shift, four on day shift and five patients."

"Five patients? In a hospital? I thought you were permanently stuffed to the rafters in the NHS."

"It's Friday and we boot as many people as possible out."

"Are the five who are in, critical?"

"Nope. We're pretty much boarding them."

"Haven't they got a home to go to?"

"That's the problem. They all need to go into homes where the staff will care for them hand fist and finger." He looked her straight in the eye. "Now, they *are* stuffed to the rafters."

"She pulled out her phone and squinted at the name of her latest victim. "Was Mrs Maddow waiting to go to a home?"

"She was waiting to go to her daughter's home. However, said daughter is in Magaluf with her family for another week, so the NHS are stuck with providing room and board." His eyes clouded over. "Not that anyone minded. She was lovely. Delightful lady. Kept us all entertained."

If she was anything to do with the Horny Housewives, I am sure she did. She kept her thoughts to herself. "Was there any reason she should have died?"

He shook his head so vigorously Shona worried he might dislocate a vertebra. "None."

"Would you say she died of natural causes?"

"I'm not a doctor but I'd stake my wean's life on the fact she was helped out of this world."

"What makes you so sure?"

"I've heard the rumours. Same age. Female. Unexpected death. You've a serial killer on your hands." He leaned forward and frowned at her. "And what are you lot doing about it?

Shona matched him gaze for gaze. "Everything we possibly can, and we'll do it a lot more quickly if you stop with the attitude."

He ran his hands over his face. "Sorry. I was dragged in early and my wean's been up teething all night."

"I know the feeling, minus the teething child though." She made a mental note not to add any children, teething or otherwise, to her future. She shook herself to dislodge the horror story of zero sleep and an investigation colliding. Blinking, she said, "Can I see the room and the dead woman?" She refused to say victim until she was sure it was a suspicious death. This despite every intelligent thought she could muster telling her it was, yet, police training dictated she hold all such thoughts until proven beyond reasonable doubt.

She was ushered to the room, thanking the Gods she had coffee en route as there was narry a sniff of a cup in this place. Quite rightly so given they were dealing with an unexpected death, so they had better things to occupy them than providing refreshment to stray coppers.

Stepping into the room she took in its neatness. She stuck her head out of the door and instructed a copper to find the charge nurse. "Back in the room she stepped over to the bed.

Yet again the patient looked peaceful, sheet and blanket pulled up to the neck and tucked in tight. She glanced at the bedside table; as she suspected a copy of *A Thousand Splendid Suns* was placed neatly on the surface. This was their killer's calling card. But why? What message was being sent to them?

Balfour McPherson appeared as requested. "What can I dae yi fir?"

This was beyond Shona's translation capabilities. Jason, taking in her perplexed look, said, "He's asking how he can help."

Shona bit her tongue so hard she drew blood. She swallowed to get rid of the bitter taste and said, "It doesn't look like you tried very hard to bring her back." She swept a hand around the room. She adopted a pleading expression. "And please, could you answer in English. I really need to understand."

"It was pretty obvious to my staff nurse that she was gone and had been for some time." Resuscitation would have pretty much been a violation of her body."

"Shouldn't a doctor make that decision?"

"Aye. There was one on the ward at the time. She'd popped in for a cuppie after visiting someone on another ward. She agreed Mary was beyond resuscitation."

Tea obviously made the NHS go round as well as the police force. "Can we have the Doctor's name. We'll need to speak to her."

"Natasha Somers."

Fireworks went off in Shona's brain. That was now three times that doctor's name had come up in the investigation. Shona didn't like coincidences. It was about time for a less cozy chat with Dr Somers, preferably down at the station.

With an uncanny sense of timing, Peter appeared.

"You took your time. Given you live in Fife I'd have expected you to be first."

"Couldn't get the car started. Had to get my daughter up to bring me. Have you ever tried to get a teenager out of bed?"

Shona didn't want to think about teenagers, so changed the subject. "Do you not feel guilty about dragging your poor daughter out of her bed?"

"I'm Catholic. I feel guilty every day of the year." He grinned. "Nah, only joking. I don't feel guilty about anything, especially getting her out of her bed. Payback time."

Shona smiled. "I'm going to ask you to ruin someone else's day." She outlined the need for bringing Dr Somers into an interview room. "We're raising her level from witness to person of interest."

"I'm on it. Shall I take someone else?"

"Abigail seems to have made it here as well, so the pair of you can do it. You'll need her to drive anyway, unless your daughter is waiting in the wings." She threw him an enquiring look.

"Nae, chance. She shot off back tae her bed practically before I was out the car."

"I'll keep Roy and Jason and they can help me interview." She looked around, eyes narrowed. "As can Nina if she ever appears."

"Bridge is probably like a traffic jam."

"The rest of us managed it."

"Fair point." He disappeared in the direction of the office.

Shona stepped inside the crime scene once more. Stopping just inside the entrance she took the scene in. Then it struck her that all their victims had been in single rooms. Considering these wards only had a few single rooms why were these particular women being targeted? Yes, it was for privacy, but given whoever was doing it obviously had a reason to be on the ward, why did they need so much privacy? Saying that, they were probably erring on the side of caution. What she wasn't getting was why the women were chosen and how? The deaths were all over the place in terms of geographical location. Serial killers usually chose one geographical area and stuck to it. Then she thought back to her previous cases and wondered who she was trying to kid. *None of your blasted cases are usual or normal, Shona McKenzie. Bizarre should be your middle name.*

As these thoughts flitted through her brain at warp speed, she took everything in. The room was spick and span, or as spick and span as an occupied hospital room could be. She looked up high – nothing unusual. She bent down low and looked under the bed. What was that? Turning, she called for the charge nurse again.

He appeared looking harried and threw out a curt, "What's wrong?"

She forgave him the sharpness and said, "How do I put the bed up as far as it will go?"

"There's a remote control on the other side of the bed. The buttons are fairly self-explanatory."

"Thanks." She was speaking to his retreating back.

"Iain?" He appeared like a genie from a lamp.

"Ma'am?"

"We need a weapon's tube."

"What? Why?" He rubbed the back of his gloved hand on the edge of his hood. "Gun? Knife? Something else?"

"None of the above. It's a syringe. Needle lying next to it. Right at the top of the bed, next to the skirting board."

Iain, adopting the disappointed look, nevertheless trotted off to do her bidding.

When he returned, Shona pointed to the items under the now raised bed and asked him to crawl under the now raised bed and get them into evidence. He used tweezers for the needle, dropped both it and the syringe into the case, then applied biohazard tape to seal them inside. No use some poor unsuspecting lab tech dropping dead before their time.

"I take it you want the book into evidence as well?"

"Got it in one."

It was duly dropped into an evidence bag and joined the other package ready to be transported to the lab.

"I'm off to interview the patients and staff. You carry on here.

"Any chance of a bit of help?"

"I'll send Roy."

"He's more hinderance than help."

"He's improved with time. It will help with his professional development."

"I'm more worried about developing this case than Roy MacGregor."

"In the words of Nike fans worldwide, 'Just Do It'." She swivelled and marched from the room; she'd better things to do with her time than babysit belligerent constables.

50

Shona, having spoken nicely to the charge nurse, found herself ensconced in an office with a hot cup of coffee. Whilst it wasn't The Ritz, it was comfortable and served its purpose, that purpose being to interview the ward staff. Whilst she had to be thorough, she wanted to get through the interviews pronto, so she could return to the station and interrogate a certain Doctor. She'd no sooner taken a sip of coffee than Nina hurtled through the door. "You took your time. Did you not fancy getting out of bed?"

"They closed the bridge."

Shona, knowing that the bridge was usually only closed if someone was about to jump from it, said, "Did it reopen quickly?"

"Yes." Nina looked her in the eye. "They're safe."

Shona huffed out a breath. "Drag one of the staff in so we can interview them."

An hour later they were no further forward. As per all the other cases, no one saw anyone, no one heard anything, everyone was puzzled as to what was going on. The refrain from all staff members was, "There was no reason she should have died."

When asked if they had an alibi, every single staff member said they were in site of a colleague or patient all night, unless answering a call of nature. The call of nature part piqued her interest, as they could have used that as an excuse. She'd have to see what fingerprints were on the syringe and what contents it held.

They interviewed the patients, all of whom had been tucked up in bed fast asleep when the death occurred. No one saw a thing.

"I'm no' sure why you're asking, lassie. The place is swimming in staff. From the cleaners tae the doctors, the catering staff tae the nurses, they've all got the right to be here."

This was the nub of the problem. How do you find a killer when every single one of the staff, probably including their killer, was exactly where they were meant to be?

They left exhausted, ready to scream at the lack of progress and with a time to return and interview Matt Bagaley who had special needs and needed someone with him before he was interviewed.

Shona screwed up her face. "Was he in Ninewells recently?"

"Yes."

"So, why's he here? And before you say it, I know about patient confidentiality but we've a serial killer on our hands. Please, for the love of all that's holy, just answer my questions."

McPherson chewed on his lip and then seemed to make a decision. "He's had a colostomy. Can't go back to his original place of residence as they can't help him with that. So, he's here until we find him somewhere new to stay."

"Where does that leave us with interviewing him?"

"I'll try and get someone in from the home he stayed in. I think they can still act on his behalf." He stood up. "Leave it with me."

. . .

Shona hot footed it back to the Gulags, via a squad car and a blue light. She needed to have strong words with Natasha Somers. In this case, three was definitely not a charm; it was beginning to look like they had themselves a suspect.

Arriving back at the station she dashed to her office and fired up her computer. The fact she did this prior to firing up the coffee pot demonstrated the urgency of her search. She'd no sooner hung up her wet coat, sat down and lifted her fingers above the keyboard, than Peter sauntered through her door.

"Can't it wait?"

"No' really, unless your keen on keeping the world's press waiting." A twitch of his lips showed he was choking back laughter. "I'm no' sure the chief would be happy as he might have to step in."

"Damn. I'd managed to forget about that." She stood up. "I take it they're assembled downstairs?"

"Aye. You'd better get a shuftie on."

"Tell them I'll be five minutes." She rummaged around in a drawer and pulled out a scarf. That, some lipstick and a brush through her hair had her looking a bit more professional and less like someone who'd been dragged in off the street. She strode purposefully in the direction of the press, clutching the notes she'd thankfully prepared the day before and run past the chief.

The purposeful stride hid the way she really felt, which was let's get this over and done with. Her tolerance for the press was never high – she thought they made her life a lot more difficult – but today she was not in the mood for this at all. Someone could be plotting more murders and she had to be all 'hale fellow well met' with a bunch of hacks. Despite this she stepped in front of the podium, set her notes down and looked at the sea of faces. The flashlights practically blinded her. It was a good job she knew what she was going to say without the notes.

"As most of you are aware, Police Scotland are currently investigating a series of deaths linked to hospitals in Dundee City, Perthshire and Fife. It would appear from our investigations so far these are related crimes committed by one perpetrator. We are currently looking at one person of interest. However, our investigation will continue until we catch the person involved. Despite this situation, Police Scotland would like to say, they hold all those who work in NHS Scotland in the highest regard and thank them for the work they do. The hospitals are cooperating fully with our investigation. We will update you further as the investigation progresses." She looked at them again. "Do you have any questions?"

A cacophony of voices erupted.

"One at a time, please. I'm more likely to answer questions if I can hear them." Her voice cut through the hubbub with a tone that brooked no nonsense; they piped down. She was gritting her teeth so hard it was a surprise they didn't break. Her dentist would be having words with her. She pointed to a bloke in a multi-coloured jumper.

"Callum Smith, *Press and Journal.* Can you tell us who the suspect is?"

"We don't have a suspect; they are a person of interest and no we cannot."

She pointed again. "You."

"Maryam Saade, STV. Why are they a person of interest?"

"Again, that is something we cannot answer."

"Serena Samuels, *The Times*. Why is it taking the police so long to catch this killer? Surely, they must be a member of the medical staff? It would seem the police are not doing their jobs."

Shona swore she felt a tooth crack. "With at least fifty wards and goodness knows how many possible community venues, we are not exactly going to pin them down overnight. I can assure you we are doing everything and then some. My officers are working night and day on this case." She took a breath and snapped out, "Last question."

"Adanna Okifor, *The Dundee Courier*. Word on the street says it has to be a doctor and the victims have been poisoned. Is this correct?"

"As I have said, this is part of an ongoing investigation, so we are limited in what we can say. Listening to gossip may not be the best way for you to get your information. That will be all." She stepped from the podium and hurried towards a source of caffeine, wishing she had a shot of whisky to put in it. She wasn't paid enough for all this blasted politeness and was going to have strong words with Adanna when she next saw her.

In the meantime, she had a spot of research to do before she interviewed their person of interest.

51

Somehow, they weren't sure how, they were legally absorbed into the system of this new country they now called home. Yet, it wasn't home. They were moved; then moved again. Still their mother coughed and wheezed and faded before their eyes. She was admitted to hospital where she languished. They sent her home to die in an apartment that was not home. This was no place for a woman to die. This hospital could have prevented it. Could have done more if they had only listened to them.

She died alone while they were at work. In a strange grey land where no one knew her. No one knew the vibrant, fun-filled generous woman she was. They only knew this broken-down shell of a human.

As they buried their mother in earth that was sodden their heart broke in two.

As the days went past rage hardened their heart. The rage grew hotter and hotter as a plan formulated. Justice would be served. They were the only one remaining to avenge their family and the grief they had gone through. They would not turn back from their duty.

52

Clutching her coffee like a lifeline, she opened the notes on the case so far and scanned through them paying particular attention to the doctors who had certified their victims dead. She berated herself for not doing this sooner. Why, in the name of all that's holy, did she not think of these things at the time? Still, this was not the time for recrimination, it was time for action. As she suspected, Natasha was the doctor concerned in one other case at Narrywells. It was slightly disappointing she didn't appear on them all. It would be nice to have a slam dunk, to snaffle one of Roy's American phrases. One of the doctor's appeared beside two of the victims and the remainder were individuals. This still didn't mean Natasha was not involved. She drained the last of her coffee, picked up the phone and arranged a warrant to receive a copy of Natasha Somers' rota.

"Are you getting somewhere with this, Shona?"

"I wish. I'd like to think I've got this all sewn up but there are a few loose threads."

"Are you a seamstress?"

"Not in the slightest. No one would want me to sew

anything for them. I've no clue where the sewing analogy came from."

"Send someone round for the warrant and keep me posted."

She hot footed it to the main office. "Jason, take a blue lighter and head to Narrywells via the Sherriff's office for a warrant. HR will be expecting you to pick up Dr Somers' duty rota for the past six months."

"On it." Jason was out of the door showing the heels of his Matalan shoes. The boy left the fashion statements to Roy and Nina.

"Nina, take your Gucci clad self in the direction of Natasha Somers. Make her comfortable in the family room ensuring she has a hot drink." She had an afterthought. "And a bacon or sausage roll. She's been on night shift, so she must be starving."

"Why are we being so nice to her?"

"So she doesn't bolt and we need to up her status from person of interest to suspect."

"She's going to want to lawyer up if we keep her here for much longer."

"As is her right. I'll be praying my best prayers it's not McCluskey or Runcie."

"Good luck with that one."

An hour later, Natasha was having a snooze on the family room sofa, covered by a fluffy Christmas blanket that had appeared from somewhere while the team pored over rotas in the briefing room. Due to another blinding flash, this time from Abigail, they'd also asked for a copy of all unexplained deaths in the last six months and produced a warrant to support the request. The hospital ponied it up in a surprisingly speedy fashion. Shona assumed they were as keen to catch the killer as the police were; probably more so.

They stuck to Narrywells in the first instance, mainly because they didn't have the staff rota for the other hospitals. If a pattern emerged, they would obtain a warrant for the other hospitals as well. Heads down, red pen in hand, they applied themselves to the task like the demons of hell were circling. They weren't far wrong as they might not have been circling around the briefing room but were most probably circling around some poor unsuspecting woman's hospital room. Shona made a mental note that if she was ever in hospital, to ask for a bed on the ward. It would seem privacy came at too high a price.

The shrill tone of Shona's phone had them all leaping. And complaining in equal measure.

"You nearly gave me another heart attack." Peter clutched his chest. "Could you no' get something a wee bit gentler."

"Don't be so dramatic. You look fine to me. I'm a cop not a ballet dancer."

She looked at the caller ID – Forensics Lab. "DI McKenzie. What have you got for me?" She paused, then, "At least I hope you've got something for me."

"We certainly do, Ma'am."

The lab tech's voice was much too cheery for Shona's liking but she kept her mouth firmly closed. "Spill. The suspense is killing me."

"Your syringe tested positive to potassium ions."

"And that means?"

"It means you'd better chat to the pathologist."

Shona pressed the red button and tapped speed dial – yes, she really did have Mary on speed dial – as she hurried from the room.

"I've only just got the last victim in a drawer. No I haven't had time to do a post mortem yet."

"I'm hurt. I'm the bearer of news. Whether it is good or not only you can say."

"Sock it to me. Quickly. I've drawers full of the deceased awaiting my tender intervention."

Shona outlined the syringe and the potassium ions.

"Of course. Potassium Chloride. For years they said it was undetectable but now you can detect it in heart blood. I've got to go."

Shona was left listening to the dial tone. "Why does everyone hang up on me or throw me out of their office." No one was interested basically because she was the only one there. Until she wasn't. A yellow clad whirlwind hurtled through the door of her office and threw her arms around her. She was followed by a more sedate teenager. "Alice. Rory. How lovely to see you. Why aren't you at school?" She kissed the top of Alice's head. It was always lovely to see her future step-daughter.

"Strikes." Rory did not look impressed.

"Most kids like a buckshee day off school."

"Not when they've got exams, and they want to go to law school."

"Fair point. Where's your father?"

"Off to see the big cheese."

"You're being rather flippant about the chief."

"Not him. The big, big cheese."

"Are you telling me the chief constable is here?" Why was she finding this out from a teenager?

"According to my dad, she's here to talk to him and the chief."

Shona turned fifty shades of pale, said, "There's cake somewhere; you know where to find it," and bolted off like a fox after a rabbit.

She stopped at the squad room, which looked quite presentable. Roy was the lone occupant, tapping away on his computer. "I'm still working on it as fast as I can. It takes time."

"Noted. Anything yet?"

He shook his head. "Not really."

Roy's not really could mean many things. She hoped this time it meant, quite a lot.

"The Chief Constable is in the building. She'll probably drop in so look lively."

He tapped the keyboard with renewed vigour.

"Oh, and find out everything you can about potassium chloride and where you can get it."

The remainder of the team appeared to be equally as industrious. The cross checking was still going on. If the queen bee arrived to survey her kingdom, she would see all the worker bees hard at it.

"We've a possible hit on our poison. Potassium chloride."

"What on earth?"

"Don't ask. I've not got a clue."

Two hours and a bacon roll later they had a visit from the top dog and a pattern. Whilst it wasn't one that dotted all the Ts and crossed the Is, it was definitely a pattern that didn't fall in Natasha's favour.

"Abigail, waken Natasha up. You can interview her with me." She pulled ten pounds out of her pocket and handed it to her sergeant. "Get her a sandwich. It's been hours since she's been fed. Take her a strong coffee as well."

"Why are we being so nice to her?" Nina asked.

"Because she is more likely to be amenable to answering our questions. Honey and flies, Nina, honey and flies." With that, Shona headed in the direction of the kitchen to make fresh coffee. She needed it to tease out the correct answers from their suspect. Yes, she'd been upgraded from person of interest.

53

The plan was worked out in meticulous detail.

How could their beautiful, selfless mother die such a horrific death when evil, wanton women lived lives of luxury and debauchery? How could their innocent sisters die? No God would want such women to live, not when ones so pure had been taken from this earth in such a horrific way. It was their job to right a wrong and restore balance. A life for each life taken on that horrifying journey to get to these shores. This was their duty. Their new purpose for being on this earth. It was time for revenge.

The plan had each step outlined.

These people thought they knew better than them. Were better than them. For no other reason than their country of birth.

They did not know how someone walking the corridors, working in such an esteemed institution, saw everything. Heard everything. Took everything in. Schemed. Plotted. Smiled. Put on an act. Carried out their plan with military precision. Blended in. Barely noticed. Who would notice one more member of staff in a hospital?

54

As Shona headed towards the interview room, Douglas was headed in the other direction.

"If you want to talk weddings, I'm too busy."

"Not a bit of it. I just thought I would say hello to my gorgeous fiancé who I haven't seen in days."

His eyes and voice melted Shona's insides. "Hello, fiancé." She gave him a quick peck on the cheek. "And cheerio. I've to go and ruin someone's day."

"I'm sure you will be excellent at it."

"No doubt," she threw over her shoulder as she trotted off.

Just before she entered the interview room, Roy handed her a sheet of paper. A couple of things you might want to see.

She glanced at the sheet and added it to the pile in her hand. "Thanks."

Natasha looked slightly more refreshed and a lot more wary. She was clutching a mug of coffee like a lifebelt in stormy seas. Shona thought it was a good thing as the young woman before her was definitely going to be in stormy water before she got halfway through her coffee.

"Thank you for coming in to see us. Thank you also for your patience. I appreciate you have been here some time."

"It's no bother. I've had the best sleep I've had in ages. It's quiet here."

Quiet wasn't the word Shona would choose to describe the police station, so goodness knows where the doctor lived. "I am sure you are wondering why we asked you to come in."

"Of course, I am. You've interviewed me every which way. Are you this thorough with all your witnesses?"

"We have a few questions for you if you—"

"Is there a reason you've dragged me in here rather than interviewing me at the hospital?"

"Yes. We would like to interview you with the tapes running." Shona's short fuse was getting shorter due to general exhaustion and lack of progress. She went through the preliminaries for the sake of the tape.

"Do I need a lawyer?"

"I can't answer that for you. I will say you have the right to a lawyer and can stop and ask for one at any time."

"I'm happy to carry on. I've done nothing wrong."

Said every single suspect I've ever interviewed even when they are as guilty as sin and then some. "Having looked at the records, it would seem you certified these four women dead." She handed over a sheet of paper.

"I certify a lot of people dead."

Shona wasn't sure that line of defence was helping the doctor in the slightest. "I'm sure you do but I am interested in those particular women."

Natasha pulled out her phone and tapped a few times. She peered at the names and did a bit more tapping. "Yes, I did."

"Are you allowed to store patient information on your phone?" Shona's frown couldn't have been deeper if she tried.

The doctor threw her an are you stupid look. "It's not on my phone. I'm accessing the NHS computer system."

If the police did that, we'd be pulled up all ways till Christmas. She handed over another list of names. "Do you recognise any of these names?"

"A couple of them look familiar. I might have treated them at some point."

Shona knew full well Somers had been working on the wards where the women had died. "Were you on the ward when they died?"

"Are you trying to pin these murders on me?" She leaned forward in her chair. "I want a lawyer."

"Interview stopped while the witness phoned her lawyer."

Forty minutes later they were back in the interview room with a lawyer who was neither Runcie nor McCluskey but looked vaguely familiar. Shona did a double take when the lawyer held out her hand and said her name. "Khrystyna Alexeyev." How many Russians could there possibly be in Dundee. The place was awash with them.

"You're not related to Stephan and Igor are you?"

"I have the misfortune to be, yes." Her lip twitched and she looked Shona squarely in the eyes.

Shona swallowed down what she was going to say and merely answered, "Small world."

"Indeed. Now, why are you claiming my client had something to do with a spate of recent murders?" There was no longer any sign of lip twitching or humour. "My client is a hard-working doctor who wants nothing more than to go home and sleep.

"That will happen much more quickly if she not only answers our questions but does so fully. We are not arresting her for anything we merely want answers." She pushed the sheet of paper with the names on them across the table once more. "Were you working on the wards where these women died?"

"Yes." It wasn't a difficult question given the wards were written next to the names.

"Were you on duty when they died."

More phone tapping. "Yes."

"Is this going somewhere?" The lawyer tapped her foot giving Shona the urge to pin it down with something sharp.

"I am trying to establish patterns." She turned back to their person of interest. "Why did you not certify them?"

"They weren't my patients. Different team."

"Why were you working at King Albert's Hospital last night? Your post is at Narrywells."

"I was doing locum work. You're not allowed to do locum in your own trust."

"Why were you doing locum?"

"I've a big trip coming up and need extra money to pay for it."

"Don't you think it's a bit of a coincidence you were there on the ward when, yet another woman died under suspicious circumstances?"

"Are you accusing my client of murder?"

"I'm not accusing her of anything, but you need to agree it seems a bit suspicious."

"Coincidences happen." Natasha's foot had joined her lawyer' s in tapping a staccato beat.

Shona did a bit more damage to her teeth by gritting them again. "Is it true you were investigated following a mix up with medication where a patient nearly died?"

Natasha turned pale in front of their eyes. "It was a mistake. I was exonerated. I miscalculated a dosage."

"That's a pretty big miscalculation for a doctor to make."

"I had worked too many hours and was exhausted mentally as well as physically. You have heard the punishing hours doctors work."

"And yet, they take on more hours." She handed over a

sheet of paper with yet more names, dates and wards. "Do you recognise any of these names."

Natasha shook her head. "They aren't ringing a bell. And I didn't work on those wards." She peered at the paper again, brows furrowed. Then she looked up and gave a nervous smile. "I wasn't in the country for three of them. Look." More tapping. She held up her phone with the calendar app open. "Barbados for two of them and Prague for the other."

"I would say this absolves my client of the ridiculous notion you have that she is some sort of sick serial killer."

She was right. *Blast.* "Were you with anyone when you were away?"

"My partner, Brittany." More phone tapping. "Here. You can check out the photos on social media. It will show you the dates and places I checked in."

Shona scrolled through several of the photos. The girl was right. They were clear proof she was elsewhere when three of the murders took place. They needed time to look at this more carefully.

"I need you to think carefully, did you notice anything or anyone out of the ordinary around the time these women died?"

The girl thought long and hard before saying, "No. Nothing. I'll apply the little grey cells to it and if I think of anything, I'll get back to you.

"Thank you for coming in. We appreciate your help. You are free to go."

As they walked back, Shona asked, "Do you think she was telling the truth? You were watching her."

Abigail, who was two steps in front of her turned back. "I was looking at her the whole time and I didn't get the impression of someone who was lying."

"The fact someone else almost died in her hands concerns me."

"She didn't look shifty about it. They obviously didn't think much of it if she's still practicing as a doctor."

"You're probably right. I'll get in touch with the GMC and get the proper story."

"The what?"

"General Medical Council. The lot that keeps doctors on the straight and narrow."

When she returned to her office there was a message on her desk saying King Albert's had phoned her. They had someone to chaperone Mr Bagaley; they would be there at the appointed time.

She grabbed her waterproof and headed to the main office. It was like the Marie Celeste. She raised a quizzical eyebrow in Peter's direction.

"All gone to the canteen for sustenance."

"Did you not need sustaining."

"I ate the healthy packed lunch the wife made me. I might like my food but I'm no' stupid. The wife'll kill me if I have another heart attack and die on her."

"That makes no sense and perfect sense all at the same time. You're with me. Grab your coat."

This time they used Shona's car, which Douglas had somehow managed to get to the office, and drove at a more sedate rate. Sedate for Shona that was. She cranked up the heat as far as it would go. Summer was doing a darned good attempt at acting like winter. So much so, Shona was sure there was an Oscar in its future.

"What's your take on all of this?"

Peter pulled out a packet of mints and offered her one. "Every case we get is weird but this takes the biscuit."

"Nothing like this in your time on the force."

"No. Some Dundee residents might be right bampots, but they would never do anything to hurt the NHS."

"Well, someone is." She concentrated on manoeuvring past a roundabout that seemed to be full of drivers who got their licences from a supermarket. "Unless they're coming into Dundee from elsewhere which would be all we'd blasted well need."

"I hope not." He sucked on his mint then tried a tentative, "What's with that book that keeps appearing?"

"Good question. Hang on." She used voice control to get hold of Abigail and put it on loudspeaker. "What's the skinny on *A Thousand Splendid Suns*? Did we ever find out if all the victims had them?"

"Most of the families got back to me. Some of them had no clue as they paid no attention. Some said, yes, the book was there but they thought their loved one had just been given it by another patient. One said, their mother wouldn't read anything so literary as 50 Shades was more her thing."

"A mixed bag then. Thanks." She tapped end and said, "Definitely a calling card."

"Aye. Is it not a wee bit strange though?"

"A wee bit. Are you having a laugh? It's a big bit strange."

"I'll give you that. Have you ever read the book?"

"No. Find out if any of the others have."

55

If they were confused to start with the interview with Matt Bagaley had them even more so but, if he was to be believed, with only one shocking outcome that required immediate and drastic action.

They had to spend ten minutes chatting and getting to know him. Peter took the lead as, apparently, he reacted better to men than women. His special needs came about due to the regular beatings the poor man's mother gave him as a child.

Shona watched in awe as Peter built up a relationship with him based on a mutual love of football and gardening. Subjects about which Shona knew nothing.

Eventually, Peter brought the talk around to the ward and how it was there.

"Nice people. Nice nurses, Nice doctors. Like it here."

"Aye, they're a canny lot. I can see why you'd like it."

"Clean. Got to keep clean. Always wash your hands."

Peter glanced at the man's guardian. Shona kept quiet."

"He's been told always to wash his hands after the colostomy and to make sure the area is clean afterwards."

"Clean. Always clean. Cleaner always here. Keeps the ward

clean. Doctor always here. Keep the ward clean. Doctor. Cleaner. Doctor. Cleaner. Cleaner. Doctor" This was said so fast they could barely keep up.

The guardian stepped in. "Hey, Matt. Could you say it slowly?"

"Doctor is a cleaner. Cleaner is a doctor."

Peter asked, "Are the doctor and the cleaner the same person?"

"Same man. Doctor and cleaner. Same man."

Shona asked, "How does he take all this in?"

"He's obsessed with cleaning at the moment, because he's been told to keep everything clean when he changes the colostomy; he can rattle off everything about cleaners in the hospital," the carer clarified, much to Shona's relief.

"Do you know what time of the day you saw the doctor or cleaner."

"Cleaner daytime. Doctor night time. Two jobs. Man work hard. Two jobs. Matt work hard. One job. Matt a gardener."

"Thank you, Matt," she said gently. You've been a great help."

The man's eyes lit up. "Matt helped the police."

"You certainly did."

His grin grew to the size of Scotland. Shona couldn't help but grin back. Whilst the news wasn't the best for her, she delighted in the fact this man was delighted he had helped them in the course of their duty. Police Scotland needed more Matts in their corner.

They walked back to the car in stunned silence. What on earth were they meant to be doing with this information? Once on the road back to Dundee, Shona spoke. "That's the most mind-blowing thing I've heard since I started as a rookie cop."

"I've been at this a lot longer than you and I'd have to say, me too. Just when I think your cases couldn't get any weirder, you surprise me."

"Hang on a minute. You can't hold me responsible for this."

Peter gave a half-hearted smile. "But the chief will."

Shona was way past the smiling stage. She managed a fully powered groan. "Any ideas on what we do?"

"No idea whatsoever. Although I can see more paperwork in our future."

"Lots more. Phone the Sheriff and ask him for warrants to get the cleaning rosters for all three hospitals. Ask him if he can email them as urgent to all three hospitals."

Peter did this, phoned the hospitals to say they were on their way and could they email the rosters back to them.

"I'll ring Dr Dalhousie to ask her who her mother's cleaner was."

"Do you think oor cleaner also worked at the university?"

"Good call. Let's wait until we check everything else first. The one thing I do know is that Natasha Somers is in the clear. Matt very clearly said he was a man."

"Do you think he's a reliable witness."

"I'm sure Margaret McCluskey and Angus Runcie would have a field day with that one. My answer right now is, yes, I do think he's a reliable witness."

"What makes you think that? I'm no' so sure myself, although he does know an awful lot about football and gardening. More than me tae be honest."

"Precisely. He takes things in. The carer seemed pretty adamant he knew what he was talking about when it came to cleaning and cleaners."

She slammed on her brakes and beeped her horn. "Idiot. Keep to the bally speed limit." She pulled out and overtook someone who obviously thought twenty miles per hour was quite fast enough on a dual carriageway.

Peter, white and clutching the handle above the door,

waited until he was suitably recovered before saying, "What I don't understand is how a cleaner could get away wi' pretending he was a doctor."

"Me neither. It's a pretty huge divide in careers."

"Maybe he's a real doctor and working as a cleaner to get more dosh."

"A pretty big stretch. Most doctors would do locum work."

"It's making nae sense tae me at all." Peter tended to come over more Scottish when he was puzzled.

"Let's hope it does soon." She bit her lip, then said, "I jolly well fully intend for it to make sense soon. Let's nail this basket case once and for all."

56

There was no time to waste. "Get the team into the briefing room, pronto."

Shona hadn't even taken off her coat before she picked up the phone to call Dr Dalhousie. She flicked through her notes, then dialled. "The person you are calling is not available. Please leave a message after the tone." Blast. The most irritating message in the history of the planet. She left a message asking her to ring DI Shona McKenzie as a matter of urgency. Then she added, there was nothing to worry about, it was just part of their enquiries into her mother's death.

Now that Shona thought about it, all the places where the women had died were pristine. Or at least the ones where there had been no attempt at resuscitation. Those ones looked like the scene of a bomb blast rather than scene of crime. Usually, she would be beating herself up about the fact she hadn't put two and two together but in this case two and two were more likely to make twenty-two. Who the heck would think a cleaner and a doctor would be one and the same person? She still couldn't wrap her head around it. But they had no other lead to follow. She still wasn't fully convinced it was the answer, but it was, quite literally, the only lead they had.

When she returned to the main office, Peter had the team hard at it. SO hard at it there wasn't even a drink in site. He'd managed to inveigle a couple of bobbies from uniform to swell the numbers. Shona didn't even want to think what he'd promised his mate to perform that little trick. She didn't actually care if it made their job easier and sped up the process of finding their killer. This case was messing with her head in more ways than one. Plus, she'd barely seen anything of Douglas and the kids, or her cat, so it was also seriously messing with her personal life. She was raking it in with overtime but, quite frankly she'd prefer to have a life. She shook herself. *Get a grip woman. People are losing their lives and you're worried about missing a couple of dinner dates and a moggie. How selfish is that?*

The cross checking was gruelling, yet no one uttered a word despite the hours passing. Nor did they mention food or drink. Shona repeatedly checked her phone to see if Dr Dalhousie had phoned and she hadn't heard it. Getting a name would help them to narrow it down.

When everyone started rubbing their eyes and doing a good impression of zombies, she decided they needed to call it a day. There were too many variables, personnel, wards, hospitals, times, and a million other things. Even if he was a cleaner at the university as well why that particular group of women? Where did he get the Potassium Chloride? Where did he get the syringes? How did he know how to administer it? Maybe he really was a doctor but why wasn't he working as a doctor? Had he been struck off? All these questions made her head ache.

"Go see your nearest and dearest but I need you back here at 8am sharp. Eat before you get here. We'll be on this immediately."

They were up off their chairs and out the door as though jet propelled. She followed them at a rapid clip.

For once she didn't even have a Talisker to wind down from the stress of the day. She took two painkillers, fed Shakespeare, and fell into bed fully clothed. She didn't even think about ringing Douglas as she wasn't sure she would be able to formulate a cogent sentence never mind whisper sweet nothings. Discussing wedding plans was the last thing on her mind. You need at least a modicum of brain power and energy to talk flowers, cakes, courses for the wedding meal and what music should be played. Quite frankly, she didn't actually care. She just wanted to be married and then get on with their life together, not all the fuss that was made over one day. She wished with every fabric of her being it could just magically happen – if she could wake up and be married that would be pretty awesome.

She was asleep the minute she'd pulled up the quilt and laid her head on the pillow. Her dreams were graphic and involved cleaners with face masks, doctors' coats, mops and stethoscopes that were so huge they could be used on an elephant. Not a wedding to be seen.

57

She woke up early, disorientated and tangled in her sheets. With some amount of effort, she dragged herself up, stripped off yesterday's clothes and scrubbed herself head to toe in the hottest shower she could bear. Shakespeare was still curled up in bed, so she popped some food in her bowl for later. Then she poured a bowl of Alpen, added an overripe banana, covered it in some natural yogurt that looked a trifle suspicious and scarfed it down.

She was out the door before her shirt as her granny was wont to say. When she was around that was. Her grandmother spent most of her time gallivanting around the world. She was somewhere in the Caribbean at the moment, but Shona wasn't quite sure where, as granny dearest was island hopping. Shona felt like getting on a plane, joining her and leaving the rest of them to it.

Instead, she dashed out of the door, leapt into her car and pointed its front bumper in the direction of the Gulags, otherwise known as Bell Street Station. By the time the others appeared she had two freshly brewed pots of dark roast ready and fresh tea steeping in a pot so big it could double as a washing up bowl. Enough biscuits to feed the entire station were heaped up on plates. They would not be stopping in their task until they'd identified their killer.

Every single one of the team arrived before 8am and bums were on seats before they had time to take off coats. Apparently, the whole team felt the same way as her. It was time to put this reign of terror to an end. Pronto.

They were startled out of deep concentration by the shrill tone of Shona's phone. Shona pulled it out hoping it was Dr Dalhousie. It was Mary.

"I've got a result from that heart blood sample I did on your latest—"

"And?"

"Give me a chance." There was a tinge of sharpness in her voice.

"Sorry."

"The heart blood samples came back positive for Potassium Chloride."

"Then we definitely have ourselves a killer. One who knows about medication."

"Seems that way."

"Any clue as to where we start catching them?"

"Good luck with that one. Thankfully that part of it is your problem and not mine. Why do you think I'm a pathologist?"

"I'm rapidly wishing I'd followed that path as well."

Her next step was to ring the Sheriff and ask for a warrant to take to the pharmacy at Narrywells. She needed to find out if Potassium Chloride was being ordered in a way that was out of the ordinary.

She left the others too it and went herself. The pharmacy staff weren't keen on giving out the information despite the warrant. Once more she found herself waiting for Stella Barrington-

Smythe to appear and give approval. Once more the woman took one look at the warrant and said, "We will need our lawyer."

Shona took a deep breath. "No, you don't." She looked the woman straight in the eye. "This quite clearly states I have the right to speak to your head pharmacist and I am going to do it now. I was willing to give the staff the benefit of the doubt, but I will arrest you for hindering a police officer in the course of her duty."

"You can't do that."

"Yes, I can. Now get out of my way before I march you out of here. In handcuffs." She'd had enough of this pompous fool. She pulled out her phone. "I'm sure the press would love a picture of that."

Seriously, more people could die whilst they hung about waiting for all the red tape to be sorted out. She didn't have time for any of this.

"I'll be reporting you."

"Please do. While you are doing it, I will be catching the murderer who is killing your patients. I'm sure you can work out which is more important." With that she turned her back on the CEO and said to the pharmacist, "Is there somewhere we can talk quietly?"

The pharmacist threw a quick look at the CEO, then led Shona to an office.

It turned out there had been a slight increase in the ordering of Potassium Chloride by some wards over the past few months but nothing that would lead to panic or investigation. They were keeping an eye on it. Shona asked for a list of the specific wards and the staff members doing the ordering. The pharmacist opened up a computer programme, tapped several keys, peered at the computer and then the printer started to churn out the results. She handed them to Shona. "Am I in trouble?"

"Not at all. Not from our perspective anyway." She wouldn't like to hazard a guess as to how much trouble she would be in from the hospital trust's perspective. An increase in sudden deaths and an increase in the dispensing of a drug that could cause those deaths did not look good by anyone's standards. The hospital might not throw just the book at her but also her P45. If nothing else she was going to be on special measures for many months to come.

Shona grabbed the sheets of paper, thanked the pharmacist and disappeared out the door. Time, tide or investigations waited for no woman. She tried looking at it while she hurtled along the corridors but could make no sense. She threw it on the seat next to her in the car. This would have to wait until she returned to the station.

As she shoved open the front door of the station her phone rang. "DI McKenzie." It was Dr Dalhousie. "You wanted to speak to me?" There was an undertone of anxiety in her voice.

"A strange question I know but who was your mother's cleaner?"

"You what? My mother is lying in the mortuary and all you're worried about is finding a cleaner."

"I appreciate it's odd but please we need to know. It could really help us in our investigation. I promise you this is not personal."

"His name was Kevin Hari."

"Is that Harry spelled H A R R Y?"

"No. H A R I." There was a slight pause and she added, "I thought it was an odd name for someone with an accent like his."

"You mean he wasn't Scottish?"

"He wasn't even British. I've no clue where he was from. He was a superb cleaner though although he never once smiled.

Didn't say much either. Not that we cared because we weren't employing him for his scintillating conversation."

"Could you hazard a guess as to where he was from?"

"No, I wouldn't even know where to start. What has this got to do with my mother's murder?"

"We aren't sure ourselves at the moment but the minute we are you will be the first to know. I can assure you, however, that we are following every line of inquiry."

And where does this fit into everything we're doing? She hoped against hope it would lead somewhere. They needed something to go into in this infernal case.

58

As she plunked herself into a seat in the briefing room, Nina poured a coffee and slid it across the desk to her. She took several large gulps before saying, "Has anything come up?"

Blank stares gave her all the answers she needed. "I've a name for you to look for; amongst the mounds of paperwork did anyone come across the name Kevin Hari?"

Jason looked eager. "Yep, a couple of times."

"Me too," Abigail added.

"Do you know what ward he worked on?"

The team just shook their heads.

"Then, check it out now."

She hurried to her office to get rid of her wet coat and make a phone call to the university. As she thought HR were not keen on coughing up any names without a warrant. Ten minutes later the warrant was emailed through to her, and she was on her way to the university via a squad car with lights flashing and sirens blaring. It would appear that Kevin also worked at the university. This still wasn't giving them any information as to how a cleaner could manage to get such a dangerous medication officially. She didn't know much about hospitals but surely cleaners didn't have access to the drugs cabinets. If it was Kevin, then he had help.

She made a quick call to both of the other hospitals involved in the case and they were happy, given the current investigation, to confirm that Kevin was, indeed, a cleaner at the hospital. It would appear they had their murderer. Or did they? She still couldn't get her head around the fact a cleaner could do all this.

As the team fact checked wards and times, Shona took a look at the paperwork she had been given by the pharmacist. One name leapt out loud and clear. She sat bolt upright and said, "Jason. Iain. Get Dave Carabiniere in here, stat. If he refuses drag him in here in handcuffs." She explained that it would appear to be him who was ordering the excess potassium chloride. "He's either up to his eyebrows in murder or is an accessory to murder. One way or the other he's going to be arrested and thrown in one of our cells where he will be taking up room and board until we find out which it is."

"Roy. Find out all you can about Kevin Hari. Use any means possible or impossible."

"Peter, find out where we can get a hold of Kevin."

They all scattered to the four winds. Shona headed in the direction of our office to phone Margaret McCluskey. She knew her client would be asking for her and this would speed up the process. Her clients were not the only ones who had McCluskey on speed dial; Shona did too.

Dave did not come quietly. In fact, he did arrive in handcuffs kicking and screaming like a toddler. Only louder. "This is preposterous. You've dragged me away from a world full of patients. My lawyer will have something to say about this."

Shona was not surprised to see that Jason seemed to be

nursing his hand. "Another injury? You know the drill." She turned to Dave Carabiniere. "For the sake of all our heads, shut up. I haven't got time for temper tantrums."

"I was on duty. You have left the ward short staffed."

"Well, the world will just have to cope. I'm dealing with a murder. Whether you are my murderer or not remains to be seen."

"Are you accusing me of murder? I want my lawyer."

"I'm not accusing you of anything and your lawyer is currently waiting for you in an interview room."

She took him to the interview room to speak to Margaret McCluskey. She did not offer them coffee and biscuits. The time for niceties had long passed.

She gave them twenty minutes to talk before walking back into the room with Peter.

McCluskey, looking like a galleon berthed at a dock, said, "Why have you arrested my client? He's done nothing. This is false arrest."

Shauna did all the preliminaries for the video before saying, "He's been arrested for impeding the police in the course of their duties. However, we are also looking at whether we should arrest him for murder."

Dave shot from his chair so fast it toppled over. "I didn't murder anyone. How dare you accuse me. I'm going to sue you."

Shona's voice took on a tone that could crack glaciers. "Pick that chair up and sit on it. Do not push me."

Dave did as he was told, sporting the demeanour of a petulant child. He was going to look more than petulant by the time she'd finished.

Shona went straight for the jugular. "Why have you been ordering so much potassium chloride over the past few months?" She pushed the paperwork over to Margaret McCluskey who snatched it up and read it.

She watched as Dave turned pale.

"Well?" She didn't have time for this.

He tried a bit of bravado. "We needed it. That's not a crime."

Shona had had the presence of mind to contact the ward and ask them about the use of that particular drug, so she was prepared for that objection. "Not according to the other nurses on your ward. They say they've only had one patient requiring that particular drug in the last six months." She watched as he took this in and added, "So, why have you been ordering so much potassium chloride?"

Dave did a good impression of a stranded salmon. He looked like he was trying to formulate words, but none were making it past his vocal cords.

"You'll understand then, why I think the only reason could be is that you've been murdering female patients on your ward."

She knew this wasn't the case because Dave had been nowhere near the other two hospitals, but she was trying to frighten him into spilling the beans about selling these drugs to someone else. If that someone else had the name of Kevin Hari that would be even better. He may not have been the person to murder the patients, but he was definitely the supplier. She leaned forward and looked him straight in the eye. "Give me one good reason why I should not arrest you for murder."

Dave tried for the macho approach. He leaned back in his chair and draped one arm over the back. "Because I didn't do it. Take me to court and my lawyer will wipe her backside with you."

"Brave, aren't you? I'm sure you won't be quite so brave when your tucked up for life with a bunch no hope lifers in a particularly unpleasant nick."

"And that's not going to happen."

"Trust me, Macho Man, it is. Unless you give me evidence to the contrary. You had the means, motive and were in the right place. I'd say we've got us a slam dunk to borrow an American phrase. How are you going to support your family..." She paused. "Sorry, families, from prison. You're not going to be getting handouts from anyone then, are your"

Dave Looked a little less brave."

"I want to speak to my client in private." McCluskey looked like she was about to hand out the death penalty.

Shona was happy to oblige. "I'll give you ten minutes." That would give her time to stock up on caffeine and painkillers for the headache that was forming like a particularly ominous thunder cloud on her brain.

Back in the interview room, the lawyer had a face like four day old road kill. She heaved her enormous bosom by taking a deep breath – it was almost mesmerising - and said, "My client would like a plea deal."

"That's down to the prosecutor but I would certainly be amenable to what he has to say and we'll put in a good word for him." She stopped, looked Dave straight in the eye, and said, "if I like what you have to say. You had better be telling me the truth, the whole truth, and nothing but the truth."

"My client wants to cooperate."

"Then he'd better get on with it, because, if he's not the murdered, then I have a murder to catch."

Dave spilled the beans and then some. He'd been providing the drug to someone he met in the canteen. A doctor who wanted to run some private experiments. He had a funny accent, Dave couldn't tell where it came from, but his English was impeccable. He had shown Dave paperwork as to why he needed it but said his research was so time sensitive he needed extra potassium chloride to run his experiments.

"And you fell for that?"

"He was offering good money, and I was desperate." He

looked even more desperate now. His face had taken on a yellow tinge as the full force of the situation he was in slammed home.

Shona was willing to bet he did not realise the full enormity of how desperate his situation really was.

"Did you give him syringes and needles as well?"

"No. Just the drugs. I swear."

"Do you have a name for this mythical being who is going to get you out of this enormous hole you are in."

"Kevin Hari. He works at the hospital."

"He certainly does. As a cleaner. You've been handing dangerous drugs out to someone who isn't licensed to use those drugs for anything other than cleaning them up off the floor."

"What, no." Macho man started to tremble. "He showed me—"

"Dave Carabiniere, I'm arresting you for conspiracy to murder and culpable homicide, you do not..." She rattled off the rest. "Sgt Johnston process our prisoner and take him to the cells." She stood up and walked out the room.

"You said I'd get a plea deal."

"I said I'd put in a good word with the prosecutors. That's a different thing all together." She fully intended having a word with the prosecutors. Whether it fell in his favour was another matter.

59

It looked like they definitely had a suspect, so catching him was uttermost in their minds. They also had a suspect who had access to dangerous drugs and seemed to use them in the most arbitrary fashion. What on earth was going through his head? If he was from another country, why target women in Scotland? Why Dundee? As far as she knew the city had never been involved in anything nefarious abroad.

These thoughts got her nowhere, so she went to find Roy. Maybe he had a few answers.

It turned out he did have at least one answer. She supposed the remainder would have to come from the man himself, if he chose to tell them.

"Are you going to tell me or keep me in suspense?"

"Turns out Kevin Hari is actually Khaled Hawari an illegal immigrant."

"How did an illegal immigrant end up in Dundee and changing his name?"

"Westminster helped him change his name." Roy leaned back in his chair and watched her face.

"Westminster?" Shona was lost for words. "You'd better tell me the whole story. And fast."

"Khaled Hawari was a doctor in the country from which he fled. I couldn't find anything about which country that was. He flew a regime so terrifying, our government wanted all the intel on it they could get. So, they made a deal with him. If he told all he would get a new identity and new home. He had to find a job himself. That job could not be as a doctor as it would have identified him."

"So, he got one in a hospital where he would feel at home. Not."

"You'd think he'd be grateful for the new start, not go on a murder spree."

"You'd think." Her eyes narrowed. "Where did you get all this information? Was it legal?"

"Better not to ask."

"You're going to get this unit into serious trouble one of these days."

"No, you are. You always give me permission." Roy grinned.

Shona didn't have the oomph to smile back. They needed to move with the utmost urgency if they were to catch a killer and stop him murdering anyone else.

60

Blue lights flashing and sirens blaring they headed in the direction of Kevin Hari's flat. Shona banged on the door. Nothing. She banged again. Nothing. "Break the door down."

A couple of brawny coppers they'd brought along for just such an eventuality did as requested. They entered the flat and, taking the utmost care, searched each room. A small child, who looked to be about five, huddled on a bed in a sparse bedroom, sucking her thumb and clutching a ragged teddy. It was the only toy in the room. In fact, it appeared to be the only toy in the whole flat. It was difficult to say whether it was a boy or a girl. "Hello, sweetheart, where's your daddy?"

The child stared but did not move or utter a word.

Given the child was alone in the flat, this was also child neglect. "Get social services. We need him or her to be moved to a place of safety. She looked over at Abigail. "You're good with kids. Stay until social services get here. Iain, you stay as backup in case our killer turns up. You've got your tasers?"

They both nodded, yes, they had their tasers. Shona had said a firm no to guns. The likelihood of them having to hunt down a killer in a hospital was high and shooting some poor sod who'd done nothing more dangerous than be seen by a doctor, was not a good look for Police Scotland's finest. Especially if they managed to up the body count in the process. Abigail moved over to the child, spoke gently to them and touched the teddy bear. She spoke some more, and Shona saw the child's face soften. Confident they were in safe hands she gestured to the remainder of the team to follow her.

The next stop was the hospital. They phoned in advance, and it was confirmed Kevin or Khaled was working, although they weren't exactly sure on which ward.

"How on earth can a hospital not know where a member of their domestic staff is working? Seriously, it's a miracle anything gets done in that place."

"That's no' fair, Ma'am. They do lots of good work in there. It's a great hospital." Peter looked the perfect example of what high dudgeon should look like.

Shona gave a grudging, "You're right," before turning her brain towards where he was likely to be.

"When we get there, we'll head straight to the wards where the women were killed."

Shona pulled out her phone and dialled the CEO. She'd better give Barrington-Smythe the heads up or they'd be tapping their heels waiting for permission.

"I'm not sure you can rampage around our wards trying to find a staff member."

Shona gritted her teeth and then thought, sod it, if I get sacked it will be worth it. "You may not be sure of anything but I'm completely sure, if this maniac, who you've allowed to roam the wards of your hospital kills anyone else you will be entirely culpable." She took a deep breath. "So, to stop that I am only letting you know out of politeness. The police will be going anywhere they want. A warrant will be winging its way to you, so check your email."

She hung up without giving the woman a chance to respond. "That woman needs to be sacked."

Peter decided the best response was no response.

Phone the Sherriff and get a warrant for Kevin Khaled's arrest. Peter pulled out his phone without saying a word and made the call.

"He's emailing it to you and the CEO of the hospital. Apparently, he already has her email address."

"Why does that not surprise me?"

Arriving at the hospital they screeched up to the main door. They hurtled up the main concourse where members of the public gave them a wide berth as they watched open mouthed. It wasn't often you saw several police officers, in stab vests, running in a hospital. Shona could almost feel the tsunami of gossip following them. She had better things to worry her than the good citizens of Dundee's feelings.

Shona indicated they should slow to a more sedate pace when they reached the ward. They didn't want to frighten the life out of any actual patients. "Stay outside. Peter, Jason, you're with me."

They walked at a brisk pace towards the information desk. "Is the Charge Nurse on?"

"You'd be better at the police station seen as you've got him in chokey."

Damn. She'd forgotten about that. "Well, who is in charge?" Her voice was sharper than she wanted it to be, but she didn't have time to be all nicey nicey.

"You've got a cleaner called Kevin Hari."

"Are you having a laugh. We have a different cleaner every day. How the heck am I meant to keep track of their names?"

"Is there a cleaner on the ward just now?"

"Yep. Have a shufty and you'll find them." The nurse dashed off faster than Shona's team on a bacon roll run.

The first cleaner spoke little English. The second, a young student with a Glaswegian accent, thought she'd heard the name.

"Hang on. Shona tapped a few buttons on her phone. "DI Shona McKenzie. Can we have a picture of Kevin Hari? Yesterday." She rattled off her phone number and within a few minutes, her phone pinged indicating an incoming text. She showed the picture to the cleaner. "Aye, that's Kev. Right barrel o' laughs. Not."

"Is he on duty?"

"Should be. He was here an hour ago, but he's disappeared."

"Any clue as to where he might have disappeared to?"

She leaned her mop against the wall. "Aye. Follow me."

She dragged them down into the subterranean corridors of the hospital at what felt like a glacial pace.

"Any chance you could speed it up a bit? This chap could be a murderer."

Their witness stopped dead and Shona ran into her back. "What? Hang on. You never said anything about murder. There's nae way I'm getting involved wi' that."

Shona prodded her back. "You're already involved. We can arrest you if you stop helping now. So, get a move on before you find yourself in a cell next to our murderer when we catch him." She glared at the woman. "And make it fast."

"I'm studying tae be a doctor. I never signed up for any o' this."

"Do you think I signed up to be running around the basement of a hospital, chasing a lunatic who thinks the best way to kill time is to murder women?"

She stopped dead again and yelled, "I'm a woman. He'll kill me."

"You're far too young for him, love. The boys and girls in blue will protect you." She indicated her team, all of whom sported a tough and serious demeanour. "Look, they've got guns." She was sure the woman didn't know the difference between guns and tasers and Shona wasn't going to explain the finer points of these to her.

This seemed to reassure the young woman and she bolted forward with Shona and her team in hot pursuit. She veered to the left and led them to a door which looked identical to every other door they had passed. Shona was left wondering how she knew which one it was. She didn't have to wonder for long. "Unofficial break room come overnight bedroom for the cleaners and porters."

"What the..." Actually, she didn't really want to know. "Don't go. We'll need you to get out of here but stand right back." She indicated a point halfway down the corridor. The cleaner scurried off keen to get out of harm's way.

They knocked and got no answer. Shona indicated to Roy he should open the door. They all stepped back ready for anything. Most had their hands poised near their tasers. "One taser at a time," she whispered. "If we all do it, we'll fry the man before we've a chance to interview him."

The door opened slowly if not silently. "Jason, check it out."

Jason pulled out his taser and approached with caution. The tension in the air would need a meat cleaver to cut it, never mind a knife. He switched on the light and entered taser at the ready. "Nothing. Not a soul in here.

They let out a collective breath.

Shona hollered up the corridor. "Anywhere else he might be?"

"Haven't got a scoobie. He doesn't exactly check in with me."

The words echoed and bounced off the walls, making Shona feel like a right prat.

"Ma'am" Nina's voice had an edge of sharpness.

Shona swivelled so fast she nearly lost her balance. Nina pointed up the corridor in the other direction. A figure, fitting the general description of their suspect, was pounding up the corridor away from them.

"After him." Shona and the team, using every ounce of energy and adrenalin they could muster, darted after him.

Jason and Roy were out in front with Shona barely a half step behind them. "Stop. Police." Roy's words bounced off the walls but made no impression on the man they were pursuing.

"What about using the tasers." Jason pushed the words out between laboured breaths.

"Too far away, we need to get closer." Shona picked up the pace and the others followed her example. She knew all those early morning runs would come in useful one day. The man disappeared. They came to a junction of a few corridors. He definitely wasn't straight ahead, so Shona indicated half of them right and the others left. She bolted down the right hand one with Roy, Nina and Peter. They kept up the fast pace, even Peter seeming to manage it. Having a heart attack had done wonders for his health and fitness levels. The pounding of their feet echoed in the empty corridors as they put one foot in front of the others. Shona caught a movement out of the side of her eye and then a bang was heard. They all dived to the floor and peered ahead. Nothing to be seen. "I think that was a door, Shona," said Peter.

More collective exhaling.

"Check every single door. Peter, take Nina and do the left-hand side. Roy and I will do the right. If it's locked, kick it down."

"My door kicking days are long gone."

"Mine never started." Nina had the look of a hangman

who'd lost his noose. Probably the thought of ruining her designer shoes, even if they were flat.

Shona rolled her eyes. Roy and I will do the kicking. They yanked open every door and looked inside. Door, after door, after door. Nothing other than what looked to them like clutter. "How many rooms does this place have?" Anxiety had given Nina's voice a soupçon of petulance.

"Stop whining." Shona wasn't in the mood for babying her team.

Only one door was locked; Shona knew with every fibre of her being, their perpetrator was inside. It was almost visceral.

The stood back as Roy gave the door a few good kicks. It flew open and as they moved to look inside a man charged towards them with a needle capped syringe in his hand. He headed straight for Shona who leapt to one side and toppled to the floor. She could hear the discharge of a taser and the others scurrying about, followed by, "Kevin Hari or Khaled Hawari, you are under arrest for the murders of..." Peter reeled off all the names without resorting to a note.

Shona was impressed as she wasn't sure she could have managed it. By the time she clambered up the syringe was in an evidence bag, and Kevin in handcuffs. All the fight had gone out of him, and he just looked devastated. He came with them without a murmur, saying not one word all the way back to the station. Neither did the others. No one knew what to say.

61

Back at the station and once in an interview room, Shona asked Kevin if he would like a drink. He asked for water, a bottle of which Peter found and supplied.

"Do you know why you have been arrested?" Shona's voice remained gentle as this man in front of her, rather than looking like a serial killer, looked like he was about to break any minute."

"Yes. Yes, I know."

His English was impeccable and only slightly accented, but she thought she had better ask, "Would you like an interpreter?"

"No. I do not need."

At least he was being compliant. She wondered why someone who had carried out so many horrific crimes, would be quite so compliant. It was a tad unnerving.

"Would you like a lawyer?"

"No. I am ready to confess my crimes and face the consequences."

This was weird. She wondered what he had up his sleeve.

It turned out he had nothing up his sleeve. The dam broke

and through sobs he told the whole sorry tale. His childhood, his family, his life changing, escape, death, his mother and the way he eliminated women who were wicked and vile. Every last, sorry word was forced through sobs, so much so, Shona tied to stop the interview, but Kevin would not let her. When he finished he laid his head on the table and wept some more

For the first time in her life, after Kevin was safely in the cells, Shona felt heart sorry for a prisoner. What a mess. How could anyone endure such suffering? She was left wondering if this was really the job for her.

62

Chapter 69

Shona was reaching for her coat and thinking of visiting Matt at King Alberts and taking him a box of chocolates – he deserved to know he'd helped the police catch the bad guy - when Roy dashed into her office. "Ma'am, there's been a development."

She sank into her chair. "For heaven's sake, we've a suspect in the cells. And his sidekick. What more can there be?" She'd had enough and the story of this poor man's life left a sour taste in her mouth. Sometimes she hated her job.

"I've to take you to the Friary. They want to speak to you."

"Can't it wait? This is the first early knock off we've had in weeks."

"Apparently it's urgent."

"Fine. Where's everyone else?"

"Managed to get away before this happened. We're it. Is it

worth us going to find out what's going on before we call them?"

"Fine. Let's go."

Roy drove like the demons of hell were nipping at his Gucci clad heels and screeched to a halt in front of the railings of an imposing red brick building. The Friary was a Dundee institution and most people in the city had attended a christening, wedding, funeral or function there at some point in their lives. It had also been the scene of at least one murder in Shona's past investigations. She sighed and stepped from the car before trudging past the playpark to the side door. The door opened as she approached, and the secretary ushered her into the office. Shona entered, then stood stock still her jaw dropping so far it almost hit her toes. Nina stood in front of her sporting a beautiful evening gown in a gorgeous heather shade of purple.

"What's going on?"

Nina thrust a wedding gown into her hands and said, "You're getting married today. Quick, get this on."

While Shona took this in, Nina pulled out her phone and sent a text. Two minutes later Abigail appeared clutching a makeup bag and brushes. She pulled over a chair and said, "Sit." She pushed Shona, who hadn't uttered a word, into the chair, then brushed, combed, styled and sprayed her hair into a beautiful chignon before applying flawless makeup.

Shona found her voice. "I can't get married today. Nothing's arranged."

"You can and you will." Nina's voice brooked no argument. "Everything's arranged. Your dad's waiting at the top of the aisle to walk you down it and your future husband is waiting, nerves tearing at his insides, at the bottom."

"Who did all this?"

"I did. Along with Douglas. The church have been in on it

for weeks and were poised for action." Her mother entered the crowded office, a smile splitting her face. She, too, was a vision in a heather silk suit. Heather seemed to be the colour of choice. One of Shona's favourites. Shona stood and threw her arms around her mother. She was hugged tight; her mother wiped a tear from the corner of Shona's eye. No crying, you'll ruin your makeup."

Shona was once again handed the dress and this time she put it on. A beautiful sapphire teardrop necklace was carefully placed around her neck. "That's gran's. She never takes it off as grandad gave it to her."

"Something old, something borrowed, something blue." Her mother handed her a box and Shona opened it. A beautiful silver wristwatch lay nestled inside. "Something new."

Shona put on the watch, and a brand-new pair of Balenciaga shoes, before being spirited through the cloisters to the back door of the church where her father awaited her arrival. Alice, also in heather, ran up and gave her a hug. "You'll be my mummy soon, Shona." Then Nina, Abigail and Alice, in their role as bridesmaids, and Fagin, in his role as ring bearer, stepped through the door and the band and bagpipes struck up Highland Cathedral. Her father took her arm, gently kissed her cheek, and walked her through the door. Everyone stood but Shona's eyes were on the face of her fiancé who waited for his bride, love shining from his eyes, with Rory at his side, at the other end of the aisle. Shona took the first step towards her future. She was ready.

If you enjoyed this book please leave a review in your favourite bookstore. I love hearing you enjoyed the book and reviews help other readers choose the right book for them. Thank you for taking time to read the books, it means the world to me that you chose one of my books.

ABOUT THE AUTHOR

ABOUT THE AUTHOR

Wendy H Jones is the award-winning, international best-selling author of the *DI Shona McKenzie Mysteries.* Her Young Adult Mystery, *The Dagger's Curse* was a finalist in the Woman Alive Readers' Choice Award. She is also The President of the Scot- tish Association of Writers, an international public speaker, and runs conferences and workshops on writing, motivation and marketing worldwide. Her first children's book, *Bertie the Buffalo*, was released in December 2018 with *Bertie Goes to the Worldwide Games* following in May, 2021, *Motivation Matters: Revolutionise Your Writing One Creative Step at a Time and Marketing Matters: Sell More Books* are the first books in the Writing Matters series. She also produces T*he Writing and marketing Show* weekly podcast and is a partner in Auscot Publishing and Retreats

She lives in Scotland where her books are based. She loves reading, travelling, and meeting new people, preferably all at once and is spreading her wings in this direction once more. Wendy also loves helping others to follow their writing dreams. She believes writing is the best job in the world.

ALSO BY WENDY H. JONES

DI SHONA MCKENZIE MYSTERIES

Killer's Countdown

Killer's Craft

Killer's Cross

Killer's Cut

Killer's Crew

Killer's Crypt

Killer's Curse

CASS CLAYMORE INVESTIGATES

Antiques and Alibis

WRITING MATTERS SERIES

Creativity Matters

Motivation Matters

Marketing Matters

BERTIE THE BUFFALO PICTURE BOOKS

Bertie the Buffalo

Bertie at the Worldwide Games

Bertie the Buffalo Colouring Books

Printed in Great Britain
by Amazon